© 2011 by David Workman. All rights reserved.

Cover art by Melissa Williams. To see more of her fantastic artwork, visit www. *http://mwcoverdesign.blogspot.com*

No portion of this book may be duplicated or used without written permission. All characters and events are fictional and are the product of the author's imagination. Any similarity to real people or events is purely coincidental. All real locations are used in a fictional setting and are not intended to depict any actual events.

Absolute

Authority

David Workman

Hayf,
Enjoy the video! Thanks
for your friendship & support!

To my wonderful wife, Stephanie, plot-twister extraordinaire, who encouraged me to complete this even when I didn't feel like it. You were right, as usual.

"Now this man [Judas] acquired a field with the reward of his wickedness, and falling headlong he burst open in the middle and all his bowels gushed out. And it became known to all the inhabitants of Jerusalem, so that the field was called in their own language Akeldama, that is, Field of Blood. For it is written in the Book of Psalms, 'May his camp become desolate, and let there be no one to dwell in it' and 'Let another take his office.'"

-Acts 1: 18-20-

Prologue

Long Beach Harbor, CA, July 1988, 0257 hours local time

The black-hooded team had been in place behind the crates for over an hour, waiting for the radio cue to move in. Impatience was starting to set in as each member checked and rechecked his weapons, making sure they were loaded and ready. Silence was imperative, as each man knew. A sneeze, a cough, a slip on the metal scraps on the ground, and the whole operation might be over.

Over the micro earpiece, he heard, "Talon Six, this is Leader. Check in." Talon Six, squatting with his back against a crate, his MP-5 cradled in his lap, clicked his mike button twice in response. All was fine, and he was anxious to get the operation underway. Leader checked in remotely with each man in order of his position to the target, each clicking in clear.

The light ocean breeze wafted the sewage smell from the *Queen Mary* permanently docked across the harbor. Unusually hard rain the previous night had washed all of Long Beach's sewage into the ocean, the current forcing it to settle around the stoic ocean liner. The Long Beach *Press-Telegram* had featured a photograph on the front page of the morning edition showing the brown ring around the boat, the waveless early morning tide not helping at all to remove the eyesore.

Tonight's target was the *China Angel*, a tanker supposedly carrying automobile parts. Its real cargo didn't make anything drive or spin or steer. It made things explode. And it was about to be offloaded onto the third busiest dock in the United States.

"Leader, Talon Six," he whispered, "I have a possible contact at the rail."

From their positions, each member of the team strained to take a look around the crates and forklifts on the dock while maintaining cover. Darkness helped, but there were still a few dock lights in all the wrong places. The six commandos, dressed in black, were spread out at twenty-five to thirty yard intervals, concealed behind large crates and equipment. Each member had a pair of night vision goggles, a silenced MP-5, a Glock 9mm sidearm, and other miscellaneous gear, including flash and stun grenades. For the moment, the night vision goggles were stowed, as the dock lights surrounding the gangplanks were more than sufficient.

A figure appeared, leaning on the starboard bow rail, the orange dot of a cigarette floating in his hand. Smoke wafted from his mouth as he turned to look out onto the dock.

"Okay, he's faced this way. Everyone hold your positions." Leader uncovered his watch and checked the time, the crate concealing the green glow display. It showed he was running about three minutes behind schedule. *Damn. Where the hell are they?*

The figure on the deck removed his stocking cap and waved toward the stern of the tanker. Leader shifted his weight as he glanced down the pier and caught a pair of headlights heading his direction.

"Talon Team, Leader. Headlights at three o'clock. Should be our target. Watch for my lead." Six sets of double clicks confirmed everyone had heard him.

The headlights became a half-ton truck with a canvas cover on the back. It ground to a squeaky halt at the bottom of the stern gangplank, two men jumping out of the back, followed by two from the cab. The driver quickly scanned the area with his eyes before barking out orders to the others, who immediately peeled back the opening of the canvas and started pulling green crates out.

"Leader, Four. I have a good look into the back of the truck. It's packed exactly as we expected."

"Four, hold your position and wait for my signal. Keep an eye out for weapons."

"None so far." They were too smart for that. Only in movies were covert operators stupid enough to carry machine guns in the open.

3

Leader didn't need to respond. They all knew what Four didn't say: *but there could be any minute now.* If there was one lesson the instructors had stressed above all others it was to always assume your enemy has access to weapons. And tonight was no different. Just because he couldn't see them didn't mean they weren't there.

Ten minutes later, Four reported, "Crate offload finished. Starting to haul on board."

"Can you see any weapons yet?" Leader asked.

"Negative. Wait. Up on the rail."

Sure enough, Leader thought. "We have weapons in the onboard hands." He had planned on this, so he was actually a little relieved to see the men with semi-automatic rifles appear on the rail. Not that he minded killing unarmed scum, but the boss looked down on it." Outpost, do you have a fix on the rail?"

"Affirmative," came the slow, measured response from the sniper positioned three hundred fifty yards behind and above them, in the cab of a large container crane perched high above the ground, right on the perfect level to see the entire port side of the *China Angel* deck.

Leader swallowed, took a deep breath, visually checked his MP-5, and toggled the microphone." Let's do it. On my mark." He counted five seconds silently, then, "Team, Leader, move out! Go, go, go, go, go...! "

Out of the shadows, the six black-clad men emerged, slinking along between boxes, their steps timed perfectly to put them at exact intervals. Three was the first one to leave the shadows, his rifle drawn tight inside his shoulder and eye as he clipped off two short bursts of silenced fire. Six bullets hit two of the rail guards square in the chest, knocking them back, the men having never known they were about to die. Another man at the rail noticed his companions fall and started to shout out an order to the others, but the words never made it out. Three rounds struck him the upper chest and neck, spinning him limply to the deck. A man struggling with one of the crates suddenly dropped his end and drew a semi-automatic pistol from under his shirt.

"Two, gun on the gangplank!" Outpost warned into Team Talon's earpieces.

Two yanked his rifle up and clipped off a quick burst, which exploded in the man's chest, sending him flailing off the gangplank and onto the concrete dock below.

Suddenly the man on the other end of the crate fell silently to his death, a shot that could only have one source." Nice shot," Leader commended.

"Anytime," responded Outpost." You have two more emerging from the superstructure, starboard side, heading to the gangplank."

Without reply, Five leveled his weapon and flipped off two bursts. Two bullets from the first burst missed, but the third found its mark, exploding the man's shoulder. The second burst landed all three bullets squarely in the second man's face, tearing the back of his head off and leaving a crimson spray against the white outside wall of the wheelhouse as he slumped to the deck.

"You only wounded the first guy. I'll take care of him," Outpost called.

A whiff of a bullet going over Five's head told him Outpost had connected. As he reached the top of the gangplank, Five glanced toward the structure and saw both bodies in a collective pool of blood. *What a gruesome game we play.*

Leader keyed his mike. "Outpost, what do you have on thermal?"

After a moment, the radio crackled and Outpost replied, "No one in the structure, and no one on deck. The truck is empty, and no one emerged from the water. I'm having trouble seeing inside the hull. Too thick."

"Good enough. Talon, Leader. Let's regroup on deck and prepare to go below."

Quickly the team gathered on the deck by the wheelhouse, and huddled to begin the insertion, Outlook watching them through his thermal scope, scanning the deck and windows for any sign of threats. There were none. Satisfied, he radioed, "Deck clear. Move in when ready."

"Clear," Leader replied as he signaled the first Talon member in line to lift the handle on the deck hatch in front of him. Slowly, the lid came up as the other Talon members surrounded the hatch, weapons poised, fingers on triggers. The room immediately below the hatch appeared empty, bare bulbs illuminating the damp floor and walls. Two latched his harness to the rope held by One and flung his feet over the edge of the hole, one hand to grip the rope, the other firmly gripping the trigger and handle of the MP-5 strapped around his shoulder. Four had a flash bang grenade at the ready just in case, but it looked like he wouldn't need it for this room.

Two slid quickly down the line, twirling in mid-air to scan for hostiles on the way down. Hitting the floor, he released the rope, slid it from the D-ring on his belt, gave his team a thumbs up, sprinted to the nearest wall, and crouched down to cover his teammates as they descended single file. As the last team member touched down quietly and safely, Leader approached the hatch on the far wall and touched the handle. Locked. Leader hand signaled to Five that they would need to blow the door. Five shrugged his backpack off his shoulders and undid the top flap, extracting a chunky block of C-4 – just enough to damage the hinges – divided it in two, placed one blob on each hinge pin, and inserted a detonator cap in each. Talon Team slumped away from the door as Five unraveled the electrical cord and connected the battery pack. Safely away, Five clicked the ignition switch and the explosive set off with a loud BANG!

The heavy steel door bucked under the pressure, detached from its frame, and fell with a loud thud to the metal deck, tipping backwards and landing flat.

1

Present Day

Costa Mesa, California

The irony wasn't lost on Max Preston. With an MBA from Harvard Business School, not much got past him – and this was no different. He sat in a lounge chair by his pool under a pair of tiki torches, the houselights from both stories reflecting off the still blue surface, glowing from the underwater lights. Preston's athletic fingers danced across the laptop's keyboard, pausing only long enough for him to look up into the dark night sky, contemplating his next words carefully. The *Foggy Daze* program received every keystroke, turning it into ciphered code in its internal workings and adjusting the combination each time Preston added or changed a single key stroke. If he erased a sentence or reworded a phrase, the software made the appropriately random adjustment and re-encrypted the new material. The program not only encrypted messages that were sent, it coded messages Preston wasn't ready to broadcast yet as well and would recode them when they were sent. If anyone got hold of his laptop, either by theft or by warrant, they would admire the pretty pictures but not have a thing to read that would tip them off about anything out of the ordinary. It was the genius of his designers – the ones who had a little extra money in their wallets each month.

Smoke wafted from the long, thick cigar clenched in the side of his mouth. Returning his attention to the screen and taking a deep inhale, the ash at the tip of the fat stogy lit bright red before he balanced the cigar delicately on the edge of the glass ashtray on the wrought iron table beside him.

He had to proofread it one more time before sending. Every phrase, every word, every letter had to be exactly right.

It was.

The cigar found itself squeezed between his lips again, the ember glowing brightly as he inhaled to relax his nerves. Satisfied, he fingered the keyboard scratch pad and clicked Send.

And with one simple action before bed, he awakened a stirring monster that would not let the world rest ever again.

2

Mesa, Arizona

Gina Lapoli closed the laptop, tucked it away in the nylon case, and headed for the door, depositing her empty coffee cup in the trash can on the way out as she dropped the sunglasses perched on the top of her head onto her nose. Outside, the bright sun struck her face, causing an unexplainable "sun sneeze," the one thing she hated about sunny days. Of course, living in Arizona was a bad choice to avoid it, but it was only the sneezes that bothered her. With a golden tan and highlighted blonde hair, she was a self-proclaimed sun goddess. Coppertone was her best friend, a string bikini her favorite relaxation. And unlike a lot of sunbathers, she had the killer body for it. At twenty-eight, her maturity said forty, but her looks screamed young party girl.

Today was supposed to be a light day. She'd taken the day off, telling her boss her sister was in town visiting for the first time in three years. It sounded like a good excuse – and a believable one. And what normal boss would deny her the time off? She had worked for one who would, but her new boss was much more understanding.

And much easier to play. She had been hired because of her fantastic credentials: an art degree from UT-El Paso and six years working at the Dallas Museum of Art. Her move from Texas had come with the addition of a new boyfriend, Greg. He'd officially lasted three months once she'd moved to Mesa, but that was only on paper. No one at her office had stopped to wonder why they had never met Greg. Must have figured her private life was exactly that, she reasoned. It made it all that much easier to hold a cover story, when people around her never asked questions. Not that she couldn't have answered them convincingly. She had a story and all the documentation to back it all up. It was all false, of course, but you couldn't tell by looking at it.

The sunlight baked her young skin, giving her new life after spending the last two hours inside the dark coffee house. She had wanted to sit outside, but there were no plugs for her computer, and she wasn't sure how long her battery would last. But now her own batteries were recharging as she strolled along the small shops in downtown Mesa. Her solace was only temporary, though. The time spent at the coffee shop allowed her to download the latest instructions and a few highly encrypted files she would need for her next assignment at her real job, which was slated for two days from now.

Reaching her car, she hopped in, lowered all the windows, and blasted the air conditioner. She liked the sun, but the oppressive heat she could do without. Even in December, Arizona often feels like summer elsewhere.

The parking spot right in front of her apartment was conveniently open, so she pulled right in, gathered her computer bag, and headed up the outside wood staircase. Inside the apartment, the air conditioning greeted her as she set her keys down on the kitchen counter bar and turned to head toward the hall. And stopped.

Something was wrong. She could feel it. It was the lighting. It was too dark where she was standing. Why? She turned toward the living room sliding glass door that opened to the balcony, except she couldn't see past the shadowy figure that blocked the middle of the light. He raised a hand that spit two flashes right at her, the first bullet catching her square in the chest right above the lace edge of the white camisole sticking up from under her shirt. The second shot sliced into her chin, spinning her against the cabinet, her head bouncing off the counter top as she dropped to the floor, taking a bar stool down with her.

Long Beach, California

Parker's Lighthouse had always been Ben Mitchell's favorite restaurant. The light blue Cape Cod clapboard exterior and the beautiful view of the harbor and the retired majestic ocean liner *Queen Mary* permanently docked right across the water had always set the perfect mood for his first choice of dinner: seafood. It didn't really matter what kind of seafood – though his favorite was shrimp. It just had to come from the ocean. Crab, lobster, shark – he loved it all. Tonight's selection was shrimp scampi, prepared in melted butter with lots of garlic. Had to have lots of butter and garlic. An appetizer of calamari had begun the meal, along with a fresh seaweed salad. The light vinaigrette dressing was just the right amount of tart to set off the kelp.

He opened the black bill folder on the table and removed his credit card, took the pen and signed the receipt, slid out his copy of the charge ticket, and folded it neatly back together before leaving. Outside, he headed across the parking lot toward his car, the ocean breeze ruffling his shirt sleeves. His shoes ticked along the pavement as he rounded the end of the trunk and fished for the keys in his pocket. They keys jangled as he thumbed the remote control and the black Mercedes chirped and blinked its turn signals in answer as the door unlocked. He reached for the handle but never got in.

Sudden weakness caused his knees to buckle as he reached for the door handle, sending him limply to the asphalt, doubled over. After a few short gasps his breathing stopped. He was found a half hour later by the people who owned the car next to his.

New York City

Cacophony was really the wrong word for it. It had been called music, but Peter Jacobs sure didn't understand why. The conductor didn't even have a score in front of him. The tuxedo-clad musicians – if they could be called that – just stood in the middle of the polished wood stage, holding their instruments. Not playing, just holding them. Until one by one the so-called conductor would point to each one, and then one note at a time would ring out, usually off-key from the previous player's tone. This carried on for almost ten long, weird minutes. It was all very detached, disconnected, strange. None of it made sense. It wasn't supposed to.

Peter left the small concert hall, his lovely Molly at his side, confused, perplexed, and not really wanting to dissect what he'd just heard. He was trying to decide if it was worth the effort. His young, beautiful fiancée was far more important to him right now as she walked beside him down the sidewalk, their arms intertwined. She looked her usual smashing tonight in her sleeveless black dress, sheer black stockings, and heels. Her soft shoulders were covered by an elegant black topcoat to ward off the night chill. Peter, no slouch himself with his *GQ* physique and chiseled jaw, always admired her in whatever she was wearing – she had the classic looks that made any fashion complete – but tonight she was especially stunning. Her wavy raven hair bounced lightly on her shoulders as her heels clicked happily along the pavement. The symphony was over, and now it was time for him to concentrate on her.

Molly rested her head on his shoulder as they strolled down the city sidewalk toward the parking lot. The car was parked only a few short blocks from the theater.

"Is it just me, or was that just plain weird?" he asked as they crossed the vacant lamp-lit street.

She chuckled against his shoulder." Yes, honey, it was weird. Even with *my* taste in music it was weird."

"Good. I'm glad I'm not so far removed from your social scene that I missed that one."

"Are you still upset about what Daddy said to you?" she asked.

"A little. I know I shouldn't let it bother me, but I can't help but think about it. He seemed so serious."

"Peter, he was only kidding with you. He really likes you. He just has a peculiar way of showing it," she said, hoping he'd accept her explanation. "He's always been that way. Every guy I ever dated got run through the wringer."

He still wasn't convinced. All through dinner the night before, Molly's dad had made indirect comments about how Peter wasn't from the "right breeding" for her and how he sure hoped Peter could provide for her the way he had when she was growing up. He was partially right.

Molly had come from "good stock," a long line of northeast aristocracy, politically connected for several generations to the industrial and governmental leaders of the area and Washington, DC. Her uncle on her father's side was still a state senator, a post he'd held since the election of 1966, longer than Molly had been alive. She had been raised with the trappings of wealth – the mansion on Long Island, summers on Martha's Vineyard, trips to Europe, a brand new Mercedes at age 16, Vassar. To the outsider, she was untouchable unless you rode around in the same atmosphere. But to people who were lucky enough to know Molly Hindan, they saw a girl and then a woman who didn't believe in letting her money define her. Sure, she enjoyed the luxuries that life afforded her, but she never let it all create a barrier between her and rest of the world. She rarely told anyone about her family background until after her newfound friend had known her long enough to feel confident in their friendship. She never bought her friends. And she never accepted "friend" invitations from others who tried to buy her loyalty. She wanted real friends, real family, real relationships, based on genuine love, not money or influence. Her parents would have loved her no matter how much money they had. Not that they were affectionate parents. They rarely hugged her or told her they loved her, though she knew they did. They just had a very standoffish way of showing it. In her view, she was the first generation of her family to truly understand genuine love, complete with all the outward signs.

After college, with a degree in finance tucked under her arm, Molly turned down several offers from her dad's friends to come join their large Wall Street firms, opting instead to work for a small investment firm in lower Manhattan. A smart dresser with a professional attitude, she cultivated a loyal customer base that impressed her boss. She quickly moved up from an investment counselor to the territory manager and was now on her way to running the office after only six years. Her co-workers could easily have been jealous and hateful, but instead they admired her hard work and devotion. Any of them would be proud to work for her.

Following a long day in the middle of last winter, Molly had taken a rare opportunity to stop by a local watering hole, a slightly out-of-character move on her part since she hated the bar scene. She had gone in with no intentions other than a nice glass of wine while she checked her e-mails and responded to a few. She sat in a back booth, her attention firmly engrossed in her laptop, when a handsome man in a dark suit with a red tie and black wool overcoat, hands buried in the pockets, approached her table. He cleared his throat and waited for her to realize he was standing there. She held up one finger for him to wait as she pressed the last couple keys and hit send before she looked up.

She didn't recognize the man but felt comfortable enough after a few words were exchanged to invite him to sit down. They shared dinner, a wonderful conversation, and a couple more glasses of wine, exchanged phone numbers and e-mail addresses, and embarked that evening on a very unexpected relationship that landed them back at the same booth six months later as Peter slid a diamond ring onto her finger and she cried tears of joy. After several kisses, they ordered the same wine and meal they had had that fateful first evening, sharing memories of all that had transpired over the last half a year and looking forward to a lifetime together.

Peter was not from the same social gatherings that Molly's family floated in, and he didn't fit the mold of what he was sure her dad would have liked for his one and only daughter. But that didn't matter to Molly. He would be able to provide her with a comfortable living. And she didn't demand anything more. That was one reason Peter loved her so much.

Tonight they had met Molly's parents for a nice dinner at a nearby Italian restaurant and then bid them goodnight as Molly and Peter hopped into his BMW and headed to the concert. Now that the concert was over, it was time for a nice relaxing night at Peter's brownstone.

They turned out of the alley and rounded the corner to the parking lot but never saw his car. The knife sliced across Peter's throat and he grabbed for his neck as he gasped for air. Blood squirted on Molly's face as she started to scream but was cut off. A gloved hand swiped across her mouth, spinning her off her high-heeled feet and down onto a pile of full trash bags on the concrete, her coat twirling open. She tried desperately to kick at the shadowy figure of the man above her, hoping to catch him with the pointed toe or heel of her pumps, but her ankles were clenched in his hands. He twisted her legs together, flipped her on her stomach, and struck her in the back of the head.

3

St. Louis

Every Monday for twelve years, executive recruiter Gordon McAllister walked casually past the gray metal lamp post at the corner of the busy intersection like the many other sharply-dressed office workers scurrying around him. But it had nothing to do with his job finding top-notch bosses for Fortune 500 companies. McAllister's spent his work days recruiting and placing top executives either in thriving companies or in dying endeavors desperate for new direction. Finding good executives was difficult, especially if you wanted the exec to actually help the company and not just collect a hefty paycheck and retire early with a lucrative pre-negotiated package. McAllister Management, Inc., one of the top executive recruiting firms in the country, had clients in several Fortune 500 companies and many of the lesser-known corporations all across the United States, in every industry.

But that was his day job, his cover, although ironically he made more money – a lot more – doing that than performing his real job: hunting down and killing people for the President of the United States.

McAllister flipped his coat cuff back with his other hand and checked his watch as his leather-sole loafers clipped along the cold concrete sidewalk: 11:30. A dedicated creature of habit, he always ate lunch before the restaurants got full with the regular crowd. Plus, getting to work so early, he was always hungry for lunch before noon. Parking in Clayton – St. Louis' "second downtown" – was a bear during lunch time, since it was mostly parallel spaces along the streets or pricy garages attached to the tall office buildings, so most people parked their cars once in the morning and walked anywhere they needed to go during the day, especially any of the great places for lunch.

He took a quick sideways glance at the lamp post, looking for the tell tale white chalk mark strategically placed somewhere on the post. The placement varied slightly each time is was marked, so as to make the pattern less obvious, which is exactly why it had been so easy for the other agent to anonymously brush past the lamp post along with the rest of the crowd, leaving a small chalk mark across one side of the otherwise clean metal, low enough that the average passerby would never notice it. Today the mark was exactly where McAllister expected it. The slight downward left to right white chalk line meant the dead drop was full. He had an errand to run. There were actually three dead drop locations he kept in play, and the placement and angle of the chalk mark told him which one. This time it was the primary site.

He called his admin assistant Rita from his cell and told her he would be late, headed back into the parking garage – a welcome break against the cold wind outside – hopped into his Saab 9^5, and drove out onto the street.

He cleared the edge of Clayton and hopped onto westbound Highway 40. Fifteen minutes later, he exited at Mason Road and turned left. As the two-lane road got farther from the highway, it wound into a residential area with large trees and even larger homes behind wrought iron gates with key pads. The gates weren't mean to keep anyone in, like a prison. They kept the riff raff out.

Finally, on the right was the turn he was looking for: the entrance to Queeny Park, a large county park with walking paths, large trees, and plenty of grass. Normally a great place for a picnic, today the cold didn't lend itself to any sort of outdoor recreation. The wind had stripped the trees clean of all their leaves a month ago, and they'd been dutifully raked up and disposed of – most likely mulched – by the parks department, leaving only a few stragglers on the ground. Now the bare limbs stretched out in every direction but held nothing except the occasional squirrel's nest, visible through the void. The grass, now brown, was clean and trimmed.

McAllister guided the black sports sedan into the empty parking lot and pulled into a space under a tree, double checking that his black wool overcoat was buttoned. He slid on his gloves, stepped out into the gray day, shut the door behind him, and pocketed his keys, clicking the remote once so the alarm would arm silently. Visually scanning the area for anyone else around, he walked briskly down the cold, narrow asphalt foot path that cut across an open field, toward a collection of steel picnic tables standing up at an angle for the winter, huddled together on a concrete pad. *Sort of a table fort*, McAllister thought as he passed. *Also a decent tactical position,* another part of his brain noted, assessing how the wood planks and steel bars could work as a temporary shield against bullets, if the need arose. He hoped he wouldn't have to test his theory. The leather soles of his black dress shoes clipped along the path as he passed the tables and neared the edge of the woods. The path went on without him as he stepped onto the grass, its dark green color lightened by the winter cold, and into the first layer of woods. As he moved, he glanced everywhere, but only with his eyes, looking for anyone who might see him. Head motion would give away his tactic. Today, someone would be easy to spot, since there was no one else around.

As he rounded a large oak, he spotted the edge of a plastic bag sticking out from beneath some mulch at the base of the tree. One last glance around to clear the area and he bent down to carefully uncover the book-size clear bag, revealing the tape around it for waterproofing. He would open it later. Right now he needed to sneak it into his jacket and get back to his car.

Parks are a great choice for dead drops because they have so many places to hide things – and no video cameras. The only worry was the occasional eyewitness. But McAllister wasn't concerned about that in the bitterly cold weather as he lifted the bag, brushed off the loose mulch with his gloved hand, and crammed the small bag into his outside coat pocket.

THUNK!

The bark above him on the tree popped and showered wood chips on his head and shoulders. Flinching for cover, he glanced up to see the damage on the tree trunk, a small hole and surrounding area stripped of the dark bark, revealing the naked soft fleshy wood inside. The quick glance also revealed more than the damage to the tree. It pointed McAllister to the direction of the shooter: behind him and to his right. Staying low, he dashed farther into the stand of trees, taking cover behind another large oak, one wide enough for him to hide behind completely. With his back against the tree, he reached inside his coat and pulled out his Walther PPS pistol, its grey frame almost hidden against his gloves. He held the gun up and saw the small sliver of brass inside the chamber, thumbed the magazine release to be sure the clip was full, jammed it back inside the grip, and assessed his situation.

The car was to his left – tactical right because his back was to the shooter – across the open field. Whoever was shooting at him was behind him, also across the field, but in the opposite direction, at an angle. *Were there trees over there?* He carefully peaked out from behind the tree. Yes. Mostly likely that was the shooter's perch. Question two: Could the shooter still see him? Probably. He had to be using a scope, which meant he had a definite advantage – the bare bones advantages any sniper has: distance and stealth – which makes snipers such an amazing tool.

The cold bit at McAllister's exposed cheeks and nose. He cupped his gloved left hand and blew hot air into it, deflecting the warmth onto his face. A brief moment of relief, gone as quickly as it had come.

McAllister flinched as a chunk of bark exploded next to his head with a resounding thump from the left side of the large oak tree. He was pinned. Go to the right, the sniper had him. Go left, toward the car, he might have sufficient cover in the woods, but then he'd have to break into a dead run to the car sitting isolated on the empty parking lot. *Think!*

The picnic tables. He knew they were between him and the car, but how far away? Could he get there safely? He looked back to his left and tried to spot them. There – about thirty yards away. Exposed. He'd have to break out of the cover of the woods to get behind them. And even then, he wasn't sure if they'd stop a high caliber round.

A high caliber *silenced* round.

That's why he wasn't hearing the report of a gun shot! That meant the shooter was using a sound suppressor, which meant his range was diminished. Silencers work great for keeping your location secret, McAllister knew, but it also decreased the effective range of the weapon, sometimes by a hundred yards or so, depending on the design. Apparently the shooter was close enough that the diminished range wasn't affecting his accuracy. Good and bad. He was close enough that McAllister might have a chance to spot him and take him out. But close enough that the shooter has better vision than if he was far away.

He listened for any small sound that might give him badly needed information, but all he heard was the whistling of the brutal wind through the barren trees. He didn't even have leaves to conceal him.

He'd have to rely on speed and maneuvering. Looking over his shoulder to his left – the direction of the car and the picnic table fort – he found an escape path that offered a good number of thick trees – probably oaks, he assumed from their size – to provide at least a little protection from a shooter who would have to hit a moving target in the woods. He decided that was the only chance of any sort of advantage.

McAllister tightened the grip on the pistol, took a deep breath, and darted to his left from behind the tree. A bullet thumped into a tree behind him, shattering the bark, as he sprinted headlong, struggling to keep solid footing with his leather-soled shoes on the slick grass. As he weaved among the trees, two more bullets found woody landings, each leaving behind shredded debris and a deep hole in the trunk. The edge of the woods – and the end of his cover – was only ten yards away. Each cold breath tore at his lungs as he bounded from tree to tree, careful to watch for low branches that could rip at his face and fallen limbs that could trip him up.

At the edge of the woods, he hesitated, almost stopped completely. And waited for a beat. *Thump!* The tree in front of him shook as the bullet slammed through the bark. McAllister had worried the shooter was adjusting his timing to compensate for a moving target. He was right. By pausing, McAllister had faked out the shooter, causing him to overshoot his intended target. McAllister turned immediately to face the direction the bullet should have come from, knowing the shooter would likely need a second or two to rack the bolt on the rifle to put a new round in the chamber.

And there he was. A hundred yards to the northeast, just inside a tree line. He was well concealed, but the arm movement of loading another round gave him away. McAllister knew he couldn't hit him from this distance with his Walther, but he had an idea. He started on a run again, toward the stand of picnic tables. He was hoping the shooter would assume he'd stop behind them. He assumed right. Another round came hurtling toward him, clanging a metal support tube with a resounding crash.

McAllister was already past the other side of the stack and only twenty yards from his car, key fob in left hand, Walther in the right, in a flat out sprint. He aimed the remote at the Saab, thumbed the unlock button and then the trunk button. The lid flung up and open as he skidded to a stop behind the black sedan. Tucking the Walther back inside the holster inside his jacket, he lifted the carpet from the floor of the trunk and opened the hatch to reveal a false bottom. From inside the now-open box he pulled up a composite-skinned rifle with a scope attached to the top, silencer screwed onto the end, and a folded up stock. He unfolded the black composite stock and clicked it into place as a sniper's bullet clanged against the trunk lid, making the trunk lid vibrate but ricocheting safely away. *Won't the park rangers have a good time piecing this one together!* He knew from the location of the sound that the high powered round would have struck him in the head and killed him instantly if it hadn't been for the armor he had ordered custom installed not just in the trunk lid but throughout the car, including the specially-designed windows. Even the tires were armored, thus negating the need for a spare and freeing up room in the trunk for weapons.

He checked the chamber and found a round safely tucked inside, ready for action. A clip slid right into the receiver and locked into place. McAllister kept the trunk lid open, using it for cover as he leveled the rifle and put the scope to his eye, resting the barrel of the gun on the right rear quarter panel. The wind once again howled, reminding him to correct for it when he shot.

But he had to find his target first. He quickly zeroed in on the spot where the shooter had been and looked for some sort of movement. *There.* The shooter was looking down at his gun, as if he was clearing a jam or reloading. Perfect. McAllister gently squeezed the trigger, so slightly as to not upset the barrel and cross hair alignment, and felt the rifle thud against his shoulder as the round leapt toward it target.

He realigned the scope in his line of sight and saw...nothing. The shooter had vanished. Had he gone down? Was he hit? Was he wounded? Dead? *Faking being dead to lure me toward him and out into the open?* McAllister knew better than to rush toward the shooter, now *his* target, not vice versa. He opened his left eye to scan the surrounding area for movement while remaining focused through the scope with his right. Nothing. He waited a second more just to be sure.

Convinced he was temporarily out of danger, McAllister shut the trunk lid, keeping the rifle to his right eye. Another quick scan with the naked eye and he set out toward the woods where the shooter was – *or at least had been,* he reminded himself – ready to shoot again if he saw his target moving. The light weight and perfect balance between barrel and stock made the weapon easy to lift yet sturdy enough to settle almost instantly into accurate shooting position.

The cold wind continued to chew at his face and chilled the sweat on the back of his neck as he cautiously walked toward the woods, carefully maintaining both a dead stare at the shooter's last known location and a steady scan of his peripheral vision.

A squirrel darted from one tree to the next high above him.

McAllister barely noticed. The gray, fluffy-tailed rodent was too high up for him to need to react. He was focused. He had a target to take out.

The wind whipped against his ears as he edged toward the shooter's perch, a stand of three close trees behind a small patch of evergreen bushes. *Perfect cover for winter time, when the tree limbs offered no concealment but the bushes did.* McAllister cursed at himself for not thinking of this sooner. He should have looked for the bushes as soon as he figured out the direction of the shots. Nearing the bushes, he pressed the rifle stock firmly against his shoulder as he spotted a form in green camos lying face down among the three trees, a rifle resting on the ground to the left. The man's head was open wide in back, a mess of black and red matter inside and around the gaping hole. All around the body were tiny spots of blood spatter – on the trees, the ground.

McAllister knelt by the dead man's body, set his rifle down on the ground, and foraged through the shooter's olive green pants and jacket pockets for any identification or other useful information. He doubted he would find any, and he was right. *Who are you? Who sent you to kill me? And how did you know about the dead drop?* Whoever this guy was, he was nothing if not a pro. *Good thing you couldn't shoot straight.*

He reached over the body and picked up the shooter's rifle, and grabbed his own rifle before standing to leave. One last look to make sure he hadn't missed anything and he set off back toward the parking lot. Back at the Saab, he deposited both rifles into the trunk and pulled out his cell phone. Willard Stanford answered on the first ring – and apparently checked his caller ID.

"Now what have you done?"

"What could you possibly mean?" was McAllister's attempt at sounding sarcastically innocent.

"You know very well what I mean. What channel should I turn to for the latest news?"

"None, if you get out here fast enough," he answered, changing his tone.

Stanford noticed the sudden seriousness in McAllister's voice. "Where are you?"

"East entrance to Queeny Park. There's a dead shooter in the woods right across from Crypt" – the code name for the main dead drop – "waiting for a pick up. And we have another problem, maybe even bigger."

"What's that?" Stanford asked.

"Someone knows we exist," McAllister answered and flipped the phone closed.

4

Back in the parking garage by his office, McAllister examined the chip on the Saab's trunk lid, determined it looked more like a rock or something else had hit it, not a high powered bullet, and headed up the elevator to the sixth floor.

"You had two calls while you were away," Rita said from her desk just inside the office door.

"Thanks," he answered, pausing to take the pink slips from her outstretched hand. Even though he had voicemail, Gordon preferred to have hand-written messages. One was from a man he knew in Dallas whom he had recruited to head a large telecommunication conglomerate, the other from a man named Jack Russell – like the dog. *What were his parents thinking?* he thought as he headed into his office and latched the door behind him.

McAllister dropped his coat onto the rack by the door and extracted the plastic bag from the outer pocket. Settling into the leather chair behind his desk, he unzipped the transparent bag and pulled the thick black plastic case from inside, setting the empty bag aside on the desk. The box was showing its age, weathered and beaten from many days sitting outside in dead drop stations, surviving rain, snow, wind, heat, and time as it patiently waited for its recipient, each time cradling secrets inside that only a privileged few were allowed to know. The lid was sealed shut with black electrical tape – one piece only with a small triangle in one corner, a clue that it was authentic. Each detail meant something to McAllister as he examined the box carefully to verify it was safe to open it. Six months earlier, a CIA officer had been killed in Budapest when a dead drop box had been rigged with a tiny explosive charge, triggered with an old-fashioned mercury switch by the motion of lifting the lid. The dead agent had been following a quick-moving chain of leads and, in his haste to take the next step closer to catching his prey, had skipped normal protocol and popped open the box without checking it thoroughly first. It blew up in his face, almost tearing his head off his shoulders.

Gordon slid his lap drawer open and took out a polycarbonate letter opener – non-metallic so as not to complete the circuit on any potential electrical explosive device, but sharp enough to cut quickly through the electrical tape. Once the seal was safely broken, he removed the lid and found a single letter-size envelope with no writing on the outside. Careful not to touch it, he set the whole box to the side and opened his right-hand desk drawer and extracted a pair of latex gloves from a small box. He wanted to preserve any fingerprints and other evidence that was on the envelope and not contribute any of his own. Snapping the gloves on, he turned his attention back to the box and carefully lifted the envelope out. The flap was unsealed, so he didn't have to worry about using the safe opener again. He carefully lifted the flap and extracted a single sheet of copy paper, which he unfolded and held with both hands. On it was typed a very simple note:

Mr. McAllister,

If you are reading this, you must have survived the little ambush in Queeny Park. Congratulations. Enjoy it while it lasts. As you are probably aware by now, your entire team has been eliminated, one by one, until you are the last remaining member. That will soon change. You and your team have become somewhat of a nuisance, an impediment to our progress. We are too close to victory to let you continue to stand in our way. This is in no way intended as a threat. Think of it instead as a demonstration of how you have lost what little control over your team you had in the first place. You're obsolete. The world has changed and no longer needs your services.

As Gordon expected, there was no signature. He examined the letters and paper, looking for anything that might give him a clue as to who wrote the note and where it came from. Obviously whoever planted it knew where to put it and how to signal to him it was ready. His cover had been severely blown somehow. How did it get blown and who now knows? And why did it matter? He had to get this note to Stanford so he could have his inside contacts process it for evidence. He dialed his cell.

5

December is always hit or miss in St. Louis. Some years it's freezing; other years it's warm enough to fool the crocus into blooming too early. White Christmases are few and far between, but occasionally they happen, much to almost everyone's delight. Almost everyone, that is, except shoppers, who have enough to worry about already battling lines in the stores. The last thing they want is to get stuck in traffic on the way to and from. This year they got lucky. The weather guessers were predicting snow tomorrow, but not today. Today was just cold. And it offered a great excuse to wear gloves.

Which is exactly what Brandon Rashid was hoping for as he locked up his car and walked toward the Galleria mall entrance, lunch box in hand. The store front restaurants in the lower level food court would have been satisfactory for other shoppers and noontime eaters, but that wasn't why Brandon was there today. He wasn't hungry at all, having eaten right before he left home, needing nourishment for the mission.

He hoped the extra weight of the unusually heavy red lunch cooler was concealed by his strength. The added pounds of the gear inside the box made him list slightly to the right, forcing him to grip tighter and adjust his walk slightly to avoid looking awkward and drawing attention to himself. To the shoppers and lunchers, he was just an ordinary guy carrying his noon meal through the slight, cold mist falling on the large parking lot. No big deal.

The automatic door swished open, letting a blast of warmth surround him as he entered the sterile environment of recirculated air and annoying piped music from at least two decades ago. Women with bags and kids hustled around him, zipping in and out of stores as he made his way around the first floor walkway that surrounded the food court below and around toward the glass elevator. The atrium was in the center of mall, the only spot that had three floors, thus the need for the elevator. Mall management had recently built new staircases and rerouted the escalators to make up for a poor original design. Now both the stairs and escalators topped off at the second level, on either side of the elevator. Traffic moved well through the walkway, but it was still full, being the center of activity. A perfect target.

Rashid had noticed the elevator car was on the bottom level, so he tapped the down button and waited. When it arrived, the doors opened and out stepped a young mother and two children: one holding her hand, the other tucked safely inside a stroller.

Safely, he mused. Not today.

Rashid stepped into the elevator, followed by five more shoppers and all their accompanying shopping bags and purses. A lady in front tapped the "1" button and down they went. Rashid always found it amusing that perfectly fit people would ride an elevator down just one floor. He wasn't here for the luxury of a convenient automated ride. He was scoping one last time, making sure he had the right spot.

He did.

At the bottom, the bell dinged and the doors opened, letting the six passengers out. Playing the part of a confused man, Rashid first exited the elevator and then got back on, being careful not to draw too much attention to himself. Back inside, the doors closed and he set the red lunch cooler on the floor of the elevator car, pushing the handle to start the silent timing trigger inside. He had urged his handler to allow him to use a cell phone trigger, where he could call a pre-determined number and the detonator would receive the cellular signal and activate. But they decided it would be too easy to trace the call back to the phone. So a physically-activated trigger would have to do this time. It just meant he had to worry about getting out of range faster.

At the middle level, the doors opened once again, letting more shoppers on. Again, he played the part of the confused man.

"Excuse me," he said as he wormed his way between the new tenants. "Forgot which floor I was on." He sheepishly offered a slight wave back toward the ladies as he disembarked and the doors closed.

Toward the exit he walked, briskly enough to get decent speed, now lighter, but not fast enough to draw attention to himself. He knew he had a couple of minutes to get out.

He quickly found his car, hopped in, and drove as conservatively as his rushing adrenaline would allow, careful not to draw attention.

Shoppers in the elevator and in the immediate area never saw it coming as the red cooler burst open with its destructive power of its contents. The windows shattered, instantly blown out by the flames and pressure of the explosion, as the BOOM tore concrete, glass, and flesh up, down, and across the open space of the atrium. The explosion killed all twelve of the elevator riders instantly, tearing them to pieces in less than a second. The force of the blast also took out six shoppers waiting to board, only the thick closed doors preventing more loss of life. The half open elevator shaft buckled, pitching the car outward before the cable snapped, releasing the carriage to fall crashing to the floor below, trapping three more shoppers and killing two more from the impact and flying debris.

The concussion of the explosion caused glass to shatter all through the atrium, including the large skylight that covered the entire middle section, two stories up. Razor sharp chunks and shards came crashing down, slicing open several patrons who less than five seconds earlier had been enjoying lunch.

6

McAllister's cell phone chirped to life as he wheeled the Saab past the stone pillars at the end of his driveway, happy to be taking the day off. The caller ID showed Willard Stanford.

"Yes?"

"Have you been watching the news?"

"No, I'm just pulling into the house. Why?"

"Turn it on when you get inside and call me back."

McAllister breezed through the kitchen, leaving his computer bag on the island, grabbed the remote for his big screen LCD TV in the living room, and flipped to cable news. The very serious blond beauty queen reporter with her perfect makeup and low cut pink suit showing just the top of cleavage was standing outside what appeared to be a mall, with emergency vehicles behind her, lights flashing. The caption at the bottom of the picture read *Opry Mills Mall, Nashville.*

"The explosion occurred right around noon, as shoppers and the lunch crowd were gathered in the food court. The mall was very busy today, so close to the holidays, the peak shopping season. We are hearing preliminary reports of at least twenty-seven dead and over a hundred wounded from a blast that apparently came from under a table near the center of the food court. Police and emergency personnel have not confirmed that location, but a woman who witnessed the blast said it looked like it originated from the center of the food court."

The screen split to show a male studio reporter with perfect hair and a gray suit with a red striped tie. "Heather, how similar was this incident to the ones we are hearing about from other cities, such as St. Louis, Chicago, Orlando, Milwaukee, and other places?"

"Rick, it appears this explosion is very similar. Obviously, we don't have final death tolls from any of the eleven of the locations, but the explosions at least on the surface seem to be very similar."

McAllister pulled the phone from his pocket and hit talk. Stanford answered instantly.

"What the hell is this?" McAllister asked.

"Looks like a coordinated attack."

"Yes, but who? And why?"

"That part we're still working on. We've pulled the video from all of the malls and are reviewing it right now. Did you see that the Galleria got hit?"

"No, they mentioned St. Louis but not where. Must have been on a different channel. How bad?"

"So far twenty-two, including kids and moms."

McAllister started to boil. "Do we have anything from the tapes yet?" He knew that in most cases there was no actual magnetic tape, since VHS had long been replaced with digital recording in most malls, but the term was still commonly used in surveillance circles.

"Not yet. But if you want to come over and help, that would be appreciated."

"Be there in twenty."

7

Max Preston was sitting up in bed, naked under the covers, remote control in hand as he flipped from station to station, watching the same news and assessing the success of the operation, *his* operation. Despite the excitement welling up from inside him for the past few days, he managed to temper his enthusiasm and sleep in this morning, knowing he would not need to go to the office today. He didn't go in every day anyway, one of the many perks of owning the company. Not that he didn't work hard. He did. He just chose to work from remote locations, thanks to smart cell phones and wireless internet. But today was going to be different. Plans had been put into place months ago that would be coming to fruition today, and he wasn't about to miss it.

The other plans he had for this morning had started out last night. And now the young blond beauty lying naked next to him began to stir, waking slowly from a wine- and sex-induced slumber. Preston had hired Lena Miller six months prior, first as his administrative assistant but with designs on much more. She had quickly accepted his more than generous salary package, and for the first few months her duties were simply admin support. It wasn't until they traveled together to meet a very highly sought-after client that it all changed, just as Preston had planned all along. He'd won the contract and that night celebrated with Lena. A few drinks inside her from the hotel lobby bar was all he needed, ending their night in her suite – shoes, skirt, blouse, bra, panties, all strewn along the floor on the way to the bed. It had been a glorious conquest. He knew it wouldn't last, but that wasn't what he was after. What he wanted was now.

His phone hummed on the bedside table, bringing him back to the present. He recognized the number on the caller ID: Dominic. Preston didn't say anything, just punched the talk button and put it to his ear.

"All accounted for," said the voice on the other end, with a twinge of victory in his tone.

He thumbed the end button and set the phone on the bedside table. Staring past the flat panel television mounted on the far wall, he envisioned the explosions, the fireballs and power, tearing flesh from bone, the screams cut short by shrapnel. It was a glorious vision. A vision of today. A vision of tomorrow. A vision of things yet to come.

His reverie was broken by a soft kiss on the cheek and Lena's gentle breath on this face. She said nothing. Didn't need to. Glancing sideways, he caught sight of her very sly look. She kissed his ear and neck, working her way down his chest as she reached under the covers and gently took hold of him, shooting tingles through his loins.

He closed his eyes. A glorious vision, indeed.

8

Stanford was clicking the mouse and studying the screen in front of him closely, trying to isolate an image, when McAllister entered the room. Full of monitors, computers, keyboards, printers, and televisions, some connected and turned on, some not, the room reminded McAllister of the cross breeding of a genius' brain center and a junkyard.

"Anything good yet?" he asked as he rolled a chair over and sat down next Stanford.

"Nothing obvious," Stanford answered, "but I may have something to work with. A straw, but at least something we can grasp." The image on the screen showed what looked like a half full parking lot. McAllister recognized it as the Galleria because of the highway in the background. "Take a look at this man walking toward the mall entrance." The picture clicked along on stop action, frames spaced two seconds apart.

"What's he carrying?" McAllister asked. "Is that a cooler?"

"I think so," Stanford said as he isolated the piece of the screen capture and zoomed in. The image started out grainy but focus in a few seconds.

"By the way," McAllister said, "any luck with the mystery envelope?"

"Nope," Stanford replied, his eyes still locked onto the screen. "No prints, no DNA from the glue, nothing. My man is still working on the paper, but it's such a common brand and type that it's likely to turn up empty. The typeface was Times New Roman, the most popular font on the planet. And unless we get a hold of the actual printer it was printed on, we won't be able to match any kind of ticks in the print mechanism that might have left distinguishing marks on the paper. It's like tracing ballistics on a gun. You have to have the gun barrel to match to the rifling marks on the bullet."

McAllister glanced at his watch and back up at the screen with the video feed, getting himself back on track. "This happened around noon, right?"

"Yeah."

"And this is the entrance closest to the food court, right?"

"Yep."

"So he could have been carrying his lunch."

"That's what I thought, too, at first. But watch this." Stanford moused the digital slide at the bottom media player into fast forward as cars and people zipped around the parking lot, finally returning to normal speed as he found the spot he was looking for. The mystery man now had his back to the camera, walking briskly away, back down the aisle of parked cars.

"His hands are empty. No cooler," McAllister observed.

"Bingo."

"Where does he go?"

"To that car right there," Stanford replied as the man turned right between two cars, disappeared, and a black Nissan backed out the spot.

"Can you get a lock on the plate?"

"Already took care of it. A friend of mine ran the plate and came back with an address. The FBI is on their way to raid the house as we speak. They'll let us know what they find."

They watched as the car pulled away from the camera and turned right at the end of the aisle, heading toward the mall parking lot exit. Five seconds later, the image shook for a moment before stabilizing. Five more seconds after that, the image turned to chaos as shoppers poured out of the mall.

McAllister's cell began to ring. Ignoring it for a moment, he said, "I think his lunch just exploded." And then he answered the phone.

9

The small brick house sat on a heavily populated street in Maplewood, among a row of similar brick houses spaced close together, all built around 1940. There was a driveway between each pair of houses leading to an alley that ran the length behind. Each house sat slightly above the street, perched atop its own small mound of lawn, the upward perspective making it look larger than it really was. The mounds also made the tiny front yards a bit of a challenge to mow, with their quick incline from the sidewalk. Mowing wasn't an issue this time of year, since it was too cold for the grass to grow, but the slope caused another challenge instead. The FBI raiding team would have to dismount the black van below the level of the house, giving the occupant – if he was home – the tactical advantage of the high ground, a position that would allow him to shoot down on the agents. To partially counter this, the driver pulled the van up in front of the house with the sliding right side door faced away from the house so the agents could egress behind the protection of the large vehicle. It left the driver vulnerable, but it was a chance that had to be taken.

The lead agents dismounted and peeked around the front and back of the van, their black automatic MP5's at the ready, checking the windows of the house for any signs of weapons aimed back at them. Seeing none, they hand signaled to the rest of the team, who fanned out and came around the van, two agents each heading down the driveways on either side of the house and the other four crouch-sprinting up the lawn toward the front door. The front team stopped at the base of the partially-crumbling concrete steps, gave them a quick glance for any obvious signs of trip wires, pressure plates, or other booby traps, and moved quickly and carefully up to the covered front porch, aware that any surface they touched could be rigged to explode. The wooden floor boards sagged slightly under the agents' weight as the "ram man" – the agent carrying the large black battering ram – moved to the front of the pack and got into position by the front door. The lead agent nodded and the ram swung back and then forward, sending the door swinging inside as the frame splintered where the deadbolt lock used to be. Because they were dealing with a bomber, flash bang grenades had been ruled out due to the risk of their pressure triggering any explosives that might be inside the house, killing them all. Banging in the potentially-rigged door was a risk they had to take to get inside.

The agents poured in, splitting into pairs on either side of the open door, weapons raised to firing position, sweeping side to side as their eyes adjusted to the darker interior, the red laser sites strapped under the barrels slicing through the darkness and dust. Stripes of sunlight cut diagonally through the double hung windows, illuminating the small rooms. Immediately in front of the agents was the staircase leading up the second floor. To the left was the living room, to the right the dining room. The living room was furnished with the bare minimum. An over-used, tattered couch sat in the middle, with a lamp sitting on a small table. On the opposite wall hung a fairly new large screen flat panel television, by far the nicest piece of furniture in the room. The gray concrete fireplace in the middle of the far wall lay dark, looking like it hadn't been used in quite a while, if ever.

The dining room had a small oak table and a single chair tucked underneath one end at an angle. An ornate but dusty crystal and gold chandelier hung from the ceiling, its intricate arms and flame-shaped bulbs strikingly out of place in an otherwise drab room.

The black-clothed agents spread out and cleared the house, including the damp, musty basement, until they were satisfied nobody was home and there were no booby traps awaiting the unobservant. The lead agent radioed all clear and was exiting through the front door as Special Agent Tom Davis, a twenty-one-year veteran of the FBI, dressed in khakis and the standard issue blue windbreaker with the letters FBI plastered across the back in bright yellow, met him on the front porch.

"Anything?" Davis asked. Behind him, two of the breaching agents were packing up the van.

"Two of the guys found some wire scraps in the back room that might interest you, but nothing beyond that. No bombs, no explosives. The fridge is cleaned out and the bathrooms have been bleached. I doubt we'll even find any fingerprints, but we might get lucky."

"The explosive-sniffing dogs and forensics are right behind me, about two minutes out. They'll take the place apart. Everybody okay?"

"Not a scratch."

"Good job," Davis said as he thumped the body-armored agent on the shoulder plate and headed inside and past the stairway and into the back room, worming his hands into a pair of latex gloves. The small room would have been completely dark if the agents hadn't turned on the bare bulb hanging from the ceiling. The only window was covered with a black sheet and affixed with electrical tape on all four sides to seal out any sunlight. A wood plank table made from an old door and two saw horses stood on the floor against the far wall, a wood straight back chair pushed partway underneath it. The table was completely empty except for a high-strength brushed aluminum tensor light. This was where the bomb had been made, Davis was pretty sure.

"Gentlemen," he said as he entered, "what do we have?"

"I found this small pile of wires that have obviously been stripped and clipped, in three colors: red, green, and black," said the agent with "Hendricks" on his velcroed nametag. "I also found this. Don't know if it's anything," he continued, holding up a small, slightly twisted, metal half-inch wide sliver between his black gloved fingers.

"At this point, everything is something. We need all the clues we can get." Davis clicked on his small LED flashlight to illuminate the details, took the metal strip, and held it closer to his eyes. As he rotated the shiny strip and changed the angle of the flashlight, an inscription became barely visible. Leaning in closer, he could just make out what looked like Cyrillic lettering, but he couldn't be sure. He neither read nor spoke Russian, so he wasn't positive that was what he was seeing.

A forensics team member entered the room behind him. "Agent Davis?"

"Yes?" he answered, still examining the object.

"We need to get started processing this room."

Davis clicked off the flashlight and turned. "Yes, of course. Bag this and make sure it gets recorded correctly. I'm not sure what it says, but there's some sort of inscription that looks like Russian or something. I don't want to lose this." He hated to let it go, but he had to hand the evidence off to the technician. The chain of custody required that forensics take all the evidence, bag it, seal it, record it, and then process it back at the lab. No steps could be skipped, and everything had to be recorded precisely. Court cases had been won or lost based on chain of custody, leverage clever defense attorneys loved to use to their advantage. Make one mistake in handling evidence and that big flapping sound you hear will be your entire case flying out the courtroom window. "I want this whole house searched meticulously from top to bottom, paying special attention to this room."

"We'll get it all. We even brought the explosives sniffer to look for residue," the technician said with a little too much glee in his eyes for Davis' taste. *Technicians do love their toys.* The grey box the technician was carrying was designed to sniff even the slightest residue that might hint at explosives, past and present, relying on the chemical signature, room temperature, and a whole host of other factors that were way over Davis' head. All Davis knew was that it had cost the Bureau a pretty penny to outfit the team with the device. But he also knew it worked.

"Nice. Call me if you come across anything I need to know about. And let me know when you're done."

By the time Davis walked back out onto the front porch, enough news crews had gathered that the narrow street was blocked as far as he could see in both directions. Satellite dishes on telescoping poles mounted on the tops of the vans stood high above the telephone poles lining both sides of the street. Reporters and camera operators were grouped around the front of a podium set up on the sidewalk, near the end of the driveway. Special Agent Lindsay Greenwood, the Bureau's local public relations agent, was reading a statement as cameras rolled. Dressed in a light brown pants suit, Agent Greenwood had the poise of ten years of professional PR, most of it at the FBI, along with the classic looks of a news anchor, which would have been her other choice of profession to put her communications degree to work had she not decided to enter the FBI Academy right out of college. The Bureau trained her as an agent and then paid for her to go back to school and earn her masters degree in communications, knowing she would be an excellent media representative, which she was. She handled herself confidently and with a smooth wit and smile that always made the reporters more comfortable, increasing the odds of favorable coverage. She knew she couldn't control what the media reported, but she hoped she could at least influence what mood they were in when they wrote it.

Davis' cell rang. It was the office downtown.

"Agent Davis, we just got a report of an abandoned car matching the description of the bomber's car, found about four miles from your location. Local police spotted it. And there's a dead body inside."

10

 Forest Park was its typical bustling self this morning, an unusually warm winter day. Molly sat impatiently on the green park bench, a slight breeze temporarily spoiling the otherwise warm afternoon. Her raven hair was tucked inside a dark green baseball cap, complementing the form-fitting green jacket and jogging pants with white Nikes. She checked her black Ironman digital watch for the third time in the last ten minutes and scanned the area again for any sign of the man she was supposed to meet. Sunday morning joggers, most in man and woman pairs, ran by every few minutes, interspersed with the odd bicyclist.

She had wrestled with whether to come at all. The events surrounding Peter's death – murder – were all so beyond anything she had ever dealt with that she just wanted to go crawl into a hole somewhere and wish it all away. Instead, she decided it was best to get at least a few answers. So she hopped a cab to JFK and found the first non-stop flight to St. Louis, bought a round trip ticket, not knowing exactly when her return flight would be, went through all the extra security measures for walk-up passengers, and found herself landing three hours later in a strange city in the middle of the night. Getting a hotel room by the airport was easy, but she tossed and turned the rest of the night, uneasy about the events of the next day. All she had was a phone number, no name. A man answered when she called, and they agreed to meet right here. So she sat on the park bench, trying to calm herself as she waited for whoever he was to show up.

"Run with me," came a male voice from behind her right ear, the same man as on the phone.

Startled, Molly fought off the urge to turn right around and see the mystery man's face. She'd see it for sure once they got going. She rose and headed right, down the narrow asphalt path divided by a solid white line to allow two-way traffic.

Neither spoke for the first half mile, McAllister slyly checking behind them periodically for any sign of a tail. When he was convinced they were not being followed, he spoke first.

"Who are you?"

"My name's Molly Hindan," she said, stealing only a sideways glance at the man's face. "And I may have some information you need."

"Information for what?" McAllister asked, watching the winding black asphalt trail ahead.

"For the bombings," Molly said, inwardly cursing herself for suggesting they meet while running. Her legs were burning and her shoulders began to ache. The six-month hiatus from jogging was coming back to bite her.

"I don't know what you're talking about."

"Right. Of course not," she said, trying to slow the pace. McAllister kept it up, so she pushed through the pain and pulled up next to him again.

"Why should I care about information about a bombing?" McAllister asked as they passed a set of baseball and softball fields, Interstate 64 farther to their right.

Molly debated her next move as the sweat dripped from her forehead and she wiped it before it got into her eyes. She was absolutely sure she had to tell this man what she knew, but he wasn't making it easy. Did he want her help or not?

"ZEBRA," she blurted out.

McAllister hoped his face didn't reveal the shock he felt inside. *Quick, think of a come back.*

"They have lots of those at the zoo. Should we jog over there while we're here?" he asked, pointing back over this shoulder. "I've heard they have great frozen Cokes. Quite refreshing."

"That's not what I meant, and you know it. Besides, I'm guessing the frozen Coke stands are probably closed in the winter," she added, a smirk across her face.

She was right and McAllister knew it – on both counts. Clever. He finally began to slow the pace as they approached the large, white, squatted hyperboloid Planetarium looming at the top of the hill off to their right. The two runners waited for a car to turn up the driveway and cross in front of them toward the structure before they crossed to the other sidewalk and picked up the pace again.

As they entered a part of the trail that wound through some woods, McAllister finally said, "Tell me about ZEBRA."

"Why should I tell you? You already know all about him."

"ZEBRA's a person?"

"Yes, and you know it."

"I do?" he asked. "How's that?"

She slowed the pace, McAllister followed, and soon Molly came to a stop, her breathing labored, hands on her hips. Between gasps, she said, "He's you."

McAllister stopped and looked past Molly, staring off into space. He hadn't heard ZEBRA in years.

He picked up the pace again. He needed the distraction of running to help him think. How could this woman, Molly Hindan from New York, whom he had never met, know anything about ZEBRA? Who *was* she? What did she have? It didn't make any sense. All the details about ZEBRA were kept under higher than Top Secret clearance, away from the eyes of everyone but a select few of the President's advisors. And even they didn't know the whole story, only enough to make them feel like they did, to boost their egos. It was also by design to make tracking a leak easier. Each advisor was told one lie about the program, so if that detail ever made it outside the inner circle it would be easy to figure out who finked. And kill him.

But here was this total stranger jogging beside him, telling him she knew a code name that was associated with only the most covert of operations. Not even the Director of Homeland Security nor the

Director of Central Intelligence knew about ZEBRA. At least, they weren't supposed to. McAllister hoped his nervousness was adequately concealed by his focus on running while they talked. It was time to dig deeper and see what exactly Molly knew.

"You said on the phone that your fiancé was somehow involved. Explain."

"Well," she said between what were now turning into gasps as her legs continued to burn. "When Peter was killed that awful night after the concert, I didn't accept the official explanation that it was random. The police said it was a senseless crime committed by thugs, but I didn't buy it."

"Why not?"

"First, they didn't kill me, too. Why not? Why only kill Peter? Didn't make any sense. Second, why not rob us? We had just come from a concert, and we were all dressed up – Peter in a suit and I was wearing a nice dress. Even wore heels and stockings that night. We looked like we had money. But they didn't even take Peter's wallet. And my purse was lying next to me when the police arrived."

"How did the police explain it?"

"They said the robbers must have gotten spooked and run away before they had time to steal anything."

"But you don't buy it?"

"Not for a minute. It's too simple an explanation, especially since it would have been easy for them to at least take my purse. Not taking Peter's wallet I understand. He was lying on his back, which means they would have had to flip him over to take it out of his back pocket, but my purse was just lying there." She spotted a bench on the side of the trail up ahead. "Can we take a break?"

"What's the matter? Out of shape?"

"Desperately."

He smiled out of the side of his mouth. "Yeah, we can stop at that bench." He knew that outward body shape was not always an indication of whether someone was in shape. Molly was slim, trim, and beautiful, but it didn't mean her heart was strong. He'd take it easy on her from here on out, as she'd already established enough credibility to take it to the next level.

He slowed the pace to a walk as they neared the bench but continued to stand as Molly plopped down and grabbed the back, breathing heavily, one leg tucked underneath her. Looking around to make sure nobody was following them, McAllister finally sat at the other end of the bench and faced her, his right leg up on the seat. He gave her a moment to slow her breathing before he asked his next question.

"So what do you think happened?"

She looked contemplatively down at the ground for several seconds before raising her eyes right at McAllister.

"I think he was targeted."

"By who?"

She looked away thoughtfully. "That part I don't know exactly, but I'm working on it."

"Well, what's your theory so far?"

"I was hoping you could tell me."

He furrowed his brow. "Why would I know anything about it?"

"Because Peter had your cell number in his speed dial on his cell phone."

"That's what you said when you called me. But that doesn't mean I'd know who killed him."

"No, but it does mean you knew him, something he didn't tell me even after all the brouhaha about the hijacking back in July. You'd think he would have at least mentioned that he knew a national hero."

There was that *hero* thing again. He wished that part would go away. It made his job more difficult.

"Yeah, you'd think."

"Which is why it raised a red flag when I noticed it. Why would he have your number and not at least brag a little back when you were all over the television and internet? I would have."

McAllister looked up as a couple of joggers passed, neither looking down at them.

"Molly, we need to talk more about this, but not here. What are you doing for dinner tonight?"

"Nothing."

"Good. Be at my place at six," he said. "Call me later and I'll give you directions." McAllister continued, "From here we're heading in different directions. You continue down the path until you reach your car, and I'll go the other way. Call me later." And with that, he stood and took off down the path, vanishing from sight in a few seconds.

11

Ten years ago, McAllister's house was in the boonies. But now, Wildwood was a thriving community, very much a part of the St. Louis area. Its charm, however, was still its country feel, and even though tightly spaced subdivisions were popping up all the time, there were still pockets where you couldn't see your neighbors. That's where McAllister lived.

Modeled after a French chateau with a steeply pitched roof and tan stone exterior, the house measured almost five thousand square feet. McAllister had done well for himself in the executive recruiting business and splurged on his biggest luxury, which also happened to be his most expensive and most lucrative asset. If he ever sold it, he'd make a fortune, even in a down market. But selling the house wasn't on his agenda – not now, not ever, so far as he was concerned. With a price tag well over a million dollars for the five-bedroom, four-bath home, complete with a lower level entertainment room with surround sound and plenty of space surrounding the handmade pool table and bar, it was by far his biggest indulgence: a fitting reward for building his own highly successful business. Not one to have much free time, however, McAllister had paid a hefty sum to have the home professionally decorated. What little spare time he had, he wanted to thoroughly enjoy, not waste it on home maintenance or decor, which was why the house was wired top to bottom for multimedia, and every television was large, with surround sound, including HD LCD screens in the master bedroom and downstairs entertainment suite. To McAllister's thinking, there was nothing better to do on a Sunday afternoon than plant himself on the leather recliner couch and watch pro football with a beer in one hand, the massive remote in the other, and chicken wings and nacho chips on the table beside him.

One of the advantages of working for himself was scheduling his own hours. None of his clients worked on Sundays and neither did he, and he tried to limit his traveling to weekdays, with the occasional trip home on Saturday night if he wanted to tack on a vacation day to his business trip. As frantic as his work week schedule dictated, his weekends were his own.

The weatherman had been right – atypical in St. Louis, where locals joked that if you didn't like the weather, wait ten minutes, it would change. And it usually did. Gordon could recall days when the morning started out sunny and seventy degrees and by the evening rush it was in the upper twenties and snowing. Today was yet another example of why being a meteorologist in this town was such a tough gig. But this time it worked out.

As predicted, dark storm clouds had begun to fill the previously clear sky as he left the park and then greeted McAllister in full force as he pulled the black Saab into the garage and closed the door behind him. He was glad for the rain for two reasons. One, it hadn't rained in a while, so the ground was desperate for a good soaking, and two, it would be harder to eavesdrop on the conversation he was going to have with Molly Hindan tonight. Laser microphones, the most commonly used long-range listening devices, worked by tracking the vibrations off of a hard object, in this case glass, and sending them back down the laser beam to the receiver, which translated them into spoken words. Bad weather, especially wind and rain pounding against the window, damped or altered the vibration off a window, wreaking havoc with laser microphones, rendering them virtually useless. The listener might catch a few words here and there but no complete sentences and most likely not enough information to gather anything really useful. Anyone brave enough get in any closer to eavesdrop with a shotgun or parabolic microphone would be picked up by the motion sensors placed seemingly randomly in the yard. The pattern wasn't actually random at all; it was a well-thought-out grid that took full advantage of the layout of the trees in relation to the house and would confuse anyone but the designer, who happened to be a good friend of McAllister's at the National Security Agency.

On his way into the kitchen, he thumbed through the mail he'd picked up out of the box at the end of the driveway. Nothing but bills and some ads touting the fantastic sale at the local electronics store. The ads found the bottom of the trash can, and the bills went with Gordon into his upstairs office off the master bedroom. Satisfied he didn't need to do anything about any of them tonight, he tossed them into the shallow wire basket on his desk to deal with later and logged onto his laptop. He pulled up a seemingly anonymous e-mail that was anything but anonymous and sent it to the printer. Stanford had done his job.

McAllister picked up the pages and began scanning the first sheet, a brief bio of Molly, with her family, education, and job histories, as well as names and contact information for some of her friends and colleagues. Gordon was always amazed at how much personal information is so easily gained through public sources. Stanford hadn't tapped into any secret databases to gather anything the first page revealed about Molly. It was all available online to anyone who took a few minutes to click a few links.

The second page was a bit more revealing, and a little harder to research. Stanford had obviously called in a couple of favors for this one. McAllister sat and read the remaining pages until it was time to start fixing dinner.

Rain pounded against the house as McAllister's cell phone chirped. It was Molly, telling him she was at the gate. Right on time. *Good girl.* He punched the button on the kitchen wall, rechecked to make sure his concealed Walther PPS 9mm pistol was easily accessible under his shirt in his waistband, and stepped into the garage to open the door. He liked the gun because it was fairly light and easily hidden but had enough firepower for most close quarter combat situations. He had chosen the double stack magazine to give him 11 rounds plus one in the chamber, even though it made the grip slightly wider, a bit more of a challenge to conceal but doable nonetheless. He doubted Molly was much of a threat and he didn't anticipate anything more than a conversation tonight, but he'd learned the hard way a long time ago to never underestimate a potential opponent or situation. He punched the door button, and as it slid up, headlights appeared as Molly pulled her blue rental Malibu into the empty spot next to his Saab. She got out, keys only in her hand, and Gordon stepped out of the way to let her inside the house, making sure she was the only one who had come inside before watching the garage door go all the way down. Per McAllister's instructions on the phone, no words were exchanged until they got safely inside the house.

Molly had her hair in an "up do," with a plastic claw clip holding the extra hair loosely against the back of her head, revealing her slender neck, which tapered into a tan blouse and slimming brown slacks, finished off by matching alligator belt and heels. She looked amazing. McAllister had no trouble understanding why Peter had been drawn to her.

"Something smells wonderful in here," she said as he joined her back in the kitchen.

"Thanks. Chicken in the oven – oh, I forgot to ask if that's okay."

"Yes," she smiled. "Chicken is good. I am by no means a vegetarian. I love a good steak."

"Good, me too," he replied. "Vegetables steaming in the microwave, and rolls warming on the stove."

"Quite the domestic servant, aren't you?" Molly said.

"I have moments. But don't tell anyone," he said and winked at her. "Might sully my reputation."

"Right. Our little secret," she said with a sarcastic wink.

McAllister hated small talk, but he didn't want to spook her by being too hard-nosed right from the start. Better to ease into it. Get her comfortable, then ask the questions. He always found it amusing when television and movie cops would play good-cop-bad-cop games with suspects. That rarely happened in real police interviews, but it made for good drama on the screen. Good detectives had discovered a long time ago that the best way to get suspects to confess was to appear to be their best friend, someone trying to help them through this difficult time. It might border on dishonesty, but it usually worked better than grilling them under a hot light. Some of the greatest confessions in criminal history were not the least bit coerced. They just came out and said it.

"I assume you didn't have any trouble finding the place," McAllister said, partially out of a need for more small talk, but also to gauge her intelligence. He had given her excellent directions.

"No, your directions were very good. I just had a hard time looking for an obscure mailbox in the rain in the dark."

"Yeah, it can be tricky, especially in bad weather. Frankly, that's one thing I like about this place. It's out of the way, back in the woods, and hardly anyone knows I'm back here. It's very quiet in the morning. And the trees offer so much shade that I have a relatively low electric bill for the size of house."

"It's plenty big. Do you mind if I take a look around?"

The timer on the stove beeped and McAllister said, "How about after dinner? I'm starving."

"Deal."

He served the meal at the two places he had set at the butcher block island, and as they ate dinner exchanged more small talk with a few innocent-appearing questions thrown in to test the waters. The wine, a 1996 Missouri chardonnay from McAllister's basement wine cellar, was starting to relax them both, but more Molly than Gordon because he was careful to drink lots of water along with it. She wasn't paying that much attention. He wanted to be sharp and not reveal too much as he took her down the road they were about to turn onto. He needed her lucid enough to tell the truth but with defenses lowered enough to reveal more than she might have otherwise. He also needed her to understand everything he was going to say, so she would comprehend the gravity of the situation she apparently had stumbled into. Finally, Molly plunged headfirst.

"So tell me about Peter," she said, locking her eyes with McAllister's. She was far from flirting.

He broke the stare, set his wine glass down, and leaned back in the bar stool. "Tell me what you know first and I'll try to fill in the blanks."

"Oh, no, we're not playing that game," she said. "You're the one who invited me here, so you first." She was not going to be easily swayed.

"You're the one who flew all the way from New York to see me, remember? Besides, I can't tell you anything until I know what you know. Seriously. I'm not trying to be evasive. As you've probably already figured out, this is a serious situation, much more serious than you probably know."

She chewed on his words for a moment before finally saying, "All right, we'll play it your way."

"Good. Start by telling me how you met Peter Jacobs."

Molly launched into the story of how they had met at the bar, the fast engagement, the issues with her father, and how it all came to a crashing end that horrible night in the alley. She shivered when she recalled the details of the murder, what little she recalled. It had all happened so fast.

"Tell me more about Peter's relationship with your father," McAllister probed.

Twirling the stem of the mostly empty wine glass mindlessly, Molly said, "They never really got along, even though I told Peter my dad was only kidding with him. He didn't seem satisfied with that explanation. Every time they were together, which wasn't often enough in my opinion, Peter avoided discussing anything controversial, which I guess included our relationship. They'd always stick to sports or something neutral like that."

"Sports can be pretty controversial, you know. Just ask Yankees and Red Sox fans. Or around here, Cubs and Cardinals fans."

"Yeah, but both my dad and Peter hated the Sox, so that wasn't an issue with them. The hottest debate they ever got into was who was the best Yankees manager of all time. That was usually my cue to leave and go find Mom."

"How did your mom and Peter get along?"

"They were okay, better than my dad and Peter, but not great. My mom was really more concerned about whether I was happy, which I was, so she backed off and let us do our thing most of the time. Of course, she would always pull me aside and remind me that Peter didn't make the kind of money that my dad made, so I had to keep telling her that it didn't matter to me. I was doing fine on my own, and Peter had begun to take some of my investment advice and it had started to pay off for him. I knew when we were dating what kind of financial difference there was between us, and it didn't bother me in the least. We came from two different sides of the tracks and I was okay with that. I wasn't marrying him for his money."

The outside darkness suddenly flashed brilliant light, followed by a clap of thunder only two seconds away. McAllister welcomed the thunder, yet another obstacle for anyone trying to overhear. The rain continued to pound the kitchen window as McAllister caught Molly eye to eye.

"What I'm going to tell you does not go beyond these walls, do you understand?" he asked, locked onto her eyes.

Without breaking eye contact, Molly replied, "Good, that's why I'm here. Tell me what you know."

McAllister had rehearsed this in his mind since the moment he knew Molly was coming to town. What to say, what not to say. How much detail to give her and what to leave out. Stanford had given him enough information to know that she was either not connected to anything about what he was going to reveal, or she had a water tight cover story that even the best in the business couldn't crack. He doubted it was the latter.

"I've known Peter for over twenty years," he started.

Stunned, Molly asked, "You have? How?"

"We worked together."

"That's strange. Peter never mentioned you. Which is why I was so surprised to see your number in his cell phone address book."

"Yeah," McAllister said, "well, we haven't spoken at length in quite a while."

"Where did you work with him? Let's see, twenty years ago he would have been" – she thought for a second – "just out of college. Right after graduation, he went to work for a medical supply company. Is that where you met him?"

Dodging the question, he asked one of his own. "Why don't we move into the living room and discuss this? Refill?" he asked, standing with his wine glass in hand.

"No, thanks, I just want to get to the bottom of this and figure out what the hell is going on," she said as she followed McAllister into the living room.

12

The expansive living room – often called a great room, but Gordon hated that term – started with a wall immediately to the right housing a fully stocked wet bar complete with a mirror in back and hanging glasses. A two-story stone wood-burning fireplace took up the middle of the opposite wall and was hemmed in on both sides by large, stuffed bookcases. The wall that joined them was composed almost entirely of a set of enormous windows that rose from the floor to the cathedral ceiling, its large wood beams meeting at the peak. The fourth wall, the most interior, was open toward the entrance hall. An upstairs hall balcony overlooked the giant room.

McAllister motioned for Molly to sit on the brown leather couch that faced the fireplace, separated by a low, square table. He continued to stand. The fire he had lit before she arrived was starting to die, so he opened the glass doors and set another log on top. He had the option for a gas log when the house was built, but he preferred wood. Seemed more authentic. Sparks rose toward the chimney as he prodded the new log with the poker until the wood all settled together and the fire came back up to full strength. A lamp on the end table at the far end of the couch supplied the only other light in the room.

"Did he tell you what he did for them?" he asked as he turned back to Molly, now seated on the couch.

"He was in medical sales. Traveled all over the country trying to get hospitals to buy his equipment," she answered.

McAllister placed the poker back in the fireside stand and turned back to her again and said, "That's not exactly the whole story."

"What do you mean?" she asked, shifting uncomfortably on the couch, one leg tucked beneath her, not sure if she liked where this was going.

Lightning crackled outside the enormous window. McAllister glanced outside to see if he could spot anyone in the heavily wooded backyard. The flash only gave him a moment, but everything looked clear. Plus his cell phone had not gone off to indicate anyone had tripped the motion sensors.

"That was only his day job. The rest of the time he worked for me."

"As an executive recruiter?"

McAllister chuckled. "Not exactly," he said as sat down on the corner of the low coffee table, facing Molly. He looked her straight in the eyes for a moment before continuing. "You'll probably think I'm off my rocker when I tell you this, but it's all true and I can prove it if you don't believe me."

Molly pulled her legs a little closer to her as she decided how to respond. Did she believe this nut case? Or was she about to learn what she came here for? She could probably make it to her car from here if she distracted him and ran hard enough. It was almost a straight shot from the couch, through the kitchen behind her, and out to the garage. But then she'd have to fumble with the garage and he was pretty well built and would most likely catch up to her. But would he try? What a stupid move it had been to agree to park inside. Now he had her. But, no, she needed to at least hear what McAllister had to say before she decided if he was really crazy or not.

"Yes," she said and nodded. "I came here to find out the truth."

"Good," he said and stood back up and strolled over to the rain-soaked windows, the storm continuing to pound outside. Even though he'd rehearsed the speech mentally all afternoon, he wasn't sure where to begin. The gravity of what he was about to reveal weighed heavily on him. Stanford had run a full background check on Molly and had given McAllister the go-ahead to bring her into the fold, which should have eased his mind, but he was still leery about giving away too much information and exposing the whole operation. He had decided he was only going to tell her what pertained to Peter, and nothing more. But how? How was he going to give her enough detail about only one operation without exposing everything? He went with his gut.

Still facing the window, he said, "What Peter told you about his day job was true, but what he kept from you might have altered your opinion of him and made you change your mind about marrying him.

In fact, we had just spoken on the phone about it earlier in the afternoon the day he was murdered. That's why my number was in his cell, on the just-called list. He didn't know how to balance what he was doing with marrying you and potentially putting your life in danger. I told him it probably wasn't possible to do both and that he needed to make a tough choice about whether his service to his country or his love for you came first."

"His service to his country? What are you talking about?" Molly asked, her eyebrows scrunched.

"Peter was a trained assassin," he said, letting the words hang there as the rain continued to blanket the large window. He watched for her reaction in the reflection in the glass. She looked down and through the coffee table, processing what he had just said, her eyes darting left and right as she grasped for the words.

Finally, her face and body steeled as she looked up and said, "I don't believe you. Prove it."

McAllister turned and took a step toward her but was interrupted by a crack of thunder erupting, followed by the crashing of glass as the window where he'd just stood shattered and crumbled out of its frame. He knew it wasn't the thunder that had blown the window in. Instinctively, McAllister ducked, yanked the concealed Walther from under his shirt, and lunged straight for Molly, landing on top of her to protect her from any additional shots. With half his body still covering hers, he flipped over and pointed the pistol toward the empty window frame, scanning for targets. Satisfied there were none, he bolted up and grabbed Molly by the arm.

"Move!" he yelled as he pulled her toward the kitchen, Molly barely able to keep her feet beneath her.

13

The gun in his right hand and Molly's arm firmly gripped in his left, McAllister sprinted through the kitchen and toward the garage, careful to stay as low as he could while maintaining speed, pulling to keep her down with him. They collided back to front as he stopped abruptly at the closet and threw aside the sliding door. Reaching inside, he smacked the left wall and it swung open, revealing a small cubby containing a black duffle bag. McAllister tucked the Walther back inside his waistband, ripped the bag out of its secret storage, and grabbed Molly's arm again.

Another shot from outside tore through the small window in the back door that led from the yard, shattering the entire pane before thudding into the wall to their left. McAllister glanced at Molly and saw that she was terrified but not frozen. She could move. Once inside the windowless garage, McAllister released Molly's arm.

"Grab whatever you need from your car," he said. "Keys, cell phone, purse, whatever. And hurry! We're not coming back here." While Molly rummaged through the front seat, grabbing her cell phone, purse, and raincoat, McAllister tossed the black bag into the back seat of his Saab and hopped behind the wheel. He already had the engine going when Molly jumped into the passenger seat and slammed the door shut tightly.

"Toss those things on the seat behind you and hang on."

She had barely gotten herself turned back around toward the front when he slammed the car into reverse and blasted through the thin metal garage door, tearing a gaping hole and laying the thin steel open. Out on the driveway, he jerked the wheel to the right, centered the car, slammed the gearshift into drive, and shot down the concrete pavement, guided by his headlights and the low white lights that bordered the pavement – he fondly called them runway lights – down the hill toward the wrought iron gate. He punched the button on the remote to swing the gate open. The car burst through the opening between the stone pillars and out onto the street. He slowed just enough to avoid skidding on the rain slicked pavement and then floored the accelerator as the asymmetrical turbo charged sprang to life under the hood, propelling the sports sedan quickly beyond the 45-mile-per-hour posted speed limit.

McAllister checked his mirrors to make sure nobody had followed him away from the house before he picked up the cell phone and dialed. Stanford picked up on the second ring.

"How come you're calling me on a Friday night? I thought you were having dinner with the lovely Molly," Stanford said nonchalantly.

"Because I just got shot at, that's why."

Now he had Stanford's attention. "What happened?"

"Son of a bitch shot my living room window."

"The big honkin' one?"

"One of them."

"Who did it?"

"Don't know. Didn't have time to ask."

"Where are you now? And how's Molly?"

"She's fine," he answered out of order. "A little shaken up but otherwise okay. We're heading – not sure where. Just had to get away from the house and keep her safe. I'm sure it's raining inside my living room about now. And whoever shot at us might be rummaging through it." McAllister didn't like the idea of leaving his house so fast, but he was prepared in case it happened. Anybody determined enough could get inside if they really wanted to, and now the living room had suddenly become a new, gaping entrance point. But any intruder, no matter how skilled, would have a tough time finding anything of any worth on the espionage front. And good luck getting the laptop off his desk without losing a limb or two. The explosive rigging would probably propel the thief out the window, which led to a three-story drop.

"Did you have the motion sensors set up?"

"Yes, *Mom*! What do you think, I'm an idiot?" he answered incredulously.

Stanford chuckled. "I've been called worse."

"Yeah, by me," McAllister answered, grateful to have a little levity infused in the conversation.

"I was still up anyway, figuring I'd hear from you after dinner. Why don't you head over to Raven and I'll meet you there in about thirty minutes. Should give me enough time to gather some things."

"See you there," McAllister answered and flipped the phone closed. He set it down in the center console and stared out between the swishing wiper blades into the black night. After several minutes, Molly broke the silence.

"Okay, so what just happened back there, besides the obvious, that we got shot at? Who shot at us?" she asked tentatively.

"I'm still trying to piece it together." How did the shooter get inside the perimeter? Why didn't the sensors pick him up? McAllister was sure his cell had not failed to receive the signal. "The shooter must have shot from long range, a hard shot in good weather, but almost impossible in a storm if he wanted to be even reasonably accurate."

"You mean like a sniper?" Molly asked.

"Yes," he answered, his attention divided between the road ahead and what had just played out.

"You're telling me that a sniper almost shot me through a window in the middle of a rain storm in a city I just arrived in while I was sitting in the living room of a man I just met and hardly know?" she protested.

"That pretty well sums it up, yes."

Molly leaned back in the tan leather seat, one hand on her forehead, the other still tightly gripping the door armrest, and stared out the side window at the trees whizzing by, the rain streaking the glass. More glass. She couldn't get the image out her head of the large pane shattering and falling into the living room, McAllister lunging toward her. To protect her? She wasn't sure, but she guessed so, since he did get her safely out of the house. But now what?

"Where are we going?" she finally asked the side of McAllister's head.

"To meet a friend."

"One who won't shoot at me?"

"Not yet, anyway," he said, his mouth curled slightly in a smirk.

14

The rain had diminished to drizzle as they crossed over the border into Franklin County and headed west out a winding two-lane state highway. Many ups and downs later, they turned left onto a gravel road, the headlights splitting the darkness and reflecting off a cave of tall, dark trees. They emerged on the other side to find a long, sloping gravel driveway heading off to the left. A two-story, white farm house sat down the hill at the far end of the drive, a single argon lamp perched high atop the main power pole illuminating the corner of the house and the base of the gravel drive. Off to the left about a hundred yards, lay a five-acre pond, the surface disturbed by the rain drops and wind. A barbed wire fence supported by wood posts ran the length of the right side of the drive, an open field with tall grass beyond leading to the woods.

As they slowly approached the house, one window was illuminated from within, a light on in the kitchen. Gravel crunched under the wheels as the car ground to a stop inside the carport, away from the glare of the outside light. McAllister grabbed the black bag out of the back seat and they headed inside the side door that led from the carport.

Stanford was inside the narrow entrance hall, gun drawn, as they entered. Molly's breath caught when she saw the gun pointed at her, the barrel looming larger than life. Stanford quickly lowered the weapon and tucked it into the concealed holster on his belt.

"You must be Molly," he said, smiling. "Sorry for the start. Had to be sure it was really you. I'm Willard Stanford, Gordon's keeper," he said, smiling as he reached his hand out to her.

She took it. "Nice to meet you, I think." She was still reeling from the last two days and felt like she was about to be overwhelmed. Everything inside her told her she was way in over her head, that she needed to run as fast as she could and not look back. But to where? Where would she go? Why give up now? She was determined to get to the bottom of all this, no matter how wacky it got.

The entrance hall dumped into the kitchen, rustic but modern, with older but functional appliances. Straight ahead was a hallway that led to first floor bedrooms and stairs leading to the second floor. To the left was a large living room with windows wrapping around the left and far sides and a wood burning stove in the far left corner and a dormant ceiling fan. McAllister set the bag on the kitchen table and motioned for Molly to follow him into the living room, where she sat on the couch and he chose the wing chair cattycorner.

"I was going to give you the long, drawn-out version," he started, "but my timetable just got a swift kick in the pants, so I'll cut to the chase. In the late eighties, President Reagan saw a growing trend in terrorism and a need to put together a team that was dedicated strictly to stopping it and, more importantly, from letting it spread to the United States. You see, prior to September 11, the US had never been attacked on our own soil. We'd been attacked overseas before: Beirut, Africa, and so forth. But never here. The President didn't want to see that happen. But he knew there wasn't a lot of support in Congress to either form a new branch of covert operations on the books or add another role to an existing organization, such as the CIA or the military."

"Why not?" Molly interrupted. "Didn't anyone see the growing threat?"

"Not really. The President saw it, of course. He understood it better than anyone. But the folks in Congress didn't believe him, and the American people felt safe enough that he knew he'd never get enough pressure on senators to get anything passed. We were still fighting the Cold War with the Soviets, which was where everyone's focus was. Nobody was watching the Afghans or the Middle East very closely."

"But it was on the news all the time."

"Yes, which is how a lot of intelligence is gathered. But you have to remember, the US intelligence agencies only have so many assets at any given time, and during the Cold War the majority of those assets were tasked to battle the Soviets. They were our main enemy. The President realized the uphill battle he was fighting and knew it couldn't be won through the normal channels, so he launched an expedition to see how he could fight both the Soviets and the terrorists while not burdening the CIA or NSA with additional responsibilities. Remember, we didn't have Homeland Security at the time. That came much later.

"He finally figured out the only way was to go behind their backs. See, the CIA is legally restricted from conducting operations inside the borders of the United States. All their activities have to be overseas or at least outside our borders. Inside the US is the FBI's territory, but they don't officially dabble in intelligence gathering unless it pertains to a crime. Terrorism is not a crime. It's an act of war, which is beyond the FBI's jurisdiction. So what do you do about it, you might ask. The answer is pretty complex. But what you *don't* do about it is try to persuade Congress to appropriate more money for another quote" – he made the symbols in the air – "'war' if all your resources are focused on the first war and nobody believes there's a need for anything else. In fact, you could argue that we actually helped them because we were funding their anti-Soviet efforts in Afghanistan and other places without thinking about what might happen if the Soviet threat ever stopped, because nobody thought it would. We never saw the disbanding of the Soviet Union coming until it happened. And because we were so focused on the Soviets, the terrorists were getting their organizations funded and ready pretty much unnoticed."

"Until September 11," Molly interjected.

"No, even before that," McAllister explained." The bombing of the Marine barracks and the US embassy in Beirut in 1983 caught his attention first. He knew something had to be done. But when the

President figured out he couldn't go to Congress and get another black ops group approved, he formed his own, with only a handful of people knowing about it."

"How?" Molly asked. "Wouldn't somebody notice it? I work with money all the time and know that accounting folks are too detailed to just overlook an entire organization, even if it is the government."

"You'd think, wouldn't you? Well, he knew he couldn't keep it a secret very long. What would happen to his presidency if someone discovered he was funding an off-the-books covert ops team without Congressional oversight? A lot of black operations take place, but at least someone in Congress knows about them."

"So what happened? Did it get blown?"

"Yes, but on purpose. After a couple of successful operations, the President decided to cover his ass and get at least some semblance of Congressional approval for the group. So he told a couple of key members of the Senate Intelligence Committee and the House Appropriations Committee just enough detail to make them feel a part of something without letting them in on too much, so he could still operate covertly and have control."

"So what exactly does this group do? I thought it was against the law for the United States to assassinate people."

McAllister glanced sideways at her, hoping she was kidding. She wasn't. "I didn't say this group was totally legal, did I?"

Her hands twisted nervously. "Is that where you and Peter come in?"

"Not yet," answered Stanford as he suddenly materialized, leaning against the archway between the kitchen and living room.

"Perimeter set?" McAllister asked his close friend.

"Sensors up and running," Stanford answered and then circled back to the topic at hand. "You see, Molly, neither of them was old enough to be involved yet officially when the group was organized, but we'd already identified them as potential operatives. So when the time came, we recruited them."

"How did you know you wanted them?" Molly asked, shifting her glance between the two men.

"That," Stanford said, "we can't tell you. It's a rather unconventional recruiting method, one that would not pass muster in any other government departments. So it remains our little secret."

Molly stared through her feet as she digested all that she had just heard, her mind racing back through the events since she landed at the airport and met this mysterious man in the park who was now sitting beside her on a couch in the living room of a farm house in middle-of-nowhere Missouri after being almost killed with a sniper's bullet that had come flying at them through a pouring rain. It would not have made much sense, would have been way too far fetched, except for the part about getting shot at. That part was very real.

"So, let me ask you, Miss Hindan," Stanford said, moving into the room and taking a seat in the chair on the opposite wall. "Why did you feel the need to hop on a plane and fly all this way just because Gordon's number was in your fiancée's cell phone directory? Seems like an awful lot of trouble and expense just to put a face with caller ID."

Molly folded her hands on her knees and looked at them both. The wood stove crackled and popped in the corner, its heat losing the battle to keep Molly from shaking ever so slightly, yet her palms sweating as she wrestled her fingers together.

She took them back through the events the night Peter was killed. The concert, the walk back to the car, the discussion about her dad and Peter's unease with their differences, and finally the murder, closing her eyes as she described the scene after he had been killed.

"After I came to, I looked around to see if they were still there, to make sure I was safe. They were gone, and the alley was eerily quiet. I had fallen on some trash bags, so I struggled to push myself to my feet, but as I was trying to get up I saw Peter. He was lying on his back, a giant open cut across this throat, and blood everywhere. Some of it had gotten on me, on my hands and face. I was wearing black, so it wasn't until later than I discovered blood on my clothes, too. I found my purse, grabbed my cell phone, and called 911." Tears began to well up in her eyes. McAllister snatched a tissue from the end table and handed it to her. "Thanks. I'm sorry I'm such a mess."

"It's okay," McAllister said, not sure whether to try to comfort her or let her be. "Take your time," was all he could come up with.

Molly dabbed at her face, wiping tears from under both eyes, and returned to the story.

"I wanted to hold Peter, to comfort him, but I knew I shouldn't touch him since he was evidence. I tried to move as little as possible to preserve the scene."

McAllister and Stanford shared a look. This was one smart lady.

She continued. "When the police arrived, I told them what little I knew, since I'd been knocked unconscious. It wasn't much to go on. I never saw a face, couldn't say how tall the attackers where, didn't have much to tell them."

"You said there were attackers? Plural?" McAllister asked, glancing sideways at Stanford.

"Yes, two. One came right at Peter while the other came after me. It all happened so fast there may have been more than two, but I only saw two. Anyway, my father came and picked me up from the precinct and took me home to their house. There was no way I could stay in the city after what had just happened. I was too upset. And confused. Why would anyone want to attack Peter? What had he done? And why leave me alive?"

Survivor's guilt. The questions, the burden, the feeling doubly sorry for the person or people who died. *Why them? Why not me? How come I get to live while they got killed?* McAllister was fully acquainted with it. More than one operation had gone bad, leaving somebody dead and others alive. He'd seen it twice himself. Only for Molly, it was from the victim's standpoint. She never fired a shot, didn't stab anyone, wasn't left holding the bloody garrote as the target gasped for air while your partner lay bleeding to death ten feet from you and there's nothing you can do but get mad. Molly didn't have that luxury.

Stanford leaned forward in his chair, cupping his hands together and asked, "Why did they leave you alive? Why not just kill you too and make sure there were no witnesses?"

"That's what I've been asking myself. I've been playing that question over and over in my head. It doesn't make any sense to me either. Why only kill Peter when they know I could easily identify them?"

"But you can't," McAllister said. "You just said you didn't get a good look at them."

"Yeah, but they don't know that," Molly answered. "So far as they know, I got a good look and could pick them out of a lineup."

"No, I'm pretty sure they're confident you can't." Stanford shifted forward. "Didn't you say you were lying face down and hit on the back of the head?"

"Yes."

"They did that deliberately. These guys aren't amateurs; they're trained killers. They know all the tricks. They're ruthless to a point, but then they hold back. They're not just a couple of thugs. They may have wanted to kill you, but then their training kicked in and they couldn't do it because you're an innocent life. Peter was their target, not you. Pardon the expression, but you were an inconvenience, a hiccup in their plan."

Molly was floored. "So you're saying that these cold-blooded killers aren't monsters? That the men who slit Peter's throat in a dark alley in the middle of New York City and left him for dead simply knocked me unconscious into a pile of garbage bags because they lived by some sort of code of conduct? Like they had a conscience?"

"Not a conscience," Willard clarified. "Training. Which leads me to believe they aren't rogue operatives. They're probably ex-military and still report to someone inside the government or at least someone who used to be. Like a former military commander. See, trained soldiers don't kill indiscriminately. They take out their targets and leave everyone else alone. Sometimes collateral damage can't be avoided, but when it can be, it is. Soldiers don't like to kill civilians. They'd rather leave them alone and just take out the military targets only."

This was all getting a lot bigger than Molly anticipated. She was losing control and hating it. Peter, a military target? But why? Rogue – or not, if Stanford was right – agents committing murder in a dark alley? It all seemed so surreal to her. Like a movie. Things like this didn't happen in real life, did they? And they didn't happen to her. She had a nice little existence. Good job, loving soon-to-be husband, great family. But now Peter was dead and she was about to enter his bizarre world, a sphere unknown to her and, so far, unliked. These things happened to other people. Not that she would want them to happen to anybody, but she'd find it easier to believe if it were someone else.

"So you're saying they left me alive but unconscious because I was in the way?" she asked.

"More or less," McAllister shrugged, his eyebrows raised. "Wrong place, wrong time, right attackers. But if you'd seen anything, or they at least thought you did, you wouldn't be sitting here tonight."

"They'd have slit your throat and left you for dead, too," Stanford added for emphasis. It was about time this girl understood the severity of her situation. The water was about to get deeper.

"But why did they kill him?" Molly finally asked.

"That, my dear," Stanford answered, knowing his age allowed him a certain level of latitude, "is the reason we're all sitting here, isn't it? Every crime has to have two elements: motive and opportunity. Take either one away and you don't have a crime. The dark alley late at night was the opportunity, but what was the motive? Have the police found anything?"

"According to the detective I spoke with before I left, they don't have any clue as to why. All they know is how. They're running his bank accounts, interviewing co-workers and family, all the typical things. But so far, nothing. No motive."

"I guarantee you," Gordon said, "there's a motive somewhere."

15

Faint blue light illuminated the face driving the speeding dark blue rental sedan as the Blackberry's GPS screen scrolled, showing the car's progress down the state highway. Dominic Rippon's plane had landed only hours before and he was already in pursuit of his target. He'd been careful as usual not to leave a trail. From LAX, he'd flown into Salt Lake and Dallas before finally setting down in St. Louis, each stop designed to reduce his chances of being followed. The pseudonym he traveled under, Chad Burnside, rented a car, checked into the hotel, and used his credit card to pay for gas and an early dinner. Cash would have been too obvious in this case, and the alias allowed the transactions to be untrackable to a real person, much less him.

Getting into position at the target had been tricky. Following Ms. Hindan out to McAllister's house had been the easy part. She was an unsuspecting amateur and didn't have any idea he was behind her. Once she'd driven up McAllister's driveway, Rippon simply drove past, found a dirt road nearby, pulled out his Blackberry, slung the hard black plastic case containing the rifle over his shoulder, and worked his way on foot through the rain around the edge of the property until he had a good view of the back of the house. Despite the cold, the rain allowed him easier egress to his position, as the moisture had softened the brittle leaves underfoot and the downpour muffled any other sounds as he made his way carefully along the back of the property. Aerial photos from an online satellite service had been enough to find out where the property lines were drawn and which way the house buried in the woods faced. All he had to do was get back there and set up. Though he couldn't see them, he knew McAllister had motion sensors set up all over the property. He was no fool. So Rippon dared not venture too close to the house. To avoid this, he brought along his favorite toy, a silenced Springfield .308 sniper rifle, a weapon with more than enough range to cover the distance between his perch and the back of McAllister's house. *And right through the front of his head.*

Except he had missed.

He'd done everything right until that agonizing split second between the trigger pull and the bullet leaving the gun. The scope was centered correctly he knew, because he had already practiced the shot back in California. The cross hairs were firmly planted on the target's head, McAllister's thoughtful stare so close to the shooter's eye, floating deep into the woods. Rippon slowed his breathing as his right index finger found its way to the rigid trigger, lightly grazing the inside of the first knuckle as it settled against the cold metal. Slowly and methodically, he squeezed the curved trigger toward his palm, finding the familiar break point where the mechanism would free the firing pin. The trigger tugged gently against the release point, snapping the firing pin into the back of the large bullet, the gun bucking only slightly as bullet and gas hurdled down the barrel, spinning rapidly clockwise to maintain accuracy and velocity.

What Dominic couldn't have planned for was the sudden wind gust that caught the gun and the bullet just as it left the end of the barrel, moving its trajectory ever so slightly right, just far enough to miss its mark and strike harmlessly into the large window. The shattering was spectacular, but Dominic hadn't fired to make special effects. He'd fired to kill his target, who was now more than aware of his presence.

Rippon had counted on McAllister's not trying to find him in the pouring rain, especially when it would mean leaving the girl behind unprotected, an easy secondary target. So when he saw them move together to the mud room, Dominic reset and slid a new round into the bolt. Taking aim again, he launched a second bullet toward the back of the house, this one entering the small window in the back door, but thumping innocuously into the wall inside, missing both human heads.

After McAllister's car smashed through the garage and headed toward the street, Dominic considered altering his plans slightly and pillaging the house for any information he could find, but he was under strict orders to follow and do whatever it took to kill him, collateral damage or not. So he slogged back through the rainy woods to his car and was now following the GPS coordinates to a place he knew only as Raven, a farmhouse with four outbuildings somewhere out in the middle of fucking nowhere.

As he drove, he continued the never-ending conversation in his head that had begun the day he met Max Preston – the one about why in the world he let that arrogant son of a bitch push him around instead of killing him when he had had the chance so many times. At any moment, he could snap his neck and feel it crumble between his hands, or take him out with a bullet to the skull from a hundred yards and get away without a clue. Yet every time Preston called, he dutifully obeyed and did exactly what he was told, like a fucking lap dog. Of course, his real loyalty lay in the payoff. Preston had so far made good on every monetary promise and had financed every operation with plenty of play money as added incentive. Rippon was financially well situated to retire anytime he wanted. But he knew that Preston would never allow his secrets to outlive his payroll, making Dominic very aware that he had a choice. Be an asset or a liability. If he retired, Preston would have him killed, sure as the sun set in the west. Dominic wasn't concerned about his own ability to stay alive against Preston; it was Max's minions that made him nervous. He knew Max had other agents working all over the country, but he didn't know how good they were or where they operated. That was how Preston had been so successful for so long: spread out the network so nobody knew what the others were doing. Only Max Preston saw the whole picture. Everyone else only saw their slice.

Finally, he found the obscure road and turned slowly down the gravel lane. In his headlights appeared the end of the driveway, but he dared not turn down it, for fear that this place also contained motion sensors. He tucked the car under an overhanging willow, killed the engine, and covered the remainder of the distance on foot, gray gravel crunching under his black boots. He stayed as close to the side of the narrow road and on the grass as possible, both for concealment and noise deadening. At the top of the driveway, he nestled into the underbrush beside a large maple and pulled a pair of small but powerful binoculars out from the pouch he had slung on his side. As he peered through the lenses, light shown through the curtains of the farmhouse four hundred yards away, but he couldn't see any movement. That didn't mean no one was home; it just meant he couldn't see them. He switched to thermal mode and found what he was looking for: three warm bodies showing up bright red against the various cooler colors of the rest of the house. The room with the heat signatures glowed warmer than the rest of the house, which Rippon figured out must have been from what appeared to be a stove on the left side. The oval object glowed the hottest, a bright red bordering on faded pink, its narrow pipe exiting out the roof, the cold outside air quickly cooling the smoke. He scanned the area surrounding the house for other warm signatures, the telltale sign of additional personnel, but only the Saab in the carport registered any heat, which was dwindling fast against the cold outside temperature.

As he surveyed the distance to the house, just enough ambient light shone to give him a hint of what lay between his current position and the target. The satellite photo had also given him a detailed layout of the farm, with distances measured from building to building. He could go back to the car and get his rifle to take a long shot, but he wasn't sure which of the digital red shapes inside the house was McAllister. And he knew he only had one shot, so he had to be right the first time. A one-in-three chance was not good odds in an operation that demanded absolute certainty. Hitting the wrong target wouldn't do him any good. He wasn't getting paid to kill anyone but McAllister, who had already shown he was too quick and too good to allow him a second chance. Miss him with the first shot and he might not get another. The fiasco back at the house had proven that, an experience Rippon wasn't interested in repeating.

For a fleeting moment, Dominic considered moving in closer but chose instead to back off and head back to the car. Much as he would have liked to stay and finish the mission tonight, he knew McAllister and whoever else was in the house had the advantage. Despite the dark and the weather conditions, surprise would not be on his side, and the distance to the house was too great to risk being spotted before he was ready to attack. For now he would have to be satisfied with a recon and back off tonight to formulate plan B, whatever that ended up looking like. Slowly, he edged his way from the top of the gravel driveway and back to his car.

16

Traffic was always bad in DC, made worse by the forecast of an approaching snow storm, the kind that always shut down the entire city. The slightest hint of impending snow was enough to paralyze the entire metro area and bring the entire government to a screeching halt. The outside temperature had been steadily dropping all afternoon, and now as the evening set in and the sun went down, it plummeted even faster until the freezing mark came and went.

Senator Franklin Stevens' limousine crawled along the slick streets as the rain began to change to snow, the large white flakes landing on the darkened bullet-resistant windows and evaporating instantly from the heat inside, turning them into water droplets that slid silently down the glass. The senator sat back in the black leather seat, nursing a scotch he'd poured for the long drive to his house in Georgetown. Since he had to be back on the chamber floor in the morning for a crucial vote on a new appropriations bill, one that he had co-authored with Bill Hodges, the senior senator from Minnesota, he had considered curling up on the leather couch in his office to save himself the slow drive in the morning. But he'd already spent enough nights on the couch and needed to get home and spend at least one night this week in his own bed. Besides, with the weather being what it was, the vote might get postponed and he would have to make the drive home anyway. Washington was notorious for a lot of things, one of them being its propensity to wimp out in bad weather. Government departments would shut down at the mere hint of impending bad weather. Add actual snowfall and the whole city shuts down. Stevens always found it ironic that "non-essential" services would get shut down during those times. *If they're so damn non-essential, why are we paying for them in the first place?*

Stevens and Hodges had been friends since the day Hodges took office after a long battle, including a recount that was finally certified by the Minnesota secretary of state after almost three long months of controversy. Way back almost thirty years ago, Stevens recalled as he settled into the plush leather back seat and sipped on a freshly-poured scotch. It had been a long road since then, through several administrations, tremendous upheaval in the junior senator ranks, scandals of all sorts on both sides of the aisle, wars, conflicts, peace. Through it all, their professional and personal relationships had grown stronger. Their wives had become best friends, spending time together whenever their husbands were taking care of governmental business. Christmas was usually spent with both families in either snowbound state.

This bill was the latest in a long list of legislation the two had introduced together, a list so long neither one remembered how many they had accumulated. Most bills failed, as the majority of legislation does, but a few had seen the light of day, though highly modified once they made the arduous journey first through the House of Representatives, where the process was officially started and taken through committee and voted on, then to the Senate, where it was chewed apart again and usually spit out in a form neither senator recognized anymore, back to the House if needed, and finally to the President, if it had the necessary votes, for signing or veto, usually the former.

But that business had been concluded for tonight, as the senator listened to the sounds of city muffled by the thick limo doors, the hissing of the tires as cars and trucks made their way home or to more work. He reached for the radio to turn on the top of the hour evening news break when his cell phone chirped. He pulled it from his coat pocket. The caller ID showed a blocked number.

"Hello?"

"We have a problem," said the disembodied voice on the other. It was familiar, but he hadn't heard it months.

Stevens tightened his grip on the phone and said, "What is it? Can you take care of it?"

"Yes, I can take care of it. BISON's girlfriend showed up and is talking to ZEBRA."

"I thought you got rid of her!" Stevens spat into the phone. "She wasn't supposed to be a problem anymore."

The tone on the other end was far from apologetic. "The team didn't think it was necessary at the time. We thought she would never suspect anything."

"Well, that's changed now, hasn't it?" Stevens was furious but wasn't going to lose control. "Get rid of her. I don't care how you do it, just make sure it can't get tied back to me. Do you know where they are?"

"Yes, we have them tracked and are just waiting for the opportune time."

"Call me when it's done," Stevens said. "In the meantime, I don't want to hear from you until everything is in place. Got it?"

"Yes, sir."

Stevens stabbed the keypad to disconnect. *Damn it!* The last thing he needed now was a complication.

17

"There's more to this that you need to know," McAllister stated, as he rose from his seat, grabbed a mug off the table, and lifted the coffee pot from atop the wood stove. "Peter wasn't the only one of our group who was murdered. In fact, he was the last of three agents who were killed in the same week."

"Three?" Molly asked. "How many of you are there?" This was getting beyond her imagination. What had she walked into?

Stanford fielded this one. "If you count the three dead agents and Gordon, there were six agents and me. Now three are dead, one is standing right there" – he pointed to McAllister – "and there are two unaccounted for."

"What do you mean 'unaccounted for'? You've just lost them?"

"More or less," Stanford continued. "See, this group of agents isn't like your typical covert ops team. Each agent works fairly autonomously, spending most of their time working their real jobs – their covers – and only being used for covert ops on an as-needed basis. In other words, it's not a full-time gig. And we don't talk to each other except when there's a job to be done."

McAllister picked up the story. "These particular agents disappeared before the killings. And because everyone else was still alive, we didn't think too much about it. However, now that half the team has been murdered, we're worried that either the missing agents are dead and we just don't know it yet, or they are the ones doing the killing."

"But if that's the case, why?" Molly asked. "Why would they want to kill their fellow agents? They have to have a motive."

"Very true," McAllister answered. "Which is why we're still wondering what really happened to them. So far, we don't know why, which is the most perplexing part of all. Why were our agents targeted? Who is killing them? Or why are they killing each other, if that's what's happening?"

Molly stood and smoothed her pants legs. "I may have something that will help us figure this all out." She headed toward the door.

"Where are you going?" McAllister asked apprehensively, stepping toward her.

Molly smiled. "Hey, secret agent man, I'm just going to the kitchen to get my purse. Relax," she said and stepped around him. When she reached the kitchen table, she opened her purse and pulled out a small envelope, which she handed to McAllister, who had followed close behind her in case she pulled out a gun.

"What is this?" he asked, feeling through the white paper before lifting the unsealed flap.

"It's a file."

He opened the flap and extracted a small digital disk with no label. "Of what?"

"That's a great question. It must be encrypted because I can't get it to open."

"Did you try?" Stanford asked.

"What do you mean, did I try?" she asked incredulously. "How do you think I know what it is?"

Stanford laughed. "No, no, that's not what I mean. What computer did you use to access the disk?"

"My home computer. Why?"

"Because," McAllister said, "you may have tipped off the owner of the disk that you have it."

"What do you mean?"

"Some sensitive data is not only encrypted but also contains an auto-launch program that starts immediately when someone tries to access the file. It sends a signal to the file's owner that someone else has tried to open the file, complete with a traceable IP address so the owner can figure out who has the disk and find the location of the computer and, therefore, the user. Often it's done in such a way as not to alert the person who is accessing the file. Next thing you know, someone is shooting up the coffee shop or wherever you try to access the file."

"So you're saying someone knows I have the disk."

"Yes, which may explain how they knew you were at my house tonight. They probably followed you all the way from New York, hoping you would lead them to me, which you unwittingly did. How did you get it?" McAllister had no idea how many people were pursuing Molly, so he had to play it safe and assume it was a team.

"It was in my purse when I got home after Peter's murder. I didn't notice it until I went to change purses the next morning."

"So Peter wanted you to have it for some reason," McAllister said. "Like there was something on it you needed to know."

"But why would he give it to me?" Molly asked. "He didn't know he was going to get killed, did he? He sure didn't act like it."

"No," McAllister said, "he probably didn't know he would get killed, but he may have given it to you as an insurance policy in case he did. I bet there's something on there that will lead us back his killer."

Wise Stanford chimed in, "Listen, it's been a long day and we're probably not going to solve this riddle tonight. So why don't we all hit the hay and get a fresh start in the morning. The security traps are set up outside, and Gordon and I will take turns pulling guard duty."

The three agreed and decided to turn in for the night. Molly got set up in the upstairs bedroom, the only room with a bed and real furniture. With all the excitement from the evening, plus what she had learned at the house, she was afraid she wouldn't be able to sleep, but within minutes sleep took hold and she drifted off into a deep slumber.

Knowing they were now very visible targets, McAllister and Stanford set up a watch rotation for the night, three hours apiece. Stanford would keep watch first while McAllister tried to get at least a little sleep. He reclined on the couch and was soon snoring away. But he was far from settled. The dream came sweeping over him again.

He hunkered down in the bottom of the dry creek bed, the edge of the tall pine forest behind him and the target ahead. The two-story log cabin sat in the clearing, surrounded by pines but itself a stark isolated structure, exposed entirely on all four sides. This was not a mistake. The design had called for an easily defensible structure positioned in such a way as to allow concealment from a low angle but enough room around the house to land a helicopter. The woods had been cleared back to just behind the creek, which ran strong in the winter and spring but was now dry from the summer heat. McAllister had made the dash from the tree line to his current position on his back against the dry bank, grass tickling his neck as he lay silent listening for any stirrings from the cabin. Surely someone had spotted him. It had been too easy to get this far unnoticed. Even though he had another fifty or so yards to cover, he was way too close in his own opinion. If he'd been on the cabin's security team, he'd have killed him by now. What were they waiting for? It was all too strange.

He turned onto his belly on the dry grassy slope and poked his head above the ground, just high enough to see the cabin. It was quiet. Not a soul in sight. A black SUV parked on the gravel driveway by the side of the structure told him someone was home, but nobody poked their heads out, and the curtains were drawn on all the windows. The cabin, constructed from large logs, was completely symmetrical, square on both top and bottom, and divided by a wood-rail balcony that wrapped all the way around all four sides, creating a shadowing overhang above the first level porch. On each side, a wood stairway led from the lower porch up through the floor of the second level.

McAllister assessed the situation, scanned one more time for sentries – none, weird – and hoisted himself up over the bank and at a dead run toward the closest porch. Completely exposed, he ran his hardest, head down, sure he was going to be seen any moment, until he reached the relative safety of the porch, where he stopped abruptly and nestled his back up against the cabin wall, panting, his heart racing. His breathing back under control, he defocused for a few seconds as he listened for the slightest sounds, indications that someone had been tipped off to his presence. There were none. He edged to his right toward a window with a low sill, the glass covered on the inside by a tan cloth drapery.

Someone was near him. He felt it. Looking up to his left, he saw the tall man at the top of the stairs looking down at him, the machine gun at his side rising into firing position. McAllister raised his gun and let off three quick rounds, sure he had sighted his target in accurately. But nothing happened. His gun had fired, but the man was still standing there, the machine gun coming into line to spit its deadly metal Gordon's way.

He turned and dashed to his left, his shoes pounding on the wood plank porch as rapid fire rounds split the boards behind him. Between the gun fire and the clomping of his run, he was sure whoever was inside knew he was there now. He rounded the corner of the cabin, gun up and ready, and saw another staircase halfway down the porch. He reached the bottom, looked up, and was greeted by another machine-gun-toting shooter. Once again, bullets sprayed behind him as Gordon changed directions back to where he started.

Pinned. Caught between two shooters, both wielding fast weapons from the high ground, an automatic advantage in almost any fight. What to do? *Go either way and I'm dead. Stay here and I'm dead.* McAllister looked up. The boards were thick enough to support weight, but would a bullet from a pistol penetrate? Footsteps above him offered the chance to find out. McAllister rattled off three more quick rounds into the floor of the porch above him. But again, nothing happened. Like he was firing blanks. The popping sound of the gun rang out in his ears, the weapon kicked from the bullet – but no holes appeared in the wood.

In his peripheral vision, he saw the gunman from his right descending the staircase, so he swiveled that way and leveled his weapon, again kicking off rounds – and hitting nothing. The marksman kept coming as he raised his machine gun. McAllister's pistol sent flying more rounds, until the slide locked back, indicating the magazine was empty. Out of bullets.

The machine gun coughed its rounds toward McAllister, the flashes indicating a quick death to its target.

McAllister awoke with a start. Welcome air raced into his lungs as he bolted upright and gasped. Blinking himself fully awake, he slowed his breathing with a few deep gulps.

"Still trying to kill the guys at the cabin?" Stanford asked from across the darkened room. McAllister could barely make him out, reclined in a wing chair with his feet on a low footstool and his MP-5 resting on his lap.

"Yeah," he answered. "I don't get why my bullets never work. The gun goes off, but nothing falls. It's like I'm firing blanks or something." After the dream had become a recurring nightmare, McAllister had confided in Stanford one evening over drinks, hoping he might have a clue what it meant. He didn't.

"An analogy about your love life, perhaps?" Stanford chided, as McAllister got up from the couch.

"Very funny. My love life is fine, thank you very much."

"Right," Stanford replied. "And the sun rises in the north." McAllister's lack of romantic involvement had been the topic of many a conversation over the years, a by-product of his nomadic existence. If he wasn't traveling on legitimate executive recruitment business, he was off to some exotic locale – or sometimes a stinking hole in the ground – to make the world a safer place. He hardly had time for a date, much less a longer term relationship. And forget marriage. He wasn't about to jeopardize an innocent person's life because of his career choice. Not only would her life be in danger just because she associated with him, but she would make the perfect kidnap target, a risk he wasn't willing to inflict on anyone. In his world, people's lives were at stake and sometimes those people got hurt. Or worse.

"It's almost your turn anyway." Stanford stood and handed McAllister the MP-5 he'd been cradling for the past three hours. "Now get off my couch."

18

The pink sun rose gently over the trees behind the house, slicing narrow slits through the light fog that had settled overnight. Dew glistened on the tall grass, sparkling as a light breeze ruffled the delicate blades. McAllister was already out at the edge of the five-acre pond, loading rounds into his sniper rifle he had pulled from the trunk of the Saab. Down on one knee, he chambered a round, leveled the long barrel, and gently squeezed the sensitive trigger. The rifle barely coughed as the suppressed round ripped its way down range and over the water and sliced into one of three glass jugs sitting inverted on branches stuck in the mud. Shards of glass exploded out the other side as the bottom of the jug bobbed for a moment before falling to the dirt below, coming to rest leaning on the base of the stick. McAllister saw the new target, adjusted his aim slightly downward, and pulled the trigger again. The gun bucked slightly and an instant later the base of the glass jug resting on the ground across the lake exploded into more shards. The other two jugs met similar fates before McAllister packed up the gun and crossed the open field back into the house.

Inside, Stanford was putting the finishing touches on a bacon-and-eggs breakfast, the aroma of freshly brewed coffee following the smell through the house. Molly was already seated at the table, dressed in the same clothes she had worn last night, a coffee mug cupped between her hands.

"Morning," McAllister said. "How'd you sleep?"

"Not bad for an unfamiliar bed. And after all that happened last night."

"You know," Stanford said as he set a plate of bacon on the table and winked at Molly, "out of context that sounds so wrong."

Molly leaned back and let out a laugh. It was just what she needed. She had slept, but it wasn't deep sleep. When she'd finally stopped staring at the ceiling and allowed her eyes to shut, her mind never really relaxed, instead playing the continuous loop of the shooting, followed by all the discussion downstairs, and thoughts of Peter lying dead in the dark alley with only a faint streetlight reflecting off the wet pavement. Just when she'd seen it all twelve times, it started over again, not always in the same order. The mind plays funny tricks when it's asleep.

Gordon set the gun down inside its case on the couch and joined them at the table.

"So what's the plan for today?" Stanford asked as he sat and dug into the scrambled eggs.

Molly said, "Whatever we do, I need to get some fresh clothes, either from my hotel or from a store."

"Your hotel is out. Whoever tried to kill us last night probably has it under surveillance. In fact, your room is probably all torn up right now after they ransacked it looking for who knows what. So we'll have to buy you some new clothes. Do you have cash?"

"Yeah, I always carry some with me, especially when I travel," she answered.

"Good, because you can't use your credit cards. They're traceable, and we can't take the chance."

"So you'll have to go shopping. What else?" Stanford asked, trying to get a grasp on whatever plan McAllister had drummed up. McAllister always did his best thinking with a gun in his hand, the main reason Stanford encouraged him to go out shooting this morning.

19

Dust kicked up behind the black SUV as it sped along the dry lake bed before sliding momentarily sideways on the cracked and weed-infested concrete as the driver regained control and pointed the large speeding vehicle toward the hangar on the other end of the tarmac. Tumbleweeds and scrub brush dotted the landscape of the airfield, long since abandoned and neglected. The seven thousand foot runway was surrounded on both sides by rusted hangars of various sizes. The one they were looking for had been used for corporate jets back in its day.

The vehicle made the final turn and screeched to a halt inside the last hangar on the end, the doors closing quickly behind it. In the middle of the hangar, floodlights illuminated a large object sitting on the floor, covered by a black plastic tarp, its edges resting on the smooth concrete. Five men stood at various distances from the object, three behind and two in front.

Two of the vehicle's four doors swung open as men in tactical gear and guns jumped out and assumed positions by the doors, weapons at the ready. With a nod from one of the men, the back right door swung open and a man in a suit hopped out, surveyed the area, and nodded back inside the vehicle.

Max Preston slid out of the vehicle past the guard, straightened his tie, and strolled up to the man who appeared to be the leader of the contingent already by the tarp. The man was dressed in a black leather jacket and black jeans, the handle of a pistol barely visible inside the open jacket.

"Any trouble getting it here?" Preston, who was armed too but not as visibly, asked the man.

"Not a bit."

"What about the driver?"

"Truck was taken out, driver disposed of and hidden. It's all taken care of."

Preston looked at the man closely, searching for any hint he was lying. Satisfied he was not, he continued. "Good. Let's see her."

The leader turned and snapped his fingers and the other four men carefully removed the tarp, revealing a small, dark aircraft that looked more like a bat than a plane. Gray on top and black underneath, the V-shaped flying wing had sharp leading edges that swept back severely, finishing in precise right-angled corners then tapered back to a trailing edge with split control surfaces. A single humped air intake molded to the airframe, the slotted opening allowing air to flow freely into the front of the single jet engine buried deep inside the smooth housing that ran down the center of the top, its sides sloping seamlessly onto the tops of the wings, forming one continuous surface with no open edges or harsh curves.

At the rear, a lone exhaust nozzle capped with a movable lower slat allowed for thrust vectoring during flight to assist with maneuvering. Absent from the airframe were tail fins, eliminated to reduce radar cross section and, therefore, radar signature, to keep the small pilotless drone from being easily spotted by enemy radar. At least in theory.

The United States F-117 and B-2, the aircraft after which this much smaller mystery bird was modeled, had seen combat and had gone largely undetected in enemy territory. Only one F-117 had ever been lost in combat, a lucky shot in Kosovo that took down a plane on a daylight bombing run, a mission not exactly suited for the stealthy Nighthawk. The black plane much preferred operating where both its radar-evading technology and its shape and color would work in concert to make it doubly hard to spot. During the day, enemy forces still found the stealth fighter hard to see with the naked eye, but once they spotted it, they were able to lock onto it and try to shoot it down, once successfully. The only B-2 ever lost was during an accident on take-off at Anderson Air Force Base on the island of Guam. A computer malfunction caused by excessive moisture sent the large, bat-like aircraft slamming back into the ground at the end of the runway as it attempted to lift off. Both the pilot and co-pilot ejected in time. Rumor had it a B-2 was once detected during combat missions in Iraq after enemy forces figured out now how to triangulate what little radar signature the massive bomber put off, but that was only a rumor, one the Pentagon had never confirmed or denied.

But what made this strange aircraft different was that no pilot would ever be lost if it crashed. The Russians had built a version with a cockpit for testing, but this one wasn't it. Instead, the Russian "Skat," as the American Defense Department called it, could fly one of two ways: remote control from the ground or another plane, or on a preprogrammed flight pattern using GPS and terrain-following technology similar to a cruise missile. So why not just use a cruise missile? They are too easily spotted and leave too much evidence. For this mission, absolute secrecy was the only way to succeed. The target should never see it coming until it was too late. And they should never know who really caused the destruction.

Preston walked slowly around the aircraft, lightly touching his fingers to the sharp edges and smooth surfaces, careful to not damage the delicate skin and ruin its stealthy character. He knew better than to press too hard. Even though the structure could probably take it just fine, Preston knew that even the slightest change in the skin of the airframe could enlarge its radar signature, spelling disaster and jeopardizing the mission. He could not afford that, not now.

"Is it prepped and ready?" he asked his leather-clad tour guide, who was shadowing him nervously.

"Yes, sir."

"And the missiles?"

"Also here and getting prepped."

Preston paused and examined the man, again looking for any indication he was lying. In his business, Preston could not afford to let his guard down or assume anyone was on his side. If *he* could turn someone, so could other people. Enough money or power could change anybody's mind. He had recruited too many people in his time not to have learned that lesson all too well. He always had a mechanism in place to verify what he was being told, but he only wanted to use it if he had to.

"Good," he said confidently as he peered into the movable exhaust nozzle. "Are all the teams in place?"

"The first team is set up and awaiting your orders. The second ran into a small snag at the border and is behind schedule but racing to catch up."

"What sort of snag? Something I need to worry about?" Crossing the supposedly porous border from Canada to the United States wasn't so easy after all, even with all the holes and gaps in security. The Homeland Security Department had tightened the rules and placed more boots on the ground, but with over five thousand miles of real estate separating the two countries, people crossed over every day away from the checkpoints. But if you wanted to appear legitimate, you had to cross at a border patrol station, which was exactly what the team in question had to do. They needed to have the Immigration and Customs Enforcement agency have record of their crossing for part of the plan that would play out later.

"One of the passports was questioned, but one phone call and your man in Washington cleared it up and they entered."

Preston thought for a second. "That actually might work out better for us that way. Okay, where's the controller box?"

"Right this way," the man answered as he led Preston to a box sitting on the floor along the hangar wall. He popped the latches of the grey hard-shell case and lifted the lid, revealing an assortment of communications and computer gear packed tightly into foam padding, including a black nylon case about the size of a VHS tape.

"The Russians still have a ways to go with shrinking down their electronics," Preston remarked as he pulled the case from its form rest. "They can shove sophisticated avionics into an aircraft, but they sorely lack when it comes to making the controller small enough to hide. Even with the Chinese helping, they still can't seem to shrink it down enough."

"Yes," the man agreed. "I pushed my contact to get a smaller one, but he said it's the only size they make. He said you can't exactly get one of these at Radio Shack."

"No, I suppose not. It'll have to do," Preston said, turning the device over. "Is it fully charged and ready to go?"

"Yes, sir. And you can take this entire case with you that has all the rest of the charging and signal equipment."

Preston waved over a member of his team, who came over and hefted the heavy grey case and loaded it into the back of the SUV.

"Does it contain all the tracking and control equipment?" Preston asked.

"All of it. Everything you'll need to run the operation," the man answered.

"Excellent," Preston said.

"I assume you've taken care of the money transfer," the man stated.

"Happening as we speak," Preston answered. He had prearranged a signal with his assistant who had loaded the crate into the SUV that once he was confident of its contents, he would complete the transaction on the laptop set up on the tailgate.

"How can I be sure?"

Preston nodded and said, "Follow me."

The two came around the back of the black vehicle, where the assistant was waiting with the account record on the screen. The leather jacket-clad man scanned the screen and saw the correct account numbers and dollar amounts. Satisfied, he turned to Preston and extended his hand.

Preston took it and said, "I'll expect to see a test flight before you get the rest. Once that's over, we'll transfer the balance."

"Good enough. See you back here tonight."

Preston and his team loaded back up and left the hangar. On the way out of the rusted and sagging airport fence, Dominic turned slightly in his driver's seat and asked, "When do we take them out?"

"After the flight tonight. We need them to get the bird off the ground the first time, but after that they're expendable. Get the gear ready when we get back."

20

Gordon and Molly returned to the farm house a few hours later, having driven a different route home to throw off any would-be tails. Of course, he knew, someone could already be in position near the property and didn't need to follow them. But he also knew the chances of that were slim because they would have most likely been attacked the night before if someone really wanted them dead.

Stanford was waiting inside, sitting at the kitchen table scanning the laptop screen.

"How'd it go?" he asked, not taking his eyes off his work.

"Everything's fine," McAllister answered as he set the shopping bags on the kitchen table. They had stuck to low-key fashions and low prices. Molly was used to high-end clothes, but she understood the need to not draw attention to herself.

"Tail?" Stanford asked.

"Not unless they were a whole lot better than I'm used to," McAllister answered, a wry smile creeping across his face.

Stanford looked up through his eyebrows. "You know I hate when you get like that. You're gonna make a mistake one day with that cockiness."

"It's not cocky; it's confidence."

"There's a huge difference and you know it," Stanford rebutted before he went back maneuvering the mouse. "So how come Miss Molly went upstairs when you came in without saying a word to me?"

"We had a pretty frank discussion on the way back. I think the whole clothes buying expedition really did a number on her, like it's finally registering with her exactly how serious this is."

"But she already knew that after our discussion last night," Stanford said.

"Yeah, but I think today lent a whole new weight to it, like somehow having the sun come up made it more real," McAllister said, a look of concern now replacing the smirk. "She's more upset about Peter today, like his death is more angering than tragic to her now. She told me she feels like she didn't even know the man she was about to marry."

Stanford peeled the half-rim glasses from his nose and set them on the table very carefully with both hands. "You need to be careful with her, Gordon. She's a wounded spirit."

Stunned, McAllister furrowed his brow and said, "Look, Willy, I'm not dating the girl. She's only here because we need her to figure out what's going on."

"I'd be careful about saying that to her," Stanford counseled. "She may decide helping us isn't in her best interest if you treat her like a tool, a convenience to help you do your job. She just lost the man she loved and is finding out there was a lot more to him than she thought. Stuff she doesn't want to know. That's a whole lot harder on her than it would be on you."

McAllister was stunned. "You know as well as I do that Molly is a tough girl. She's always been that way and now she's more so with what's going on now. She'll be fine.

Stanford paused and then in his typical fatherly way said, "It's a façade, Gordon. She's still a sensitive soul. Be careful how you handle her."

21

The bat-like aircraft sat quietly at the end of the runway, idly awaiting instructions from its controller in the hangar. With the engines buried deep inside the fuselage, only someone standing directly behind the mysterious plane could hear it. Taking its design cues from the F-117, the Russians had built the exhaust nozzles to help the stealth characteristics. Not only could radar not see it, but anyone on the ground wouldn't hear it until it had passed them, which by design was too late. By that point, the bomb or missile it delivered would have already struck the target. Its victims would never know what hit them. They wouldn't even know they were getting hit until it was all over. And that was exactly what Max Preston was counting on tonight.

Heat waves from the engine grew behind the drone as the controller throttled up the engines, and the black wing began its speedy roll down the runway. Once airborne, the landing gear quickly sucked up inside the fuselage, creating a smooth surface on the belly and rendering the aircraft virtually undetectable. The Skat climbed effortlessly into the sky, its dark frame quickly disappearing from sight.

Inside the hangar on the ground, Preston watched the screen on the controller's laptop as the dot representing the Skat moved away from the airstrip. The man at the controls manipulated the joysticks to the control box, adjusting the wings and throttle.

"We'll put her on autopilot in about 15 seconds, once she clears enough space that we can bring her back manually if we need to."

"How likely is that?" Preston asked.

The man looked at him sideways. "It's a Russian aircraft."

Preston rolled his eyes. "Keep me updated," he said before he left the controller and strolled over the leather-clad man, who was monitoring his own screen and watching the progress. The man removed his light headset so he could talk to Preston.

"So far, no radar has even come close to picking her up," he said, eager to report some good news to his customer. "Nothing unusual is happening."

That was good news, but Preston wanted to verify for himself. He slid his cell phone off his belt and punched in a speed dial number. The other end was answered on the second ring. "Yes, sir?"

"Any radar blips on your end?"

"No, sir, nothing. She's silent as can be. No one has any idea she's up there."

The leather-clad man said, "She's on autopilot now."

Preston covered the mouthpiece. "Any changes?"

"Nothing," said the controller from behind them.

He spoke into the cell phone again. "Any changes on your end?"

"Nothing. Everything's the same. We're good so far."

So far. That was Preston's concern. This test had to be perfect or the whole deal was off.

The next hour was spent nervously monitoring radars and communication channels. Apparently nobody outside of Preston's group had any idea there was a Russian stealth aircraft circling over the southwestern United States desert. Just to be sure the test was one hundred percent viable, Preston had ordered an in-flight route change to buzz within ten miles of Area 51, Groom Lake, the officially undisclosed top-secret airbase that everyone and his brother knew about. Known for housing highly classified "black" project aircraft, Area 51 had some of the best detection equipment in the world. If there was an aircraft nearby that could be detected, it would be. But apparently the Skat was out of electronic reach. No contact. No detection.

The test was a success. On to phase two.

22

After the test, with the Skat safely tucked back inside the hangar, Preston's security detail had painstakingly disposed of all the leather-clad man's team, systematically rounding them into a conference room at the back of the hangar and shooting them all before they'd had a chance to react. The table had long since been removed from the center of the room, so it was like short range target practice. The walls, ceiling, and floor had then been cleaned of all blood spatter and the bodies piled into the rental truck and hauled out into the desert for burial in a mass grave.

While that was happening, Dominic had downloaded the flight planning codes from the controller's computer onto a secondary drive just in case the original computer malfunctioned or was damaged. He kept the memory stick on its string around his neck, concealed under his shirt.

As the sun went down, a new team arrived, this one for a different phase of the mission. He had picked the best because he expected that out of them. This was a no-fail mission. If anyone screwed up, they all went down, which he had made very clear to them before they signed on. Failure was fatal, and they all knew it.

Preston could sense the tension as each member assumed his role: programmer, missile loader, airframe inspector. The plan was to roll out the aircraft after dark and get it airborne in coordination with the other three in locations throughout the country. Timing was crucial because the attack was to be simultaneous, an overwhelming shot that would have the government looking every which way, unable to determine where it came from or how to stop another one. There wouldn't be another one, but the authorities wouldn't know that for quite some time. He hoped long enough for him to make his escape. At least, that was the plan.

Preston's outward confidence masked his inward turmoil. His insides were jumping, about to burst – a condition he was most certainly not going to reveal to his team. They were dedicated to this mission and nothing was going to stand in the way of total completion.

Sitting in front of the screen, Dominic clicked the keyboard, loading the flight plan into the memory chip plugged in the USB port on the side of the laptop. When the light turned to green, he removed the chip, slid it into its protective case, and nodded to Preston that it was done. With Preston in the lead, the two men exited the closed hangar through the side door and walked quickly toward the black aircraft sitting at the end of the runway. Dominic mounted the step ladder, strategically positioned to not touch the delicate surface of the aircraft, and flipped open the hatch on top behind the nose.

Carefully, he inserted the chip until it was firmly affixed to the circuit board inside and closed the hatch with a click. He then ran his fingers over the edges of the small door to make sure it was tightly closed and formed a smooth surface. Any corners or edges protruding above the skin could create a radar signature and make the Russian aircraft detectable. That wouldn't do. Not just because it would blow the mission, but also because Dominic knew he would meet with the same fate as the leather-clad man and his team.

Back at the computer, Dominic keyed in the commands and the screen became a monitor for the on-board camera in the nose of the Skat. The color image was too dark to show anything, so he switched it to night vision and was rewarded with a clear negative image of the short runway ahead.

Preston checked his watch, dialed his cell phone, and raised it to his ear. When it was answered, he said simply, "Go," and hung up, not waiting for a reply telling him if the others were ready.

Outside, the Skat's single jet engine, concealed deep inside the fuselage, roared to life, the only way to hear it being from behind the aircraft. The black-winged plane began its slow roll and then suddenly jolted to life as the engine exhaust fully propelled the aircraft. Hurtling down the runway, the nose rose slightly and then the whole airframe followed, jumping off the ground and into the night sky. The landing gear doors quickly gobbled up the wheels, shutting fast to diminish the plane's radar signature. Being so near the ground, the plane would be too low to create a radar echo, but the designers had learned from American stealth technology how to avoid taking any chances. The Russians had learned well from the stolen secrets. Preston hoped they had improved upon them.

He stared at the screen as the camera showed the tops of the trees at the end of the runway dropping below the plane beginning its ascent. The radar monitor on the desk next to the laptop was quiet, not a single chirp to indicate anybody knew the first wave of attacks was on its way. They would know soon enough.

23

McGuire Nuclear Station in western North Carolina sits on the edge of Lake Norman, built as a four-purpose lake in 1963. During warm weather the 32,500-acre lake serves as a recreational lake for boating, and year-round as the water supply for the nuclear plant, the nearby Marshall Steam Plant, and Cowans Ford Hydroelectric Station, the dam that was built on the Catawba River to create the lake.

Built in 1981, McGuire's twin cooling dome system generates nearly half of the nuclear power for the state. In its entire operational history, not one serious incident has ever taken place that put the public at any risk. Thanks to heavy-duty construction and redundant safety features, the facility is rated to withstand a crash from a commercial jet liner and remain operational. Not that anyone had ever tested it in anything except a simulation. In fact, until the attack on the World Trade Center, nobody thought it would ever happen. It was purely hypothetical, a mathematical formula that picked a large jet liner only because it was heavy enough to demonstrate the integrity of the design. But every one thought it was ridiculous.

Not anymore. In fact, all the previously "ridiculous" scenarios had been upgraded to "possible" and added to the training manuals and classroom instruction for nuclear power plant security forces across the country. Nobody took anything for granted anymore. If you could dream it up, it could happen. And it was about to.

The targeting computer flipped on automatically as the Skat slipped through the North Carolina sky undetected, on a direct bearing for its first preprogrammed target. The plane throttled back to reduce speed for more precise targeting.

In the old days, a hit like it was about to execute would have required a lower altitude and tighter maneuvering, but with the advent of better targeting systems, including precision laser- and GPS-guided munitions, putting steel and explosives down an airshaft or through a window was almost routine. Punch a few buttons, line up the crosshairs, and watch the footage of the target blowing up later on back at the base. No need to get your hands dirty actually seeing the enemy. And now that pilotless aerial vehicles could put bombs on target as well as humans could, the operator got to stay a nice safe distance away, sometimes hundreds of miles, and not risk chipping a nail as he sent a thousand pounds of munitions screaming down toward death and destruction.

The Skat's onboard camera hidden in the nose relayed the targeting information back to the controller's display, showing the large nuclear facility coming into focus in thermal black and white –

the hotter the whiter, darker shapes illustrating the cooler contrast. The short, round-topped dual cooling towers showed as dark grey and the reactor building slightly lighter, revealing they were both well insulated and radiated minimal heat. The bomb would still be able to detect enough of a signature to find its intended target.

Destination ahead, the black bird made minute adjustments and settled its electronic sites as the bomb bay doors swung open, released the payload, and shut almost instantly, sending the 500-pound bomb on its guided course toward the station.

Engineer Cliff Braggins would never know how many lives he saved or the damage he averted thanks to his selfless, yet completely unaware, sacrifice. Thanks to a losing battle with insomnia, he decided he might as well make use of his awake time and get some extra work done, so he'd come to the plant in the dark early hours. He wheeled his red Chevy Suburban around the last corner, grabbed his choice of parking spots, shut off the warmed engine, gathered his briefcase, and stepped down onto the pavement.

High above, the bomb's targeting system was suddenly confused. Why were there two targets? Where did that hotter source come from? Not smart enough to reason, the tracking system released its hold on the first target, the large cooling domes, and instead grabbed hold of the new heat source and adjusted the stabilizing fins to redirect its trajectory.

"No, no, no, no!" Dominic shouted miles away, seeing the rapidly changing images on his screen. "That's not the target! Get back on track! " He willed the bird to break off the new target, which he could plainly see was a vehicle of some sort, not the nuclear facility, but the aircraft wasn't listening to telepathy.

Misguided, the bomb slammed into the SUV, detonating a mere two feet over the roof, vaporizing both man and machine instantly. The explosion lit up the night sky as it ripped through several more vehicles on its way to destruction in all directions. The shockwave carried across nearby Lake Norman and sent ripples across the water, overturning nearby boats and upsetting their docks.

Inside the station, alarms blared as security personnel tried to decipher what the hell had just happened and piece together whether they were even still alive. Many had been knocked to the floor, some trapped temporarily by desks and filing cabinets that had toppled over as a result of the blast. As they gathered themselves, each reported in and began the drill they had practiced so many times since Homeland Security had teamed up with them for just this sort of event – not necessarily a bomb, but at least an explosion or some sort of terrorist attack. Inside the reactor, security and engineers entered a controlled scramble to lock down the core and keep it protected, in hopes that whatever happened outside wasn't going to damage the inside.

24

Dinner had been a collaborative effort. Molly fixed the appetizer while Willard and Gordon took care of the rest. For a farmhouse, the place had a pretty good kitchen – modern appliances, decent cabinetry. Overall, not bad. After dinner, Willard logged back onto a well-redirected e-mail account, routed to make messages virtually untrackable on their way to and from. The network sent each message all over the world through a series of servers and cutouts that decrypted and encrypted each message multiple times so that no one server could be tapped to get the whole message. There would literally have to be hundreds of taps working in complete concert to decipher even a single sentence of any messages sent across the elaborate network.

Gordon clicked on the inbox and skimmed through the first few messages, most of which were phony spam with embedded information – normal messages the average user would simply delete or ignore. Instead, he saved them for later, because one particular message caught his eye. He clicked on the icon and began reading.

Partway through the message, his cell phone chimed and he grabbed it from its belt holster. The screen came alive with an alert he hadn't seen in years. He looked at it but did not answer the call.

"Willard?" he asked toward the other side of the room.

"Yeah, I got it too," Stanford replied, looking at his cell phone's screen. "I'm on it."

Stanford quickly headed for the side door as McAllister dashed out the front, leaving Molly by herself looking befuddled in the kitchen.

Outside, McAllister punched a series of key commands into the phone as each screen prompted him until the entire sequence had gone through and the screen indicated the secure line had been established and he was free to speak.

"What's going on?" he asked the man on the other end, a man he had never met but had spoken to many on many occasions, but not recently.

"McGuire Nuclear Power Station in North Carolina just came under attack by an explosive agent of some sort. Local authorities are already on scene and the feds should be arriving shortly. The entire area is on lockdown with roads closed and airspace closed off."

"Casualties?" McAllister asked.

"Don't know yet," the man answered. "The scene is still too hot to assess and they're still taking a head count of everyone who was supposed to be there. I'm sure we'll find out as soon as the media grabs hold of the story, which should be in a few minutes."

"Was the reactor damaged?"

"Don't know that yet either. Preliminary satellite imagery shows no visible sign of leakage, but that's just on the outside. God knows what's going on inside the building. The good thing, if you want to call it that, is that apparently the explosion was in the parking lot. Satellite shows a gigantic crater in the pavement."

"All right. Keep me posted. Anything I need to do right now?"

"Not until you get word from higher up." And then he was gone.

McAllister reentered the house and clicked on the television, already tuned to a cable news channel. It was exactly as the anonymous man on the phone had said. So far there was very little to report other than a massive explosion at the nuclear facility and all the typical warnings about radiation and the hazards of nuclear energy. The media were loving the big story, and this might turn out to be the biggest they'd covered since September 11. The only pictures being shown were from ground cameras because of the restriction on helicopter flight in the now-closed air space.

Flipping from channel to channel, McAllister noticed all the reporters seemed to be set up just outside the main security entrance, the closed steel gate casting striped shadows on the ground from the glow of massive flames several hundred yards behind. The area around the plant was fairly level, being right next to the lake, so nobody had yet been able to get a bird's eye view down into the facility.

25

The limo pulled up in front of Senator Stevens' large colonial home, the white Corinthian columns that lined the long front porch pointing skyward to the second story overhang. A single large wrought iron lamp, hung by heavy black chains, loomed over the front door, its three bulbs cutting the darkness to illuminate the steps and porch. Stevens exited the limo before his driver could get around and open the door.

"Senator?" the driver asked, as he rounded the trunk.

"Hmm?" he answered before snapping out of his thoughts. "Oh, thanks, Jim. I can take it from here tonight." He faked a smile and headed toward the house, leaving the driver standing almost at the car door. He strode distractedly toward the house as the driver got back behind the wheel and pulled the limo away down the street.

Stevens pulled his keys from his pants pocket, fumbled for the right one, and finally got the door unlocked. Inside the large foyer, the alarm pad was beeping on the far wall, indicating he had thirty seconds before all hell broke loose and cops from all around descended on his property. He shrugged off his topcoat, folded it over his arm, strolled across the marble floor, and flipped the keypad cover open and entered the code. The beeping stopped and he replaced the cover.

Silence resounded throughout the foyer, only to be interrupted by the clapping of Stevens' shoes as he headed toward the majestic staircase that bisected the grand entrance.

Halfway up, he stopped. *What was that?* He turned back toward the mysterious new sound emanating from the study off the entrance hall and tried to decipher what he was hearing. The clicking was familiar but not quite clear. Curiosity getting the best of him even at the late hour, he backtracked to the foyer and toward the study door, pausing outside to listen again.

The clicking continued.

He knew it couldn't be an intruder. Right? The alarm was still armed when he had walked in. A water drip from the snow melting on the roof? It had never leaked before. Besides, the study was on the first floor so any leak would have stopped upstairs. He turned the knob and entered. And gasped inside, trying to maintain complete control on the outside.

"Good evening, senator," said the man sitting in a wing chair by the dark fireplace, his legs crossed. In his hand was a pistol, a Sig Sauer P226, which he was tapping with a Monte Blanc. The clicking sound. "You look surprised to see me. Why? You knew we'd be talking eventually."

"How did you get in here?" was the only thing Stevens could think to say as he stood just inside the door, his hand still on the knob even though he knew there was no point in trying to run. The man sitting calmly before him was a professional and would likely have the gun up and the trigger pulled before Stevens could take even a single step.

"Do you really think I'm going to answer that?" the man responded. "You know me better than that. Never give away trade secrets. Ask any decent magician. Please, take a seat." He waved the gun toward the other wing chair on the other side of the fireplace.

The senator swallowed and sat in the chair, the leather sighing as he eased into it. He knew something like this might happen but hadn't figured it would be now. The nuclear facility was still ablaze and nobody had figured out what had happened. Everybody assumed it was a bomb that had been smuggled onto the property, exactly what everyone was supposed to believe. It wouldn't be until later that the true cause would be discovered, at which time all hell would break loose and everyone would run around putting their piece into the blame game. At least that was the plan.

"Why are you here?" Stevens finally asked. "Everything is going as planned."

"Yes, and we'd like it to stay that way."

"Why would you think it won't? I've done everything I agreed to do."

The man reached into his jacket pocket and extracted a small envelope, which he tossed to Stevens. It landed in his lap and he jumped a bit as if the envelope would explode. It didn't.

"Open it," the man instructed, once again waving his gun a bit too casually for Stevens' taste.

Stevens followed the instruction and lifted the flap. Inside was a thin stack of photographs, which he pulled out. The top one showed two people, a man and a woman, sitting in a living room. The picture seemed to be taken through a window from the outside. The man was unfamiliar, but he immediately recognized the woman sitting on the couch.

"Why is my niece in this picture? And who is she with?"

The man with the gun raised an eyebrow and said, "That's what we want to know. Not who he is – we already know that part – but what your niece is doing with him. We were hoping you could enlighten us."

Stevens was very much aware of the plural references the man was using. He knew he was not working alone. In fact, he thought he knew the man's employer but couldn't be perfectly sure. Part of the intrigue of this whole operation was its anonymity. Everyone thought they knew the other players but nobody was completely sure. Identities had to remain hidden for the operation to be a success.

"Who is he? Maybe I can tell you why they are together if you tell me who he is."

The man squinted at him for a moment before deciding his next move.

"His name is Gordon McAllister. He's a government operative" he finally said.

"So what does he have to do with Molly?" Stevens asked, still not sure where this was going or whether he liked it.

"What does the code name ZEBRA mean to you, Senator?"

Stevens went flush when he realized the connection. He looked back at the picture. His hand began to shake.

"McAllister?"

"Yup," the man, glaring at Stevens through his eyebrows. "One and the same."

"Does Molly know who he is?"

"We believe so," he said, not breaking his gaze.

"But I thought you got rid of him," Stevens said. "I gave your employer very clear instructions to take him out of the picture. He's the only member of the team left and the only one who can still ruin the operation."

"I know, and therein lies our problem. You see, he's the best of the best. He trained the entire team and is now the only one left. And thanks to a botched assassination attempt, he's now on high alert. Which is exactly why I've come to visit you tonight."

Stevens looked back at the man. "So what are we going to do about it?"

"*We* aren't going to do anything. You are."

"Me? What can I do? I don't know anything about covert operations. And even if I did, there's no way I could take this guy out. You just said he's the best of the best. Well, I'm not. I'm just a crusty old politician. I'd be dead meat."

"That's all very true. Which is why you don't have to pull the trigger. All you need to do is lure him to you and let us take care of the rest."

"But I can't be connected to any of this or the game is over. You know that."

"Ah, yes. Plausible deniability. Interesting concept. But does anyone ever really have that? Is that really even possible? Somebody somewhere knows something about any operation and can blow the lid off it if they want to. Which is why there is always a safety valve," the man said ominously and lifted the barrel of the gun toward Stevens.

The chair groaned as the senator sat back a little deeper. He was sure that this man wouldn't hesitate to kill him if given the right motivation. Perhaps he already had it. Perhaps that was why he was here in the first place. Well, if he were, Stevens wished he'd just get on with it. But, no, that wouldn't make any sense. Why would he draw this whole ordeal out only to pop him off in the end? He needed something. He had just said so. He needed a safety valve.

"What if I say no?" Steven asked, very afraid of the answer.

The man stood and tucked his gun away into an unseen holster inside his jacket in one swift motion. The grace with which the man moved told Stevens all he needed to know about his chances: none. The man was a hired killer. He doubted very much that any of his training records still existed, so even getting a picture on the home's surveillance cameras wouldn't do any good.

"Then this will be the last time you see your beloved niece. You know what this operation means to this country and how much it means to the future of our national security. Do as I've instructed and everyone walks away happy. That is, of course, except McAllister. He won't be going anywhere."

After the man had gone, Stevens double checked all the locks on the doors and windows and sat back down in this study, this time behind his large mahogany desk. Flipping on the green banker's lamp, he studied the pictures the man had left with him. No doubt the man and his employer had the negatives or digital files, so it was no use destroying the photos. They'd just make more. But they could only do so much with them without exposing the whole operation.

Maybe that was his angle. *What if they can't really use the pictures for anything?* Stevens thought. What good is blackmail if the "evidence" can never be used? Could this not be so bad after all? His head was much clearer without having a gun pointed at him.

He poured himself a scotch from the credenza, turned off the desk light, reset the alarm in the foyer – not that it would apparently do any good, he thought – and headed upstairs to what he was sure would be a fitful night's sleep. Exhaustion had been quickly replaced by a rush of adrenaline. He knew he'd fall asleep eventually, the alcohol helping, but just when he didn't know.

The man watched from his car parked across the street as the senator's bedroom light blinked off behind the curtains in the second floor window. Pulling away from the curb, he dialed his cell and was immediately connected.

"He got the message," he said to the man on the other end.

"Excellent. I'll see you for coffee in the morning."

26

Local firefighters had joined the on-site security and fire prevention team at the McGuire nuclear power station to both control the fire and secure the scene while they waited for the investigators to arrive. The investigative teams arrived shortly and began combing the crater and surrounding areas looking for any and all clues that might point to a cause. Terrorism had immediately leapt to everyone's minds, but it was very early and too soon to tell what really caused the massive explosion. What was known was that it had completely destroyed an SUV, which was now so black it was impossible to tell what color it was originally. Security cameras showed a man getting out of the vehicle seconds before the explosion and then getting caught up in the fireball. Everyone assumed he had been blown up in the explosion, but they still had to treat him as a missing person until they found evidence – most likely tiny bone fragments or small particles that would contain his DNA – before pronouncing him dead.

Early morning sun had revealed a crater measuring nearly seventy-five feet in diameter and almost twenty feet deep. Some of the piping and electrical lines that ran under the parking lot had been damaged or destroyed and were being traced to the appropriate apparatus inside the facility to see what systems they linked to. So far nothing catastrophic had been affected and the plant could function again if it needed to. But it had been shut immediately after the explosion, just in case the core or any of its protective concrete layers had been shaken or cracked. There was no visible damage. It would be a while before all the official inspections would take place and the plant certified to restart, but so far it appeared the building had worked as designed.

"Inspector!" came a shout from across the roped-off parking lot. It was a field agent for the Nuclear Regulatory Commission. "You need to see this!"

The Commission's agents had been called in as part of the multi-jurisdictional task force Washington had sent within hours of the explosion. Unlike local and federal law enforcement, the Commission's jurisdiction began and ended at the plant's entrance. But while on site, they had full investigatory powers and were the main resource for technical evidence gathering and analysis. Along with the ATF, the Commission's agents had been scouring the scene as soon as the fire fighters had deemed it safe, collecting parts and scraps that might hold some sort of clue as to the cause of the explosion. From explosive material residue to the shape of a fragment, each bit of evidence could potentially yield a great deal of information if looked at through trained eyes and studied within the broader range of the investigation.

Tom Phillips, a twenty-one year veteran explosives expert and now lead investigator, crunched his thick boots across the asphalt, carefully stepping over and around debris that might yield valuable clues, to where the other inspector stood holding what looked like a curved piece of shrapnel. Phillips took the metal fragment and turned it over in his latex gloved hands, looking at every angle to assess exactly what he was holding.

"Doesn't look like a car part," said the junior inspector, "so I doubt it came from the fried SUV. Could it be part of the bomb?"

"Very possible," Phillips observed, continuing to shift the scrap in his hands, using the newly risen sun for light.

He stopped turning it.

"Look here," he said, pointing to a broken edge. "This looks like some sort of writing, like a label of some sort. But it's not English, or it doesn't appear to be. Look for more pieces like this to see if we can put it back together. In the meantime, bag that one and get it into the truck for collecting and processing."

27

Preston clicked off the TV from across the room and leaned back into the plush leather couch in his immense living room. The flat panel high definition LCD blinked to black as he continued to stare at the images now faded away of the reporters covering the blast in North Carolina. *Damnit! How could this have missed?* Everything had been planned correctly. The targeting computer had been programmed correctly. The aircraft had released the bomb right on schedule and on target. Everything seemed to work as planned.

Yet, it missed.

He dreaded what would happen next. His mission had failed and there would be hell to pay, he knew. Heads would roll, most likely his being one of them. How could he have let this happen?

He needed to clear his head. The operation's schedule had wreaked havoc with his sleep schedule and now he was feeling more than a little disoriented. It reminded him of his days confined in an Iraqi prison during a failed covert operation, part of an unofficial wing of a joint Marine-CIA task force that was sent into Iraq before the air operations were to commence, when the helicopter he'd been flying in was shot down. Three weeks wasn't very long to be held prisoner, but being confined to a windowless cell without his wristwatch had been enough to completely throw off his internal clock. It took him nearly a week to get reoriented after the daring rescue by a squad of Marines. They had come swiftly and quietly during the night and methodically taken out all the Iraqi guards in the makeshift prison just outside Baghdad. The house-turned-prison had belonged to one of Saddam Hussein's chief military officers and featured a basement buried deep underground, far enough to withstand a direct hit from a rocket or mortar. It served an unintended purpose when Preston's Navy CH-53 Sea Stallion helicopter had spiraled to the ground after being struck by a pair of rocket-propelled grenades.

The operators were being flown toward northern Iraq on a rescue mission of their own when they were shot down. The RGPs slammed into the tail rotor of the large bird, causing it to spin out of control and slam into the desert floor with enough force to kill fourteen operators aboard. The three remaining survivors were quickly overrun by the Iraqi troops who had shot them down. One of the surviving Marines was barely alive but coherent enough to reach for his sidearm. He got one shot out of his Beretta, but his shooting arm had been too badly damaged by the impact to aim effectively, and before he could fire again he was quickly dispatched with by an Iraqi soldier wielding an AK-47, lowering the survivor count to two. As a captain and the commanding officer of the battalion of Marines,

Preston was the most prized possession the Iraqis could want, and now they had him. They wanted him alive for leverage.

The sight of the prison door suddenly blasting open startled Preston at first, until he remembered his training and quickly realized it was a rescue. By the time the first Marine was through the door, Preston was up on his feet and ready to go. The other survivor prisoner, a corporal, was rescued at the same time and was waiting for Preston aboard the Blackhawk rescue helicopter. Everyone loaded in, and they took off. On the way back to base, he learned the Marines they had originally been sent to rescue had engaged the enemy and had gotten themselves out of the jam, but at the cost of four enlisted soldiers and two officers. It had been a bad three weeks for the Marine Corps, but they had faced harsher difficulties and pulled through just fine. It was what they did. It was their job. And they all knew it and relished it. They were Marines.

Preston had not been seriously wounded in the shoot down, so he chose to return to duty after a brief rest and recovery. Not one to shy away from action, he immediately received his next assignment and once again went out into the field. Through three more top-secret missions, he guided F-117 bomb runs from the ground, sometimes being so close he could feel the heat off the explosions and hear shrapnel whizzing past his head. His job was to light up the target with a laser and then boogie on out of theater as soon as the target had been hit. He came close to being caught only one time, and it was only by a stroke of luck that a member of the Iraqi Republican Guard happened to turn the wrong way when he thought he heard a sound in the quiet night. Preston was able to duck behind a building a mere fifteen feet from the soldier and avoid detection until the man walked away a few minutes later.

His main task, however, was a target of a different kind. With a background in electronics, he had been assigned the job of electronic eavesdropping, spying on secret conversations among Iraqi military leaders and their troops in the field. The intelligence gathered through cell phone and radio monitoring had proved invaluable as the coalition forces decided where and when to attack for maximum effect. When going into battle, knowing your enemy's plan is always a plus. Early in the bombing, coalition forces took out the lion's share of Iraq's communications structure, blasting away at telephone sites and radio towers. But they couldn't stop all communication. There were still hard-to-tap satellite phones and the old standby: personal contact. In fact, one of the tricks often used by the Iraqi government during the opening stages of the war was to send messages via disguised couriers, many of them little children. The kids would be given a package they didn't know contained secret messages and sent on their way. American and other coalition soldiers would never suspect intelligence was literally walking right past them. However, all it took were a couple of slipups for the Americans to figure out the tactic and the game was over.

After the war, Preston stayed in country for a few more months, monitoring the occasional message but mostly setting up permanent covert installations throughout the country and working with HumInt – human intelligence assets they had hired to continue the spy work.

Finally, he returned to the States and worked with the government to set up his computer company, with his first contract being a networking solution for the Pentagon, a contract that allowed him to use his contacts within the military and covert operations world to get an inside track. It was completely outside the written rules for awarding government contracts, but that's the way many senators and representatives chose to do business. He got in with the right committee heads and got what he needed to set up shop.

He felt a presence enter the room and turned to see Lena standing in the doorway. She was a stunning picture of elegance, her wispy blonde hair pulled up revealing her slender neck, her hips now waving gently as she crossed the room dressed in a shimmering gold silk spaghetti-strapped dress that stopped tantalizingly just shy of her knees. Rounding the far side of the couch to sit, her grace filled the air as her perfume alerted Max's nostrils, invoking feelings deep within. She gently touched his arm and began to kiss his ear, stirring him.

When he was about to move toward her, she whispered, "Just a reminder, we have reservations at seven and don't want to be late."

"Why not?" he replied softly.

Between nibbles, she answered, "Because the Hendersons would be very disappointed. They came all the way out here to see you, and you wouldn't want to make them eat alone now, would you?"

He closed his eyes and wished the Hendersons back to Colorado. But he knew that wouldn't really work. So he breathed in, turned to Lena, and kissed her passionately on the lips.

"That will have to hold you until after dinner, my dear," he said. "Now I have to get dressed. Mustn't keep our guests waiting."

He got up and left the room, leaving Lena by herself. After watching and hearing the door click closed, Lena stood and walked over to the tall, lean plant standing on the floor in the corner near Max's desk and dug through the top layer of soil until her fingers found the object she was seeking – a small grey plastic box, about the same size as a lipstick case. She dusted off the device and her hands and smoothed back over the soil so it looked undisturbed. Into her purse went the little box, tucked snugly inside for use later. On a tiny chip inside the device was what she hoped was enough evidence to hang Max Preston.

28

Dinner with the Hendersons, some old friends of Max's, went fine. Everyone was so impressed with Lena and how great the couple looked together. They hadn't seen each other in over a year, so the Hendersons wanted to know all about how Max and Lena met and fell in love. It was too gushy for Max, but he played along for the sake of friendship and social graces. They all took pictures and promised to e-mail them to each other. Finally, after dinner, dessert, and a couple rounds of drinks, the couples parted ways and headed home.

Back at the house in Costa Mesa, Max tossed his suit coat over the back of a chair in the bedroom and headed toward the walk-in closet as he loosened his tie. Slipping his shoes off, his feet looked a little strange, like they were moving of their own volition. He stood still for a second to gather his bearings. Even as inebriated as he was, he realized he was drunk and needed to lie down before he fell over and hurt himself. So he eased himself out of his clothes, which he left in a pile on the floor, and headed to bed in just his boxers. Lena was just walking into the room when he hit the bed and was out in a matter of seconds. She hated when he did that because he landed on top of the covers, making it nearly impossible to get into bed herself. She sometimes slept in the guest room because of it. And that would be her excuse tonight if he woke up and noticed she wasn't in the bed.

At dinner, she had been careful to drink only enough wine to fool her fellow diners but had stuck mostly to water so she would be coherent when she got home. Now as she changed into jeans, a t-shirt, and tennis shoes, Lena lingered in the bedroom long enough to hear Max snoring. Satisfied he was out, she crept down the hall and grabbed a running jacket out of the coat closet. She knew all the house alarm codes and disarmed the alarm long enough to slip out the back door, wanting to be clear of the structure before the alarm would automatically reset itself for the night. Outside, the cool ocean air greeted her with refreshment. This she would miss; the rest she would not.

She was about to embark on a new phase in her life, a release from the captivity she'd live in for the last year. The sudden adrenaline rush gave her a quick shiver before she pulled herself back under control and took to the woods behind the house. Staying to the predetermined route she'd mapped out days before, she followed the subtle markings she'd made on the trees with dots of glow paint to help her find the exact exit point where it would be safe to get out into the open again. From a distance, the spots were invisible, but to her trained eye they were bright as sunshine, leading the way to freedom – not just for her but for the entire country, though they didn't know it yet.

Ten minutes later, she neared the edge of the woods and crouched behind a tree, listening for any indications of trouble or any movement that might indicate she'd been followed. It was highly unlikely anyone had any idea she was out here except for the one person who should be waiting for her…there. She spotted the black sedan across the road and pulled a small flashlight with a red lens cover out of her jacket pocket. One quick push of the on/off switch let the driver know she was there and ready to cross. He responded by flipping the dome light on and off once quickly. In that brief instant, she caught a good enough glimpse inside the car to know the right man was behind the wheel. She'd seen his picture in the file she had been sent in response to her signal that she was ready for extraction.

This was it. And with that, she took off at a dead sprint across the road, stopping abruptly at the car door, which she quickly pulled open and shut behind her. Inside, the car was eerily quiet. Neither spoke for a moment.

Finally, the man behind the wheel said, "You have everything you need?"

"Yes," she answered.

"Ready to go?"

"Do I have a choice now?" Lena asked rhetorically.

"Not really," he felt obligated to answer. "Your gun's on its way to your destination as we speak." And with that, he fired up the engine and they took off down the road, leaving her former world behind her for now, sure she would face the participants again soon enough.

29

Gordon and Molly had left Stanford back at the farm house and headed toward his home in Wildwood. Now that some time had passed and he was reasonably sure nobody was watching it anymore, he needed to assess the damage and see if there was anything salvageable. He also needed to know what his attacker knew and see if he might find any clues as to who it was. Normally he liked to work alone but decided to bring Molly along as a second set of eyes. Plus she'd been there the night of the attack and it might be good for her to be there this time for therapeutic reasons.

He pulled the Saab through the front gate, which was still gaping open from the car's collision with it in his hasty exit, and up the long, winding driveway. Pieces of the broken garage door still lay on the concrete in the parking area, the edges of the door clinging to rails inside the frame. Gordon parked the car in a clear space and turned off the engine. On the way up the drive, he had visually scanned the surroundings, including all the windows and the roof and chimney area, making sure there was nobody lying in wait for an ambush. All was clear.

They got out and said nothing, as Gordon had instructed. If anyone was inside the house, out of view of Gordon's initial sweep, no doubt they would have heard and seen the car and already known they were coming. He didn't want to give the extra advantage of hearing them walk in, too.

He extracted the Walther PPS from its concealed holster inside the waistband on his right hip. He motioned with his free hand for Molly to tuck in behind him as they stepped through the opening left by the destroyed garage door. Raising the weapon in front of him with both hands, he scanned the interior of the garage and saw nothing moved or changed. The inside door to the mud room was closed, the way they had left it. He pushed on the door. Still latched. Slowly he turned the knob, knowing how he could open it without being heard so long as he didn't push it to the point where he had a built-in squeak he had designed into the hinge just in case someone had tried to surprise him. They slipped inside the open doorway and into the mud room. Again, no signs of anyone being there. The closet door was slid back the way Gordon had left it, the panel inside still gaping open.

They moved cautiously, clearing each room and checking for signs that someone besides them had been there. The entire house was empty and nothing had been disturbed.

Back in the kitchen, Gordon grabbed a bottled water for himself from the fridge and handed one to Molly.

"Okay, so we know nobody was here after we left," he said. "Or if they were, they did a great job of covering their tracks. Which means one of two things. Either they didn't have any idea there was valuable information here they could have taken, or –"

"Or they already had everything they needed," Molly interrupted.

"Exactly. So that means all they really wanted was me, or both of us, dead." Shattered glass lay strewn around the living room where Gordon had been standing the night the bullet almost hit him. Exposed to the outside, the living room had taken a little bit of weather damage from the pouring rain that night, mostly in the carpet, which could be cleaned later. Much later. First things first.

Molly took a sip of water. "So what does all this tell you besides the obvious part about wanting to kill us?" she asked with a slightly patronizing raise of her eyebrows.

Gordon admired her wit and let the little insult go uncountered. Things had been pretty tense, and it was time to let off a little steam.

"It tells me they know enough about me that I may be operationally off the table. Which means they have connections somewhere inside and I have lost all my contacts. I can't trust anybody," he said, staring at the floor, taking in his own words. Then he looked up at Molly and studied her face.

"What?" she said as she swallowed another sip of water. "Why are you looking at me like that?" It was his turn to return the patronizing eyebrow, only it wasn't meant to be funny. "What, you think I had something to do with this?" she blurted out. "*I* came to *you*, remember? Not the other way around.

"Yes, that's exactly the problem. How did you know where to find me? Seems a bit too convenient to me."

"Are you serious?" she asked, floored at his accusation. "We've already been through this! I had nothing to do with any of this, never wanted to even be here. But I didn't have a choice. If you think I had anything to do with this, I'm walking right out that door and not coming back. My car is still parked out there in the garage, you know."

"Yes, but you don't have the keys. They are back at the farm house."

"How do you know that?"

"Because you left them on the table in the living room when you grabbed your purse."

She blinked twice. "You pay that much attention to what I'm doing?"

"Have to. In my line of work, I can't afford to miss details like that. I'm not just paying attention to you. I'm paying attention to the entire world around here. Details matter. For instance, did you know there is a car pulling up the driveway right now?"

Molly wheeled around, but there wasn't a window facing the right direction to see out. "How do you know that?"

"Sound. I'm very familiar with this house and can tell you what sounds everything makes. Also, I cheated."

"Cheated?"

"Yeah, my phone vibrates when I'm at home and someone breaches the sensor at the bottom of the driveway. It turns on a camera hidden in the overhang by the garage so I can see who it is." He pulled the small phone out of his front pocket and punched a button on the front as the screen came alive. "It's a small car. Can't tell anything about the driver, but he's going slowly, like he's not sure he wants to be here. Let's hope he just has the wrong house." But he knew that probably wasn't the case. Nobody knew the driveway was there unless they were looking for it. He turned the phone so Molly could see the car on the screen. "Recognize it?"

"No."

"Then we have a problem."

The mystery car came to a stop right behind McAllister's Saab. Its sole occupant, the driver, slowly emerged and looked around before tentatively entering the damaged garage.

McAllister had Molly move to the dining room as he got positioned behind the island in the kitchen for cover, gun in hand. The inside door from the garage creaked on cue and then the latch clicked subtlety as the intruder tried to close it as quietly as possible. Quiet footsteps on the tile meant he was entering the kitchen and slowly moving toward the island. McAllister double checked his grip on the gun and listened again as the footsteps stopped for a second and then slowly started again toward him.

McAllister sprang from behind the island and caught the intruder with his forearm. He had gone for the chin but missed because his target was shorter than he had anticipated. Instead, he clipped the man's forehead and snapped his head backward enough to stun him. As the man was falling to the ground, McAllister noticed a shock of long blond hair landing hard on the kitchen floor.

He was a she! Gordon grabbed her by the arm and flipped her onto her stomach, and he held her down with one leg and searched her. Finding the gun in her waistband was easy. He extracted it and laid it on top of the island. He checked by her ankles for additional weapons but came up empty.

"Who are you?" he demanded, the nose of his gun pressed against her ear.

"I have information for you. Something you'll want to know," she replied through her mouth wedged against the cold tile.

"About what?" he asked, his search over and not yielding any other weapons. He kept the gun against her.

"About the terrorist attack on the nuclear plant," she answered, wincing under the weight on top of her. Her ribs felt like they had been shoved through her lungs, straight back to her spine. Breathing came at a painful price.

"Terrorist attack? How do you know it was a terrorist attack?" He applied slightly more pressure.

She let out a shallow cough. "Because I know who did it, okay? Now let me up! " Her attempt at sounding forceful died a quick death through restricted airways.

He paused for a moment before moving the gun away from her ear and letting her stand up. She held on to the island counter and found her way back to her feet. Her gun lay less than a foot from her hand. McAllister saw her eyeing it.

"Go for it," he said. "But you better make it quick because it's the only chance you get."

Her shoulders relaxed as she pulled her hand back. "If you're who they say you are, I won't need it. Nor would I be fast enough to get it."

McAllister stared at her for a moment, looking for the littlest indication to tell what she was thinking or about to do. Seeing nothing, he walked to the other side of the island to put some space between them and asked, "Who am I?" *How much does she really know?*

Unfazed by the blunt inquiry, she answered, "If my sources are correct – and I believe they are – you are a trained killer who works exclusively for the President of the United States. You have no military background and were recruited by sheer luck after someone in the CIA noticed your superb marksmanship at an indoor firing range. You report to no one but the President, and everything you do is completely away from any congressional oversight. Nothing you do is ever known to anyone who isn't supposed to know it, which basically means only one man – the sitting President – ever knows anything about you."

So far, so good, he thought, his face passive, not giving away anything about how right she was. But you better give me more or this conversation will come to a screeching halt real quick.

She continued. "You're the leader of a team of operatives, each one selected the same way you were, through initial observation and then very careful screening. But the members of this team have recently been systematically picked off, killed one by one over the last several months. And you're next."

"Is that why you're here? To kill me?" he asked.

"Hardly. I'm here because I know who's doing it."

"I thought you said you knew who carried out the attack at the nuclear station."

"I do. They are one and the same. The people who are trying to kill you and your team are the same ones behind the attack. They also orchestrated the explosions at the shopping malls."

"And just how, exactly, do you know all this? Did you read it on some blogger's posting on the internet?"

"Hardly," she sneered, arms crossed. "I know it because I used to work for the man who organized the whole operation."

McAllister frowned. "Right. And you just happened to waltz in here off the street to my house and tell me all about it."

"No, not at all. I said I *used* to work for him." She looked down. "That was until last night, when I left and flew out here to find you."

"And how did you do that, find me? I don't exactly have an ad in the yellow pages."

"No, but you are in the white pages," she countered, smiling through pursed lips.

He smiled back. "Okay, you got me on that one," he answered, momentarily recalling his other life, his executive recruiting firm. He'd only been gone from the office a few days, yet that side of his existence seemed so far away. It always did when he was on a mission. The last thing he ever worried about was finding a CEO for a bank or a VP for an insurance company when he was out killing bad guys. His ability to compartmentalize had kept him alive. But in a twist of almost laughable irony, McAllister had been forced to list his home address and phone number in the white pages so he could maintain his cover as average Joe citizen.

"So tell me," – he glanced at her empty left ring finger – "Miss…"

"Miller. Lena Miller."

"Okay, tell me Miss Miller, who do you work for and how do you know all this?" he said, motioning for her to sit on one of the bar stools.

She composed herself and thought a moment about the best way to start. She had rehearsed this moment over and over on the plane, to get every detail right, but now she had to regurgitate everything she had learned over the past several months on cue. And she knew who she was saying this to, at least by reputation. Her lungs burned again. After being in the same bed with the man who was about to attack a nuclear power plant in the name of national pride, this should have been a cinch. Not so. She was about to reveal information that could take down a very powerful organization. She swallowed hard before she spoke.

"Two years ago, Homeland Security got a tip through the NSA wiretap program that we might have a couple of homegrown terrorists. It was just a tip, with nothing substantial behind it, but they flagged it nonetheless. With the help of the NSA's eavesdropping protocols, they were able to dig through electronic communications and cell phone calls and begin to pull all the pieces of the puzzle together. Then the FBI found a clue that finally tied it all together."

"What was that?"

"A strange new encryption technique embedded in an e-mail triggered the NSA's computers to flag a message sent from a laptop in Costa Mesa, California. At first it seemed like it might just be some software engineer messing with some new programming. But after the technician decrypted the code, the clues came together and led to a man named Max Preston, the owner of a small computer company in Costa Mesa, California."

"What's the connection to Preston?" he asked.

She told him about Preston's covert operations involvement in the Gulf War and how the government helped him set up shop.

"So where did you enter into all of this?" he probed.

"Max – Mr. Preston – hired me to be his admin assistant and then it got deeper." She told him all about the relationship. "Then one day I was out running some errands and was approached by a DHS agent, who asked me to go undercover, which I guess you could say I already was," she said with a wink. "I was leery at first, since I'd never done anything like that before, but when they explained to me why, I agreed to do it. I was scared to death, but they told me what to do and showed me how to act around him so as not to raise suspicion. Things got back to normal, and I settled into my new role. As his admin, I saw everything that came across the company e-mail and was able to figure out how to get into his personal account and work from there undetected. Pretty soon, I had built up enough information to give DHS what it needed to be fairly sure he was behind the attacks."

"So why are you talking to me? Why aren't you going back to your bosses at DHS and telling them what you found instead of sneaking into my house to find me?" he asked suspiciously.

"Simple," she said matter-of-factly. "I don't trust them."

"Why not? They're the ones who asked you to work for them."

"Yes, and it all seemed way too easy. Not only was I able to get all the information I needed, I was able to get away far too easily last night. I hadn't thought of it until I was in the air, but a man as powerful as Preston wouldn't just let me waltz right out of his house, information in hand, uncontested. He has to know."

"Yeah, I know," McAllister said. "Which is why I've been asking all these questions. I don't believe for a second that a guy like Preston doesn't know exactly where you are right now. Which means he knows where I am, too."

"And where I am," said Molly, entering through the dining room door behind Lena, who turned.

"Who are you?" Lena asked, instantly on guard.

"Molly Hindan," she answered. "The fiancé of one of the dead *operatives*, as you called them."

Lena's eyes went wide and her guard broke down. "I'm so sorry," she said as she hopped off the bar stool and hugged Molly before she could react. McAllister stood by awkwardly and rolled his eyes at this impromptu show of affection – *women!* – shrugging his shoulders as Molly looked at him wide-eyed, pleading with him. She was on her own for this one. The ladies finally parted, and it was back down to business. He was back in his comfort zone. His line of questioning continued.

"What involvement exactly did Preston have in all of this?"

"It's too complicated to explain, and nobody would believe me, which is why I put all the records on this," she said, reaching inside her collar. From inside her shirt, she extracted the flash drive she had pulled out of the potted plant and handed it to McAllister. "Everything you need should be on there. It's whatever I could extract from both his laptop hard drive and his e-mail accounts. Keep in mind I was in a hurry every time I accessed anything, so it may be a bit disjointed."

McAllister pocketed the flash drive and said, "So what's the other reason you didn't go to your bosses about this?"

Lena played her finger across the countertop in a semi-circle, took a deep breath, and looked McAllister square in the eyes. "Because this plot goes way beyond Preston. I believe the information on that drive will point to people higher up, people who have far more power than one very wealthy computer geek. They boosted his ego to get him hooked, but in the end he's just a flunky. I believe they enlisted my help not to get information to prosecute him, but to protect themselves."

30

They left Lena's rental in the driveway, figuring anyone who would come looking for it already knew she was in town and had made contact with McAllister, and they all piled into his Saab, headed toward the farm house. On the way, he called Stanford to fill him in on what happened at his house. It took a little longer than normal for Stanford to answer. Normally he picked up on the first ring. *Not a good sign*, McAllister thought.

"Go," Stanford said, his typical greeting relaxing McAllister a little. But he still had a strange feeling about things, especially after the events of the morning already transpiring.

"How are things at the house?" he asked. The normal sounding banter was actually a trick question, one designed to sniff out trouble. How Stanford answered would tell McAllister all he needed to know.

"Fine, why?" Stanford responded, sending McAllister's brain into overdrive, mental alarm ringing. Stanford was in trouble. McAllister had to be very careful about what he said next. Any slipup could make Stanford's situation worse, so he had to choose his words carefully. And he had to assume he was either on speaker phone or someone was eavesdropping. He had to act like everything was exactly that: fine.

"We're heading back to the house. Need me to pick up anything on the way?" Another probing question designed to sound innocuous. He thought he heard a voice or voices faintly in the background but couldn't be certain.

There was pause, and then Stanford answered, "No, just head on back. I'll see you when you get here." And the line clicked off.

McAllister's worry must have shown through because Molly asked, "What's wrong?"

He glanced at her and then to Lena in the back seat before turning back toward the road. "Things just got a little more complicated."

"How so?" asked Lena.

"Stanford's in trouble at the house. Probably someone followed you out here last night and now knows for sure we're connected."

"What are we doing to do about it?" Molly asked, again questioning getting involved with this whole fiasco.

"Exactly what he said. We're heading back to the farm house."

"But they're waiting for you."

"That's what I'm counting on."

"Are you crazy?" Lena said from the backseat. "Do you know what you're up against?"

"Do they?" he countered, and smiled into the rearview mirror.

Besides rescuing Stanford, McAllister's other concern now was how the person or people inside found out about the farm house. Only a handful of people knew enough about his operation to know the house even existed, much less its location. It was becoming increasingly apparent that someone was working their own operation from the inside. Not only had other operatives who were formerly anonymous been killed, which screamed *inside job*, but now secondary targets were being identified and exposed.

Of course, he was concerned about how his good friend was doing. He was obviously alive, but had he been hurt? He didn't detect any pain in Stanford's voice, which was a good sign. But that didn't mean they hadn't done anything to him. Or were doing it now. Or maybe they were waiting for McAllister to come roaring through the front door before they tortured him, hoping they could get a two-for-one deal. Wasn't going to happen, so far as McAllister was concerned. He'd been in this business too long to let something like this bring his career or his life to an end. He was going to save his friend and figure out what the hell was happening.

A plan began to gel in his head. It wasn't a great plan, but it was a plan. He had about twenty minutes to get it all in place. If he delayed too long, whoever was holding Stanford might become suspicious and make things worse. He focused on the road as the parts and pieces of his rescue operation fell into place. Used to working solo, McAllister had a keen sense for one-man tactics and how to best use all the tools at his disposal to formulate plans using the limited resources available to him. In this case, all he really had was himself, Molly and Lena – who he had no intention of involving – and the weapons on his person and in the trunk. His greatest weapon, however, didn't have a trigger. It was his awareness of the surroundings at his target, a strange way to think of his own safe house. The lay of the land surrounding the farm house was not only familiar, he had chosen the site and designed and installed its security system, giving him intimate knowledge of every sensor and trip device installed in and around the house. The property had been rigged not to keep out intruders but to give the occupants a moment's notice when anyone got close enough to be a threat.

Pulling onto the winding two-lane highway, McAllister briefed the ladies on the plan. He was going to drop them in a safe place near the edge of the property and continue solo toward the house, hoping to lure out anyone from inside. Whether they came out was going to dictate what he did next. It would give him a better of idea of how many enemy targets he would have to handle.

While still deep in the woods, he let Molly and Lena out near a grove of oaks with their cell phones – he had programmed their numbers into his speed dial – and made sure Lena had her gun before he drove down the rutted gravel driveway toward the house, his presence no longer a secret, having just crossed a sensor as the wheels crunched the gravel. If – a big *if* – the intruders were monitoring the alarm system then they knew he was coming even if they couldn't see out a window. The car was also exposed, visible in the wide open, leaving the cover of the trees behind.

McAllister had done a quick visual scan with binoculars of the house, buildings, and surrounding property while still hidden in the woods. As he drove down toward the house, he continued to survey the area as he made his way dangerously closer, trying to maintain normal speed so no one would think he suspected anything. Still no signs of movement. Stanford's car was tucked away in the carport, so he was either still in the house or had been taken away in another vehicle. He hoped for the former, but he'd deal with the latter if necessary.

He pulled the Saab into the empty slot in the carport, keeping his eye on the inside door in case someone burst through and started shooting. Nobody did. He extracted the Walther from its concealed holster, grabbed the black nylon bag from the back seat, and got out, closing the door quietly behind him. He sneaked out of the carport and under the kitchen window, peeking carefully through the bottom of the pane and into the house. Inside, Stanford sat alone at the kitchen table, his back to the window. *Okay, where's your captor? Where is he – or them – hiding?* McAllister knew there were a couple of great places inside the house for an attacker to lie in wait because he had already thought of them himself in case he ever had to use them. Now, in an ironic twist, someone might be waiting to ambush him just like he would.

Sticking to his original plan, he returned to the carport and opened the inside door casually, his gun in hand by his side. The hall was empty. He listened. Nothing. So on in he went. Slowly. By this point, all normal behavior was thrown out the kitchen window and replaced with combat mentality. He wanted to be prepared if he was about to walk into a kill zone.

The hall emptied out into the kitchen to the right and the living room to the left, with blind spots in both rooms, so he knew had to be doubly sure to not reveal his position before he ascertained his enemy's position or positions. Creeping silently along the left wall, gun down and at the ready, he reached the end of the short hall and scanned for targets. He knew Stanford was sitting just around the corner at the table, but oddly he wasn't making any noise. No computer key clicks, none of the normal, ordinary sounds. Now McAllister definitely knew something was wrong. His awareness level rocketed inside his head, and he tried to control his heart rate as the adrenaline began to rush. Over the last few moments he'd almost forgotten to breathe and wasn't about to start now.

Switching to the right wall and still partially concealed, he quickly glanced into the living room, again looking for a target. It was empty, at least the part he could see.

Across the kitchen, opposite his current position, was another hall that led to the lower floor bedrooms and another outside door. The light was off in the hall, leaving the back door with the sun shining downward through the four panes as the only light coming from that direction. It wasn't enough for McAllister's purposes, as it left most of the hall dark, so he was going to have to improvise.

Setting the nylon bag quietly on the floor, he unzipped the ultra-quiet black plastic zipper and pulled out two cylindrical flash bang grenades. Designed for noise distraction, the devices were extremely loud and would disorient anyone within a reasonable earshot, temporarily deafening them without ear protection.

Stanford was seated facing where McAllister intended to toss the grenades, so he was reasonably sure he'd have enough warning to cover his ears. Either way, there would be no long term damage.

Crouching down and laying the Walther on the floor, McAllister pulled the pin on the first flash bang and chucked it into the living room, where it thudded on the carpet. The second flash bang followed immediately and landed in the middle of the kitchen floor. McAllister turned away and put his fingers deep inside his ears.

In quick succession, the two powerful flash bang grenades ignited, forcing a shockwave of sound across the house.

BOOM! BOOM!

"Ah, shit! " came a cry from the living room.

McAllister grabbed up the Walther off the floor and darted through the kitchen and to his left, into the living room. In the middle of the room, writhing in pain, was a man he did not recognize dressed in jeans and a leather jacket. As he stammered to get up, the man's jacket flew open revealing a handgun. With the man's hands still grabbing at his ringing ears, McAllister yanked the gun out of the man's waistband and locked him into an arm hold from behind. The man was temporarily helpless to fight back, exactly what McAllister was counting on.

"Who are you?" McAllister asked into the ear that was now uncovered.

"What?" the man replied, still in shock.

"I said," McAllister continued as he applied more pressure to the arm lock, "who the hell are you?"

"I'm not telling you shit!" the man spat back over his shoulder.

McAllister pulled the man closer from behind and whispered into his ear, "Do you not understand English? I'm not asking for shit. I want to know who you are and why you're here, plain and simple. It's not that complicated of a question."

"Go to hell," the man winced as McAllister increased the pressure again.

"You'll be begging to go there yourself for a little relief if you don't tell me what I want to know. Now I'll ask you one more time politely and I expect an answer in kind, nice and polite. Who are you and why are you here?"

The man said nothing, just grimaced.

"Fine," McAllister said and swung the Walther up over the man's head from behind and brought it crashing down onto his nose, cracking bone and spraying blood onto the man's upper lip. He screamed in agony. The man started to slump down, but McAllister applied more pressure and forced him back up. "Now, shall we try this again?"

Again, the man said nothing, blood dripping from his now deformed nose, into his mouth, and down his chin.

"Here let's go into the kitchen so you won't get blood on my nice carpet." The man refused to cooperate by walking, so McAllister dragged the man across the floor and onto the kitchen tile. "There, that's better. Now, where were we? Oh, yes, you were about to answer my questions in a gentlemanly manner or else I would make you bleed somewhere else. Isn't that right?"

The man closed his eyes. For a moment, McAllister thought he might be trying to compose an answer, but after a short pause realized he was just stalling.

"Are you right handed or left handed?" he asked the man, who said nothing in return. "You gotta help me out here. With the price of bullets these days, I'd hate to waste one shooting the wrong elbow. Of course, I could just choose one, since I have a fifty-fifty chance."

The man tried to jerk away, his right hand moving first, giving McAllister just the information he needed. He rested the Walther right behind the man's right elbow and squeezed the trigger. The man let out a scream as the bullet ripped into and out of the bone and ligaments, exiting the front of his arm and landing with the thud amidst the blood splatter on the kitchen wall.

"Okay, okay! What are you going to do to me?" the man pleaded, pumping blood forming black streaks down the right sleeve of his leather jacket.

"Let me make this perfectly clear," McAllister enunciated, "so there would be no misunderstanding or confusion. If you do not give me what I want, I will systematically disassemble every part of your body until you are left with only enough parts and pieces to scream for me to kill you. Which I will not do."

Resigned, the man closed his eyes and said, "No, you'll definitely want to kill me."

"I will?" said McAllister, a bit surprised. "And why is that?"

The man twitched his head to the right. "Because of him."

McAllister looked toward the kitchen table for the first time since he'd entered the house. There, sitting perfectly still in his chair on the far side, was his old friend Willard Stanford, bruised, beaten, bleeding, eyes closed, with a yellowed rubber strap tied around his upper arm and a syringe hanging from just underneath the skin.

31

"You might want to keep that thing elevated," McAllister said, pointing to the bleeding elbow of the wounded man now sitting at the kitchen table with his ankles duct-taped to a wooden chair. The man winced as he strained to move his arm even slightly through the excruciating pain. "You might also want to think about how the game has changed now, since my friend's life is no longer at stake."

He let the words sink in before continuing.

"That was an idiot move to make, killing him," McAllister continued. "You see," he said, moving to within inches of the man's face, "now you've lost all your leverage. I no longer have anything to lose. And that's a very dangerous place to put me."

The man was visibly shaken but tried to force it back. The bleeding from his elbow increased as his heart rate went up. In spite of what he said, McAllister had to be careful how he played this. It was true the man had lost the edge by killing Stanford, but he still had to be careful how he went about applying just the right pressure to get what he wanted.

"Let's start with any easy question. What's your name?" he asked. The wounded man stared down at the table, saying nothing. McAllister hefted the pistol in his hand and leaned in toward him. "Apparently there's something wrong with your ears. Perhaps I should fix that," he said as he raised the weapon and fired a shot that grazed the man's right ear, slicing a notch and causing it to bleed profusely. The man screamed and tried to grab at his ear with his wounded right arm, doubling the pain on the right side of his body.

"Okay, okay!" the man exclaimed as he writhed in the chair trying desperately to ease the pain somehow. Finally, he collected himself enough to answer. "Name's Dominic Rippon."

McAllister stepped back. "Alright, Dominic, now we're getting somewhere. Why are you here?"

He looked at McAllister and then thought better of bullshitting his way out of this one. Getting shot twice point blank was enough for him. And he figured anything his boss would do to him would pale in comparison to what McAllister would do – assuming he even saw his boss again. Probably wouldn't work anyway. Through wincing, he answered, "I was sent here to kill you and Stanford, then get rid of the girl."

McAllister was glad to hear him say *girl*, singular. That mean he didn't know there were two. But which one did he know about?

"Why? What's so important about her?"

"She was supposed to have been killed the night her fiancé, Peter, got dumped, but the pricks screwed up and didn't finish the job. They only got him and left her."

Okay, that narrowed it down to Molly.

"Who do you work for?"

Dominic had to think long and hard about that one. Not because he didn't know the answer but because he was far more scared than he let on about how this whole thing would turn out. Should he tell him and blow the whole operation? Then again, what good would it do to hold back information now? McAllister had already demonstrated he was willing to do whatever it took to get what he needed one way or another. Dominic Rippon knew too much about the man standing over him to question whether he'd live to tell his story to anyone else.

McAllister aimed the pistol at Dominic's right knee and prepared to pull the trigger.

"Max Preston!" Dominic blurted out to save himself the agony.

The pistol lowered as McAllister said, "That's the second time today I've heard that name. Interesting. What do you do for him beside sneak around and kill people?"

"Hey," Dominic said with a sudden shot of courage, "You do the same thing!"

"But for different reasons and you know it. I don't kill innocent civilians – women and children – in the name of world domination or some other crap. That's called terrorism, plain and simple. It's also called murder. Don't ever lump me in with garbage like you! " The rage was boiling up inside him, but he knew he had to hold it back if he was going to get anything out of this interrogation. Calming himself, he said, "What *exactly* do you do for Max Preston? And this is no time for getting shy on me. I want it all."

Dominic swallowed hard, both to muster his strength and to mask the throbbing pain in his arm and ear. The wince that followed was only partially because of the physical wounds.

"I guess you might call me his henchman, like in the movies. I do the grunt work."

"Like what?"

"Like just about everything."

"Were you the one who blew out my living room window?"

Dominic looked up at him, unsure again about how to answer that one. "Yeah," he decided. "That was me."

"You're not a very good shot," McAllister jabbed, one eyebrow raised. "Didn't adjust for the conditions. Rain and wind can do funny things with a bullet."

Dominic didn't feel like bantering right now. He knew McAllister was using a classic interrogation technique of trying to buddy up to his subject, make him your closest friend, but it wasn't going to work with him. He was growing impatient and more scared by the moment. If McAllister was going to kill him, he wished he'd just get on with it.

McAllister reached across the table and turned Stanford's laptop around so he could see the screen, which was logged into their proprietary accessing program capable of hacking into just about any government file or database they needed. He knew at this point Stanford wouldn't mind McAllister touching his stuff. He entered

Dominic's name into the search engine and found exactly what he was seeking. Dominic Rippon, age 38, former analyst for the National Security Agency. Family emigrated to US from United Arab Emirates when he was age three. Joined NSA in 2002, left 2007. Exemplary reviews. Father was an exec with major oil consulting company.

"So why'd you leave the NSA?"

"The pay is better in the private sector."

"Especially if you're working for a well-financed organization like Al-Qaeda."

"Al-Qaeda?" Dominic snorted. "Are you kidding? Bin Laden couldn't pay the entrance fee to get involved with what we do."

"How so?" Al-Qaeda certainly wasn't the only terror organization out there, but in spite of its struggling finances it was still the largest. Country after country had been choking off support, at least on paper. Really they were just funneling funds through even darker back channels with more conditions attached. Fools that they were, many of the leaders of these countries operated under the illusion that their conditions would be met. McAllister always found it amusing when governments were surprised when terrorists broke their promises. It reminded him of the Johnny Depp version of *Pirates of the Caribbean* in a scene where swashbuckling Jack Sparrow is plying his craft against Orlando Bloom's character, novice swordsman Will Turner, in a duel inside a grain mill. When Turner complains that Sparrow is not fighting fair, Sparrow shrugs and reminds him matter-of-factly, "Pirate." And that's the way it was with terrorists: they only pretend to fight fair until they get what they want, all along lying to your face. Then they strap on a bomb and go blow up a bus. Or fly an airplane into a skyscraper.

Dominic stared down at the table, his mind swirling. Then he looked straight at McAllister. "What's the wealthiest organization in the world?"

McAllister thought for a second before answering, "The United States government."

Dominic continued to stare up at him, not blinking, not flinching. McAllister broke the stare and said incredulously, "Wait a minute, you're telling me the United States government has been behind these attacks? Who are you kidding here?"

Dominic said slowly, "Mr. McAllister, let me make myself abundantly clear here. Just like you, I have absolutely nothing to lose now, remember? If I manage to walk out of here alive, I'll be dead by sundown with a bullet in my head from Max Preston. I have zero reason to hold anything back."

"That is, unless Preston himself wants you to tell me all this so I'll believe you and stop worrying about him."

"Now that would be pretty clever, wouldn't it?" countered Dominic. "Except that it wouldn't get you off his back because he has his fingerprints all over the entire operation, from start to finish."

"Tell me all about it, in as much detail as you can provide. I want names and dates and targets."

"Okay, but first I need a glass of water."

"Water? Why?"

"Because I'm thirsty. And if you haven't noticed, I'm bleeding."

"Yeah, I think I remember something about that," McAllister replied dryly. "You're dripping blood on the table and onto my nice tile floor. While I get your water, you start yappin'."

McAllister was on his cell phone within minutes of Dominic's confession, waiting impatiently for the other end to pick up.

"Leonard Martin," came the voice finally.

"Leonard, it's Gordon."

There was a long pause, then reluctantly, "What do you want?"

"Stop it, Leonard," McAllister smiled into the phone. "You know it's always an adventure when I call."

"Yeah, a real joy ride," replied the voice on the other end flatly. "Who am I hacking into now?" Sigh.

McAllister always admired Leonard Martin's candor, especially since he knew he was sitting in an open cubicle in the middle of the black glassy building in Fort Meade, Maryland, known as the National Security Agency, where every phone call, e-mail, and probably casual conversation was monitored and recorded. Right now, a computer was transcribing their conversation onto an encrypted hard drive and running it through over a dozen software packages looking for anything that might be a tip off to threats to the United States, either at home or overseas. Of course, neither man was going to say anything that might cause a warning flag to pop up

– that wasn't why they were talking – but they were still acutely aware they were being taped.

"Nobody. I was wondering if you'd like to have dinner tonight with me and two lovely ladies."

"The lovely ladies part I like, but you're calling from St. Louis. You'll never make in here in time for dinner."

"Grab a snack to hold you over. Meet me at your favorite place. I'll call when we touch down."

He disconnected and put the cell phone in his pocket. He grabbed the cordless phone off the kitchen wall dialed another number. He didn't want the party on the other end to trace his cell.

"Federal Bureau of Investigation," said the man on the other end. "Special Agent Davis speaking."

"Agent Davis, I need you to pick up a dead body and a suspect. I'll give you the location."

32

The Washington night skyline stretched out beyond the tiny airplane window, the Capitol dome majestically lit in the distance and the pair of red eyeballs blinking at the top of the Washington Monument so close McAllister felt he could reach out and rake his fingers against it. He was constantly amazed at how close Reagan National Airport was to the center of government. He knew many of the buildings in the DC area had added layers of protection, with air-to-air missiles and additional communication capabilities, but it still struck him as odd that airplanes routinely flew right down the Potomac River, snaking between national landmarks on their final approach. He doubted anyone could actually take the kinds of actions necessary to stop an attack with another airplane at that point if the pilot or hijacker was really determined. All it would take was a slight course deviation on final approach and within seconds the plane would plow right into the White House or the Capitol and wreak unimaginable havoc not just across the nation but around the world. Both buildings were equipped with air-to-air missiles and orders to shoot, but it would all happen way too fast to get off a decent shot that would actually down the plane in time. The momentum alone would carry the flying fireball right into the façade of either structure. There was a reason it was a no-fly zone for private aircraft. The compromise had been that commercial airliners still needed to operate inside the zone to access National, a crucial destination for airlines serving the area.

The three had purchased round trip tickets in St. Louis, careful not to sit together, Molly and Lena using their real names and McAllister using one of many fake identities he kept stashed away for his real missions but proved useful for just such an occasion as this. For this mission he was traveling as Lyndon Miles, an international banker who worked out of an office in Shady Grove, Maryland. The real Lyndon Miles had died of natural causes at an early age several years back, freeing up his identity. Unbeknownst to his wife and three children, Mr. Miles was going to be back in the area again, albeit with a completely different face.

Getting through security in St. Louis had been a breeze, and now they were about to touch down in the nation's capital. Georgetown flashed below them to the left, followed by the Watergate Hotel and Kennedy Center, so close he could see the evening's attendees hustling back inside to catch the second act. The unusually warm winter evening allowed them to stand outside and smoke in relative comfort.

The jet's wheels chirped on the pavement and the thrusters reversed, abruptly slowing the plane to taxi speed on a runway considered by many to be too short, especially with the waters of the

Potomac surrounding three sides of the airport and lapping at each end of the main runway. There was zero margin for error, as the passengers on Air Florida flight 90 found out too late when it crashed into the river taking off in a snow storm on January 13, 1982, killing 78 people, including four occupants of cars on the 14th Street Bridge, which the plane struck before splashing into the icy water. Only five people on board survived. Of course that plane had been taking off, not landing. Gordon always found it ironic that aircraft were so hard to land safely. Taking off is easy under normal conditions, but putting a plane safely back on the ground takes skill and finesse.

McAllister was a master of surveillance, always mindful of anyone who might be tailing him or watching him from a distance. The entire flight he had surreptitiously glanced around, checking for subtle movements by his fellow passengers and flight attendants that would tip him off that he was being surveiled. While it was a good idea for the three of them to spread out in the plane, because of the last minute booking he could not seat Molly and Lena in a place where he could protect them the way he would have wanted. They were too far away for him to reach them fast enough if something happened on board. When the wheels touched down, he breathed a bit easier, knowing any trouble now would most likely not come from inside the airplane.

He met up with the ladies in the terminal. None of them had checked baggage, as they only planned to stay a short while, so off they went to the rental counter, picked up the car – also under

McAllister's alias of Lyndon Miles – and headed into the heavy Washington, DC, traffic, a constant no matter what the time of day. They could have taken the Metro, but McAllister had long ago been trained to always have control over his escape route. The light rail system was extremely reliable, but he didn't stake his life on it. Having his own vehicle at least partially assured he could safely get out of danger. He carefully drove into town, always mindful of anyone following them.

The restaurant was only a few blocks from the White House, down Pennsylvania Avenue to the east. They parked a block away and around the corner, allowing McAllister a good field of view and a chance to scan the area for tails. Subconsciously, he tapped his right hand against his black overcoat, feeling to make sure his Walther was still here. But this time it wasn't, thanks to airline regulations. He felt vulnerable without his weapon on his side. Typically he would either ship his sidearm overnight to his destination or have his on-site contact supply him with one immediately upon arrival, but he hadn't had time to make those arrangements. Instead he'd have to improvise this time if anything happened.

They entered the dark restaurant and immediately headed toward the back corner where Leonard Martin sat in a booth nursing a mostly-empty beer, white foam streaks edging their way down the inside of the thick mug. Martin got up immediately and let McAllister have the bench facing the front door, a security arrangement McAllister always insisted upon. Molly sat down next to him on the inside to give McAllister a tactical advantage as Martin and Lena slid into the other bench. A waitress materialized at the end of the table, and they ordered drinks, including another beer for Martin.

Getting down to business, McAllister asked, "So what did you find?"

Knowing not to ask too much, Martin reached into his leather jacket pocket and extracted a white letter-size envelope and handed it to McAllister. "Everything you need is right there. Phone numbers, times, names. The whole shootin' match."

"What did you find when you looked at the records?" McAllister asked, sure Martin had already perused the information.

"I don't even know what I'm looking for. All you asked for was a list of name and numbers. What does this have to do with?"

McAllister studied the man across the table carefully. Leonard Martin was a scrawny man, the type who made tight shirts look oversized. He was also a certifiable genius and knew it, proud of his membership in Mensa, having aced the test, one of only a handful of people to have scored perfectly the first time. He had commented to the proctor on the way out the door that they really should make the test a little harder, a remark that was met with a condescending scowl. Combine his intelligence with a master's degree from MIT and the government came knocking on his door one afternoon. He could have made more money in the private sector, as his skills would have fit with hundreds of IT companies all over the world, but part of Leonard Martin enjoyed the challenge of dealing with the bureaucracy of the government's way of doing things juxtaposed against its need to flex in order to combat a new and rising enemy tactic: terrorism. He might be a nerd, but he was more of a patriot. He viewed September 11 as a challenge, an affront to freedom not just for America but for the entire world. In his mind, that day the terrorists began a war they would later regret starting. Soon after he started with the NSA, he was tasked to a secret project, code named SPIDER VISION.

The project, brain child of the newly-appointed Director of Homeland Security, threw Martin right in the middle of logistical support to one of the most effective, yet hidden anti-terror projects. Through the unique technology of the NSA's Red Cell program, Martin was able to coordinate and run field operations through his cubicle, providing tactical support for eight (thus the name Spider) secret field operatives working to take down Al-Qaeda and other terrorist organizations, mostly within the United States. Foreign operations were largely relegated to CIA and military operations, even though intelligence shared among them often led to joint international and domestic operations. Staffing for the project was selected through a combination of existing personnel and new hires specifically brought in for the sort of "wet work" needed to get the job done. McAllister's selection had been a no-brainer, since he had done such exemplary work during the Cold War and was already tactically trained. He just needed a brush-up on new technologies. The others were selected because they were single and unattached, easily transportable with simple-to-concoct cover stories.

"What I'm looking for," McAllister answered, "is a connection between Max Preston and someone in Washington, beyond just his typical workings as a government contractor. I have information that someone on the inside worked the arrangements that got my team killed."

"Well, the information in the envelope might help you."

"Yes, but there's more to it, which is why I wanted to meet." McAllister pulled out the thumb drive Lena had given him back at his house and slid it across to Martin. "I can't get into this. There's a file on there that's so encrypted my system can't break into it. I'm hoping yours can."

"Of course it can! I am the wizard! " Martin bragged with a wicked smile.

"I know," McAllister agree, eyes rolling. "Now wave your magic wand and conjure up an answer."

The waitress reappeared and everyone ordered dinner before she drifted away again.

Lena picked the conversation back up, looking at Martin. "If I give you Preston's phone numbers, both his personal ones and his 'business' ones" – she made the quote in the air – "could you track down the audios and get something?"

Martin looked back at her and then to McAllister, who nodded agreement. He returned to Lena. "Yeah, but it would take a while. We have the software. It's just a matter of getting access."

"I think I can help with that one," offered Lena.

Martin eyed her suspiciously. "And just how to do you plan to do that? Do you understand how hard it is to get into NSA computers without proper authorization?"

"Yes," she said flatly. "Which is why I offered." She turned to McAllister, "Does he know about me?"

"Probably not," he answered.

"Wait a minute," Martin said. "What's going on here? What haven't you told me, Gordon?"

McAllister smiled. "What I haven't told you is that Lena was on the inside. She was working Preston from within his organization. She had access to all his files. That's how I got the thumb drive. Which is why I want you to take her with you and get inside the big black box so she can help you."

"Help me?" Martin responded indignantly.

McAllister ignored Martin's attempt to lure him in. "Look," he countered, "she's an NSA authorized agent. She was their idea. They'll let her in."

Martin sighed consent.

Dinner finished, the four parted ways: Lena with Martin driving in his SUV to Fort Meade, and Molly with McAllister, headed to the hotel. Safely inside the rental, Gordon checked his watch to make sure it wasn't too late at night, then pulled out his cell and dialed a number he hadn't used in a long time but his fingers never forgot.

The man on the other end answered on the second ring. That meant nobody else was eavesdropping. Plus, it was a secure line on the other end.

"Hello?" came the innocuous answer from the other end.

"Mr. President, this is ZEBRA," McAllister stated flatly. "You have a minute?" The long pause on the other end told him he'd caught the President by surprise.

"Just a moment," the President replied finally. "Let me move to a better location." McAllister could hear crowd noise in the background that suddenly stopped. "That's better."

"Mr. President, I need to ask a favor."

"Maybe, but first why are you breaking protocol? You're not supposed to call me."

"Yes, sir, I know, but this is an emergency. I am working an angle on the recent terrorist attacks and need your authorization." McAllister knew he was about to walk a fine line, especially when the President didn't officially know McAllister's team exists. And he most certainly didn't know McAllister by his real name.

"You know I can't authorize anything," the President replied.

"Yes, sir, I know *you* can't. It would look bad. But your administration can, through the right channels."

The President didn't like where this was going but was willing to listen. "Go on."

McAllister explained his plan to the President, asking him for clearance for Lena to have access to Red Cell and all other NSA protocols that might help Martin find the right phone calls and transcript needed to hunt down the connection.

"But why not just have Director Henderson authorize that?" the President countered.

"Because, Mr. President, I have reason to believe the director may be in on the whole thing."

"Now wait just a minute," the President said indignantly. "You're telling me you believe the director of the National Security Agency, a man I appointed three years ago, is part of a conspiracy against the United States? That's quite an accusation."

McAllister knew that wasn't going to go over well. This was one time he hated being right. "Sir, I believe it's possible. I didn't say he was. I just think it's wise to be careful about how many people we bring into this. You know the first rule of intelligence: the fewer people know, the less chance of a leak."

"And if you're wrong?" the President asked point blank.

"Mr. President, you and I go back a long way, and you know my history. I have never lied to you, nor have I have ever failed a mission. I appreciate all the times you've stuck your neck out and let me play by my own rules. I've never failed you, and I don't plan on starting now."

The President thought for a moment before answering, "Okay, ZEBRA, you have your authorization. But make sure your folks on the inside stay within the parameters you outlined."

"Yes, sir. Thank you, sir." He hung up and called Martin.

33

Lena and Leonard arrived back at NSA headquarters thirty minutes later, and her clearance was waiting for her at the door. She clipped on the badge, and, after all the necessary scans and detectors, including electronic fingerprint and retinal scans, they boarded an elevator down to Martin's level, far below the parking lot. Very few people were around the rather dark floor this time of night, allowing them some latitude to talk more openly, even though both were acutely aware that in a building known for its eavesdropping capabilities, anything they said was probably being recorded. Every computer key click, every phone call. Everything. But Martin was okay with that because he understood the need for the heightened security in a post-9/11 world and understood that the average American's life wouldn't be changed by a little innocuous listening to cell phone and landline conversations. The NSA didn't care what Grandma was fixing for dinner or how well little Johnny did on his history exam. They didn't care that Mommy was having an affair with the next door neighbor. But they did care if a terrorist was planning to blow up the White House or poison the water supply at the Super Bowl.

They swung by the break room and grabbed coffee – Lena's in a foam cup and Martin's in a ceramic mug that he grabbed off the wall hook. The bright orange mug said in black stenciled letters, "Caution: Genius at Work." The back said, "Keep Back 10 Feet."

They arrived at Martin's cubicle, where Lena pulled a chair from a neighboring cube and sat down behind him so she could watch over his shoulder. For the next two hours, they pored over data mined from logarithms Martin and several of his smartest co-workers had created to weed out any information deemed useless and crank it down to only data that might lead somewhere. Martin typed madly, pulling list after list, and Lena checked numbers and logs to find that tiny bit of information that might be the beginning of a connection.

Finally Lena stopped him. "I think I found something. Pull up this conversation here," she said and pointed to a number on the last printout.

Martin clicked on the corresponding number on his screen and up popped an audio player tied into the recording servers. They both donned headphones, and Martin clicked Play. The recorded cell call was amazingly clear, not due so much to the NSA's equipment – although it was the best in the world – but because cell technology had made such huge advances since going digital. The call quality was amazing on all carriers, with very few dropped calls, an unintended benefit to the eavesdropping program. The audio began.

"What is the status of the package?" asked the first male voice.

"Safely tucked away and waiting for you to tell us where and when to move it," answered the man on the other end. "We're ready when you are."

"Good. The delivery truck should be by to pick it up around midnight. Follow the truck to the hangar and help them unload."

"Yes, sir." There was a slight pause. "Does Frank have the codes?"

"He said he did, but you know how reliable he is," responded the caller with a sarcastic overtone.

"Yeah, okay. We'll see you tonight."

The call ended.

"Why did you flag this one?" Martin asked Lena.

"A combination of things. First, the time stamp: three in the morning. Second, the call originated from Preston's cell to the 202 area code, Washington, DC. That doesn't mean the person was in DC at the time, but it does mean he had connections back to the area."

"Yeah, but I can do you one better," Martin said as he punched some keys, drove the mouse, and pulled up a map on the screen. "This map shows the location of the caller, down to within fifteen feet."

"I thought cell tower triangulation wasn't that accurate," Lena said.

"It's not, which is why we rarely use it anymore, especially in crowded metro areas. GPS works much better. And now that most phones have navigation capability, they send out a constant GPS signal that can be turned off by the user but rarely is. Most folks never even think about it. They just see the little crosshairs at the top of the screen and ignore it. Plus, now that smart phones also have navigation capability, which requires GPS, if they turn if off then they can't use half the features on the phone. Upwards of ninety percent of callers never turn it off, which means we can track just about anybody anywhere with pretty much pinpoint accuracy and they'll never even know it."

"That's kinda creepy," Lena said.

"It is," Martin said, "but it's their own fault."

"So how can you track GPS coordinates on a recording? He's not on the phone right now."

"True, but that doesn't mean there's not a record of where he was at the time of the call. See, every data bit in a call contains what's called a metafile," he explained, "which is a little tracker that lets you go back to the moment the call was made and see exactly where the caller was standing or sitting at the time of the call. It's kind of like when you take a photograph with a digital camera. Each picture contains a metafile that can be used to get the exact location of the camera when the picture was taken. It was designed to be a useful tool for researchers trying to recreate a scene, but the unintended benefit – again – is that it allows us to track bad people."

"So in other words, you can see where he was when he called for the delivery?"

"I can see where they *both* were," he said, focusing back on the screen and keyboard. A few commands later he had a result. "Okay,

Preston was at his house in Costa Mesa, looks like lounging at his pool, while our mystery man was in…huh? According to this, he was inside Senator Franklin Stevens' office in the Capitol building at the time of the call."

Lena grabbed her cell. "How's the reception in here?" she asked Martin.

"Deliberately not that great. That way they can keep us from calling anyone with information from, say, an eavesdropping mission," he answered with an upturned lip.

She looked at her cell's display. No bars. She reached past Martin and grabbed the handset from his desk phone. "Dial McAllister's cell."

He did as he was told and in a moment it was ringing.

The number on his cell display was blocked, but he answered it this time, knowing it might be Martin.

"We have our connection," Lena said on the other end.

"Who?" McAllister asked as he glanced at Molly sitting on the couch in their suite. To maintain cover, they had checked in as a married couple sharing a room. It also meant Molly didn't have to be out of McAllister's site during the night.

"Senator Franklin Stevens, the senior senator from North Carolina."

"Yeah, I know who he is, but how do you know it's him?"

Lena filled him in the recorded phone conversation and the GPS tracking. He was convinced.

"Okay, what we need to do is get some rest tonight and then meet up for breakfast in the morning. Do you have a place to stay?"

Lena hadn't really thought about that, too busy with all the excitement of figuring out the source. In fact, she hadn't slept since the plane ride in from California. Over the past twenty-four hours she'd flown all the way across the country, met with an unofficial government assassin after breaking into his house, hacked into classified files in the headquarters of the National Security Agency, and discovered the source of a terrorist attack on the United States of America. It never crossed her mind to call Holiday Inn.

"I'll stay with Martin," she said, glancing at Martin, who shrugged his shoulders. "It's too late to get a hotel and I'm afraid someone might track me there if I used my credit card."

"Good thinking. I'll call you around six to set up a meeting place."

He punched the button to end the call and slowly turned to Molly. "I need you to tell me all you know about Senator Franklin Stevens."

34

FBI analyst Allison Crenshaw was frustrated. For two days she had been at her station in the FBI lab in Quantico examining the blast fragments from the attack in North Carolina and could not for the life of her figure out exactly what she had.

She pushed her wire frame glasses back onto the bridge of her nose, wishing she could tolerate contact lenses. As much time as she spent bent over examining evidence, she knew they would be more practical. But the idea of touching her eyes every morning and night upset her far more than the annoyance she felt from constantly fingering the nose piece. And by now she'd gotten so accustomed to it, she would almost miss it. Besides, the glasses made her look smarter – a stark contrast to what everyone who saw her strawberry blond hair assumed.

A stunning beauty, Alison had spent her whole life fighting the stereotype. Graduating top of her class in computer science helped but only for those who knew it. The average Joe on the street still lumped her into the category of the jokes and assumed she was only good for looks. She fiercely resisted using her external beauty for gain, despising other women who did. Sure, it would have been easier to get any job she wanted just by flirting and batting her eyelashes, but she refused to stoop to that Neanderthal level. She didn't date men who thought they were hunks, and she wasn't going to use her beauty to advance her career. Instead, she studied like a mad woman and finished top of her class. Her reward: a top analyst position with the FBI's Counterterrorism and Forensic Science Research Unit (CFSRU) at the main FBI laboratory in Quantico, Virginia, also home of the FBI's training academy. As the role of the FBI's crime investigation had grown, so had its need for more space, making its old location in the J. Edgar Hoover Building too cramped to operate effectively. Along with new technology and greater understanding of laboratory techniques, the new CFSRU center had the space and equipment necessary to more thoroughly conduct investigations.

The shape of the explosive device sitting on her work bench was easy to figure out. Parts and pieces from the site had been carefully gathered from the various investigators at the scene and were all finally in one location, having been painstakingly cataloged to assure they had all been accounted for. After careful examination of each part, they were partially assembled into what looked like an aerial bomb. That was the easy part. What frustrated her was its origin. Several of the pieces contained Cyrillic alphabet letters. Russian. Obviously the piece had been manufactured in the old Soviet Union or present-day Russia. But there was no date on it. And the piece was so clean – except for the explosive damage – that it was impossible to tell with the naked eye how old it was. The paint on the outside looked brand new, but the targeting device appeared to be old technology, the triggers dating back to the mid 1980's, according to her desk reference book laid out beside the reconstructed device.

So she had sent a small piece over the metallurgy and was waiting for the results to see if they could give her a chemical breakdown of the metal and paint fragments to maybe pinpoint a time period of the materials. Unfortunately, she knew, the old Soviet Union was always hard up for cash and therefore had little room for innovation or experimenting with new manufacturing process. In fact, most of their weapons were simply backwards-engineered replications of Western weapons, with a uniquely Russian accent so the Politburo could claim they had built something new and make themselves feel better about stealing the West's designs.

But the most frustrating part for her was the need by her superiors to have a report immediately that they could forward to the President. He needed something to work from, to give him some sort of direction as to actions he might or might not take against whoever was responsible for the attacks. What he got was accurate, just incomplete, and it had Alison's name on it, which meant she was handing unfinished work to the President of the United States, a foul in her own mind even if he didn't care.

Her report had stated unequivocally that her analysis was incomplete and that the FBI lab was still working on data that might yield better answers to questions she was sure he was going to ask, perfectly reasonable questions that he needed answers to before he would be informed enough to make a decision one way or another. The lab director was satisfied with her statements and promised to pass them along verbatim, a promise she knew he was in no position to make or keep. In theory, lab analyses are supposed to be presented in their entirety as they were originally written. But when they went through the hands of politicians on their way up the food chain, sometimes things got changed. Not big things, usually. No hard data. But she wrote it the way she wanted it, and that was that.

What she didn't know was that the lab director felt her analysis was so important that he had spoken with FBI Director William Longfellow, who asked for the entire file to be on his desk immediately so he could personally present it to the President.

In fact, he was on his way to the White House at that moment.

The Secret Service agent led Director Longfellow into the Oval Office through the curved side door as the President was hanging up the phone. He came out from behind the Resolute Desk and greeted the director with a warm handshake.

"Bill, good to see you. You said you had something urgent to show me. Please, sit down," the President said, gesturing toward the pair of couches and wing chairs framing the fireplace opposite the desk. Longfellow chose the customary visitor's couch while the President sat in one of the wing chairs.

Longfellow extracted a folder from his leather briefcase and handed it to the President. "Mr. President, I'll get right to the point. We have reason to believe the bomb that detonated at the nuclear facility in North Carolina was Russian made. What you have there in your hands is our analyst's report up to the present. She is not finished yet with the entire analysis because she is waiting for a report from our metallurgy department to determine the exact age of the bomb. Once we get it I will personally pass it along to you."

"How do you know it's Russian made?" asked the President.

"Several fragments have Cyrillic writing printed on the outside, and the words all point to terms used by the Soviet or Russian military. The paint chemistry also matches Eastern Bloc munitions. Without getting into particulars, let's just say the chemical signature is unmistakably Russian or Polish, the other nation where the Soviets had major weapons factories."

The President crossed his legs and studied both the cover sheet summary inside the front of the folder and Longfellow's face. He sighed and pursed his lips before raising his eyes to meet the FBI director's.

"Are you suggesting the Russians somehow set off a bomb at a nuclear power station on US soil and then slipped away undetected?" the President asked, trying to keep his cool.

Longfellow was prepared for this question and answered, "No, we don't have enough hard evidence to accuse them of that. All we know is that whoever did it used what appears to be Russian or Soviet materials to do it. A lot of materials have fallen into the wrong hands since the end of the Cold War. Someone else might have obtained it through black market channels."

"I knew nuclear materials had escaped, but conventional weapons, too?"

"Yes, sir. They are heavily traded by black market arms dealers."

"Do you have a delivery device?"

"It appears the bomb was dropped somehow, not planted on the ground. Blast patterns indicated high velocity descent prior to explosion, which would be inconsistent with the device sitting at ground level when it exploded. More likely it was dropped from altitude and the ground proximity fuse blew it up right overhead, maximizing the damage."

"So it was dropped from what? A plane?" asked the President indignantly.

"Some sort of aerial vehicle, yes. We don't know what kind yet."

Again the President looked at his longtime friend, Bill Longfellow, fellow Harvard law grad and Marine, and frowned. "So you're telling me that some person or organization has obtained Russian bombs and apparently an aircraft capable of delivering them on target and we don't know about it?"

"It would appear so, Mr. President."

The President stood and walked toward his desk and past it to gaze out the window on the South Lawn, the leaf-barren trees jutting up jaggedly against the clear blue winter sky. Somewhere in all that brilliance there was an aircraft operating undetected over the United States, *his* United States. He wasn't a king, only an elected official, but he was the leader of the most powerful nation on earth. Yet if Bill Longfellow's conclusions were even semi-correct – and he had every reason to trust them – that meant any target in the entire country could be vulnerable, including the White House. For a moment he imagined what it would be like to have a bomb come screaming in through the heavy bulletproof glass he was now peering through. He might never see it coming.

"Mr. President?" came Longfellow's voice from across the room, bringing the President back into the present.

"Bill," he said as he turned back toward the room, "I want you to brief the Joint Chiefs on your conclusions downstairs in an hour."

35

Molly was still seething at breakfast. And pacing around the suite all night added to her foul mood. McAllister had urged her to get some sleep since they had a long day ahead, but she couldn't calm down enough. Originally, she was going to take the bed while McAllister slept on the couch, but around midnight he couldn't take her pacing any longer and switched the sleeping arrangements and went into the bedroom and closed the door. With her audience gone, Molly finally collapsed onto the couch around two and slept fitfully until McAllister poked at her shortly after seven. Her lack of sleep made it even more difficult to get her head around the events of yesterday and last night and her introduction even further into this frightening new world.

Between McAllister's accusations that somehow her uncle, a trusted United States senator, might somehow be implicated in a series of terrorist attacks on US soil and her own knowledge that the case against him seemed to be adding up, she wasn't sure how to feel other than angry. Confused, maybe? No, angry. Angry at McAllister. Angry at Uncle Frank. Angry at herself. Angry at everybody who caused this awful mess, including – *how did it come this far?* – Peter for dragging her into his sick and twisted world without so much as a hint of what he was involved with.

But her anger toward Peter quickly subsided in the grand scheme, as she realized he was only trying to protect her. It wasn't his fault he got murdered, after all. He was a patriot, a warrior. Someone who worked in the shadows to make sure everyone else could live free in the light. But Uncle Frank? Now he was a different story apparently.

Molly wasn't naive about the ways of politics. She'd been around it all her life, far too long to be fooled into believing politicians were to be admired or worshipped. Many of them were low-life scum in a suit. She knew some of the worst ones, not because she hung around with them but because her family knew all the stories and told them around the dinner table on a nightly basis.

She snapped out of her trance and straightened in her chair, rubbing her hands on the napkin in her lap.

"Okay," she said to the other three sitting around the table in the half-full hotel lobby restaurant, "let me get this straight." McAllister and company stopped talking to listen. "You're saying that somehow my uncle is tied into the plot to bomb the nuclear plant. But what about the other attacks on the malls?"

"That part we don't know yet," McAllister said, "because we don't have a connection between them yet. If we can tie them all together, then we'll know whether your uncle's involved."

"But what if they're not connected?" she asked. "What if they are all separate attacks orchestrated by separate groups or individuals. Nobody has claimed responsibility for any of them yet."

McAllister appreciated where Molly was coming from. She wanted desperately to believe her uncle wasn't involved in all of this. He got it. But he also knew she was probably wrong. He set down his coffee cup.

"Terrorist organizations are normally poorly organized and poorly funded, which means the chance of these attacks being unrelated is slim. To put that many attacks together from multiple groups in such a relatively short period of time is unlikely. Nearly impossible. I may be wrong about this," he said, picking his cup back up, "but I'd put money on these all being connected somehow."

Molly's shoulders dropped. She knew he was probably right. After all, assuming what he said was true, he was far more experienced than any of the rest of the folks sitting around the table when it came to dealing with terrorists. He'd been face to face with them and knew how they operated.

She had always feared something like this would happen. No one was immune from the virus that was Washington, DC.

Suddenly the stock broker in her rose up, the determination kicking her doubt out of the way and pushing aside her hatred and anger. It was time to get the job done.

"All right," she said, placing both palms firmly on the table on either side of her plate. "Let's go nail the son of a bitch."

36

McAllister and Molly put their plan together back in the suite while Martin and Lena headed to the van he had picked up at NSA headquarters. The vehicle was equipped with an entire electronic suite in the back, more than enough to run this operation, but it was the only van they had available if they were going to be McAllister's eyes and ears for the operation. Martin had also brought along some specialized equipment McAllister had requested, all of it now installed and calibrated.

"You sure you're up to seeing your uncle right now?" McAllister asked. "You're not in the greatest of moods."

Molly forced a condescending smile. "Couldn't be happier. Are you ready yet?"

Martin had already called ahead and set up the meeting with the senator, posing as Anthony Layton, a very wealthy businessman from Stevens' home district, who wanted to talk about some pending legislation and just happened to be in town with his wife on related business. The cover was only to make sure Stevens would be in his office and not preoccupied with other business when they surprised him.

The van pulled up a couple blocks from the Capitol and the two got out, leaving Martin and Lena to monitor the audio and video devices installed on McAllister's and Molly's clothing. They buttoned their coats against the blustery breeze and walked to the Capitol, where they were greeted by magnetometers and radiation detectors, defenses against threats from the outside. McAllister couldn't miss the irony in Stevens' presence inside the building, having passed cleanly through similar devises on his way in the back of the building this morning. At least McAllister didn't have to worry about his gun setting off the detectors. He hated walking into a potentially hostile situation without his weapon, but he doubted he would need it.

Molly had only been to her uncle's office once before, so she had to locate a map on the wall to find where they were going. They found the right office and headed that direction. Every time McAllister walked the halls of the Capitol or any other building in DC, he was reminded of the great minds and hearts that had constructed the country and the wisdom it took to create such an amazing form of government. All it took was watching the evening news to bring him back to the present and realize how far the country and its leadership had strayed from the Founding Fathers' original intent.

He was so lost in his revelry that Molly had to grab his arm to keep him from walking past the door to Stevens' office. McAllister gave the receptionist the alias, and she called into the senator to tell him they were here. A moment later, the inside door opened and through it stepped Franklin Stevens, senior senator from North Carolina, toothy grin and warm handshake ready to great a wealthy campaign contributor. Molly wished she had a camera to capture the moment his expression changed abruptly to abject terror before he quickly composed himself and moved to embrace his niece. She would have nothing to do with it. As she backed away, McAllister cut off the senator's path and held up his hands.

"This might not be a good time for that sort of thing. She's liable to knee you in the nuts."

The receptionist reached for the phone, looking up to her boss for instructions. He looked McAllister in the eyes, then toward the receptionist and shook his head. She put down the receiver. Stevens backed up a step. "Please," he said graciously, "come into my office. We can talk in there."

Molly led the way. Brushing past Stevens on his way through the door, McAllister cracked, "Remind me to play poker with you, Senator."

Stevens closed the door behind them and offered them the wing chairs across from his large oak desk that he sat behind in his deep burgundy leather chair. It wheezed as he sat down. Stevens was a formidable figure, not just in politics but in life. At just under six feet tall, he didn't seem all that imposing, but McAllister could sense a sort of inner strength hidden beneath the black suit and red tie. Not that he intended to do any physical harm to the senator today, but

McAllister had a habit of always sizing up any potential threats before they became one.

"Molly, it's good to see you. How are things in the world of stocks?" Stevens asked.

Looking right at him, she said, "Cut the crap. You know why we're here."

"I do?" he said, feigning ignorance. "And why would that be?"

McAllister put his hand on Molly's arm to steady her as he took over. "Senator, I'll get right to it. We have every reason to believe you are involved with an organization that planned and executed all three of the recent terrorist attacks on this country and that you helped orchestrate them."

Stevens leaned his chair back and raised his eyebrows. "Those are pretty serious accusations, Mr. . ."

"McAllister. But you knew that already."

"Really? And how would I know that, especially since you came here using another name."

"It's all part of the business I'm in, as you also know."

"My, my, Mr. McAllister, you sure are making a lot of assumptions and getting plenty of exercise leaping to conclusions. On what basis do you intend to accuse me of these horrible things?"

The tiny plastic bud in McAllister's ear came alive. It was a direct encrypted link between him and the van outside. It was Martin saying, "The room is free of bugs. Nothing's showing. And his phone isn't recording anything. You're free to talk openly."

McAllister cleared his throat to acknowledge Martin's transmission before answering Stevens. This was going to be fun. He leaned slightly forward, a tactic used in prisoner interrogation to create a slight sense of dominance. "Senator – or rather Frank, as Max Preston calls you – I have phone logs and recorded conversations that tie you to Mr. Max Preston, who is directly responsible for the attack on the nuclear power station in your home state of North Carolina."

"I'm sorry, who is this Max Preston you speak of?"

This was playing out exactly as McAllister had anticipated, hook, line, and sinker. "Max Preston was the man on the other end of this phone call."

McAllister extracted a mini MP3 player from his suit jacket pocket and pushed play. The call Martin had recorded came through the tiny speaker. When it was over, Stevens tried to mask his unease but McAllister picked up his "tell," the sign all human beings make that reveals they are lying. Not only did he fidget in his chair, his eyes darted slightly away just for a moment, long enough to tell McAllister all he needed to know. But Stevens wasn't through lying yet.

"How do I know you didn't patch that together from various recordings? Audio trickery is rather sophisticated these days," Stevens countered.

"Yes, Senator, it is. So is eavesdropping. I assure you this is one single continuous conversation, played back for you verbatim, and you know it. Ironically, the very legislation that you voted for allowed us to capture that conversation and use it against you."

Stevens didn't like where this was going, especially the remark about eavesdropping. His greatest fear about voting for that bill was coming true in his very own office. He wasn't concerned about privacy issues for the American people. To hell with them. He was more concerned about incriminating himself. Dealing with the old-fashioned FBI wiretaps was easy. No warrant, no tap. And if they used one illegally, any evidence from it was thrown out of court almost automatically. But this, this was different. The Patriot Act, as well as other laws designed to make it easier to catch terrorists, also made it easier to foil plans like he was involved with. Which made him pause. Was it possible McAllister was taping this very conversation? He would have to proceed with caution.

Stevens leaned forward, propping his elbows on the desk blotter, and interlacing his fingers in front of him. "Tell me, Mr. McAllister, how is it you know so much about this Max Preston?"

"The same way you know so much about me. Connections." He wasn't going to tell him about his little conversation with Dominic Rippon quite yet. He'd play that card only if he needed to trump. "You have them, and so do I. After all, how else would you have known about my team and me? As you are aware, only the President and the Chairman of the Joint Chiefs know we even exist. Our identities are hidden and our records are not kept anywhere permanently. However, every one of my team members except one – me – is now dead," he lied, "and it all happened right before these operations started taking place. Coincidence? We're both intelligent men here. You tell me."

Stevens stared at McAllister. He didn't know what McAllister knew but he had to assume he probably had the whole plot figured out and had plenty of evidence to back it up. He also knew McAllister was more than capable of killing him right here and now and making it look like an accident, or at the very least self defense, and had every incentive to do so. His only play would be to pull Molly's heart strings.

"Molly," he said, turning to her, "surely you don't believe I would ever get involved with this sort of heinous affair. I would never betray my country. For Christ's sake, I'm a Marine! "

Molly's face revealed nothing except complete contempt for the man across the desk, a man whom she had trusted her entire life, apparently for no reason. If he was capable of carrying out this hideous act, what else could he do? What else had he already done? Suddenly everything in her childhood took on a whole new angle. How many times had he lied to her? To her dad? To her mom? How many people had he manipulated and betrayed – not just in the family but how about the entire country? She knew politics was often a nasty business, but her uncle? She resigned herself to this being true. She'd seen the evidence herself and was smart enough to know when someone was guilty. She sat up straighter.

"Senator Stevens," she said, deliberately not calling him Uncle Frank, "you have betrayed this country and your family. I believe Mr. McAllister has pegged you correctly as a traitor."

The room went awkwardly quiet, the only sound coming from the cold winter wind outside whipping along the side of the building.

"Well, then," he said, standing, "I suppose you have a lot of work to do if you intend to put a case together against me. Oh, wait." He moved around and sat on the corner of his desk so he was looking past Molly to McAllister. "You're not attorneys. You're not even cops. Which means that you have no legal or binding authority to make any of these claims stick. In fact, if you come out with any of this, you blow your own cover, Mr. McAllister." He leaned forward toward them and looked down his pointed finger. "You come out with this information, and your time is up. You're through. Every target you've ever hit will be open to public scrutiny. Every world power you have upset over the last two decades will know who you are. And you and every President you've worked for will have a target on his chest the size of Texas."

McAllister let Stevens have his moment in the sun, feigning panic until he thought Stevens had taken the bait. What he really wanted to do was grab the finger Stevens was waving in front of his face and twist it back until it snapped off. But he refrained. Finally he just spoke instead.

"Do you seriously think I didn't already think of that? I didn't get this far by being a fool. I can take you and Preston and whoever else I find was a part of this down in a heartbeat and never even break a sweat. It's precisely *because* of my cover that I have unfettered access to things law enforcement can't touch. It's been that way all along. That's how I've always operated. The only hope you have now, Senator, is that you get this whole mess cleaned up before I take you down."

"Are you trying to bargain with me?" Stevens asked.

"No," McAllister said as he and Molly stood up to leave. "I'm not bargaining. I'm racing. Better get your running shoes on."

Martin picked them up at a different location from the drop off, just in case Stevens or anyone else had them under surveillance. Moving from place to place decreased the chances they would be followed and had the added benefit of not being in view of the same traffic cameras for both drop off and pick up.

Once back in the van, they headed toward Stevens' neighborhood to scope out his house. Nobody in his neighborhood wanted unsightly garbage cans in the front yard, so an alleyway bisected the back yards of the row of houses where the senator lived. They made a slow, rolling pass by the front of the house and then through the alley to survey the back, McAllister taking pictures through a high-megapixel digital camera. He paid special attention to any obvious security features, like boxes hanging on the side of the house that would indicate an alarm or monitoring device, and also tried to spot any unusual or hidden features, added measures the typical burglar wouldn't spot in time. As Martin drove, McAllister downloaded the photographs to the laptop connected to the gear in back and printed out copies for everyone to examine, which they did all the way back to the hotel.

"Okay," McAllister said as he closed the hotel door behind him. "Here's what we need to do next. Obviously Senator Stevens is the Washington connection, but Preston is the mastermind of the operation. He's the one we want. Martin?"

Martin looked up from his Blackberry.

"I need you and Lena to tap into anything of Preston's you can access and see if you can find his plans. Travel, calls, e-mails, whatever you can find. I need to know where he is and where he is going."

"Got that for you already," Martin said.

"You do? How?"

"Simple," he said, holding up his Blackberry. "I set up a remote tap on Stevens' phone before we left the Capitol, routing it through my terminal and onto here. His entire call log is on my screen from the moment you walked out of his office. Not only did he call Preston about a minute after you left – from his office phone, *duh!* – he had a hard time finding him and had to call three numbers before he made a connection. Would you like to hear the conversation?" Martin smiled.

McAllister shook his head. "No, just let me know if you find out anything on playback. In the meantime, I need to see a contact of mine here in the area and get some equipment."

37

Leninsk-Kuznetsky, Kemerovo Oblast, Russia, 1985

Oleg Michelavich shoved his hands deep inside the pockets of his heavy, black sailor's coat, bracing against the whipping wind, his collar turned up against the frosty air, as his thick boots crunched on the grey, downtrodden snow, dirty from passing cars and busses and earlier pedestrians. He had to hurry. More snowfall was predicted overnight, possibly making his exit the next day more difficult, he feared. Not that fear was an emotion he dealt with very often. But tonight was different. Tonight was his last to spend in his homeland, a mixed blessing. The Americans had promised him a hasty departure once the final package was delivered, a quick getaway from the drudgery of another day cramped inside the oily machine shop of the munitions factory that had been his – and his father's – sole source of income for over thirty years. One last mission and it was on to a new life, one with singing and dancing and drinking – not like here in the Soviet Union, where everyone longed for the old days, where they would have welcomed back the freedom of a czar, but genuine freedom, where he could do what he wanted, when he wanted, and not have to constantly check around every corner to see who was watching or listening, waiting to trump up false charges and throw him in jail just to give themselves job security. Not that job security was a big problem in Soviet Russia. After all, the Politburo had promised everyone would always have a job. The vast Soviet Empire must have hard workers to provide for all the people. *Ha,* he snorted as he turned down the alley off the main road, the frigid wind slicing his face and almost tearing off his thick stocking cap. A brand new electric trolley bus, part of a city-wide initiative designed to line local politicians' pockets, passed on the main thoroughfare, providing just the right distraction and visual block for anyone who might be tailing him.

He found the small black door beside the garbage can on the side of the brick building and rapped three times, waited, and knocked a fourth time, the signal of who he was and that it was safe to open the door. The door opened a crack, sending the delicious scent of potatoes, cabbage, and other dinner items flowing out into the alleyway – and begging him to come in. He was famished. Which was part of the deal. A portion of his payment was a delicious hot meal in return for delivering the package tucked away inside the warmth of his jacket. The rest of his payment would be given to him afterwards, in the form of a roll of American cash, worth far more in the prodigious Russian black market than the ever-declining ruble.

The man standing inside the door eyed Oleg suspiciously before opening the heavy door the rest of the way and letting him in. He checked the alley before closing it.

"What did you bring me tonight, Oleg?" said the man as they entered the busy kitchen. Business was good tonight, as hungry customers packed the dining room beyond the swinging doors on the far side of the kitchen. Cooks and waiters hustled around, the stainless steel counters and tile floor abuzz with activity. "Please sit," he said, motioning to an old wood schoolteacher desk in the dark back corner, away from everyone. Oleg sat carefully in the rickety wooden chair as the other man sat down behind the desk and pulled out a bottle of vodka along with two glasses from the top desk drawer and set them up. He popped the top from the bottle and poured two drinks, sliding one glass to Oleg, who let it sit.

"You look nervous," the man said, waving toward the untouched glass. "Drink up. We have much to discuss."

Reluctantly, Oleg grabbed the drink and downed it in one burning swig, figuring it might give him the final bit of courage he needed for the evening.

"First, the package," the man said, gesturing toward Oleg's jacket.

Oleg unzipped and pulled out a small box wrapped in brown paper and held it with both hands, staring at it for a moment before looking up to the man and extending the package to him. The man took it and began to unwrap it when a waiter appeared at his side. The man looked up.

"What is it, Dimitri?" he asked the waiter.

"We have a problem in the dining room, sir. A customer is insisting that he speak to you immediately," Dimitri replied.

The man sighed. "Fine, I'll be there in a moment," he said and waved the waiter away. "I'm sorry for the interruption, Oleg. I'm sure you understand. I will get back with you later."

"You have a business to run. I'm sure it gets crazy at dinner time," Oleg replied.

The man smiled. "You have no idea how crazy it can get. Dealing with customers wouldn't be so bad if it weren't for the customers themselves."

The men laughed heartily until the restaurant owner finally sighed and looked right at his companion. "You have served us well, Oleg. You will be aptly compensated. See Dimitri for your meal and look for the rest of your compensation in the usual place tonight after you eat." And with that, the owner got up to take care of an irate customer, leaving Oleg to wait for his meal.

CIA station chief Walter Simon sat in the study of his Moscow dacha sipping tea from an ornate Russian cup his neighbors had given him as a welcome-to-the-neighborhood gift when he arrived in Moscow three years earlier. The tall two-piece glass and pewter set was a passable replica of a much more expensive cup owned by Czar Nicholas II before he was unceremoniously deposed and killed in 1917 during the Bolshevik Revolution. The weather in Moscow was just as brutal tonight as it was all across the Soviet Union in the dead of winter. Only the brave or stupid dared set foot outside if they didn't need to. And he didn't. Instead, he had come home from the embassy an hour early because he knew the importance of the evening's events. While several of the embassy staff were attending the ballet tonight, he would be up late working on final preparations for the extraction of HOPPER, the CIA's last remaining of the three native agents imbedded in the Leninsk-Kuznetsky munitions plant. Air transport had been readied and verified from the local airport, as had ground transport backup in case it got hairy. Once at the coast, a Los Angeles-class submarine would be waiting to pop its head up and deploy a Navy SEAL team in a Zodiac to make the final leg of the extraction under the cover of the early morning darkness. They had chosen a spot far away from any known Soviet sub pens to reduce the possibility of being spotted either visually or on sonar. Now all Simon needed to hear was a signal from CINC-ANT (Commander-in-Chief, Atlantic Fleet) that the sub was on station and ready to accept a guest. Once that signal arrived, he would put the ball in motion and get his undercover team in Leninsk-Kuznetsky moving to get the agent out of Dodge.

His belly full of potatoes, beef, and vodka, Oleg Michelavich strolled back out into the alley and headed for home. As he clipped along the sidewalk, head down against the cold wind and impending snow, he dreamed about his new life: winters in Florida or Hawaii, no more snow, no more harsh weather, no more begging for a warm meal that he couldn't otherwise afford on his paltry hourly wage making missile parts. The Soviet military was large and mighty, but it was built on the backs of drastically underpaid workers, who foraged for every ruble they could make. Nobody was paid overtime, and workers had no choice but to put in the extra hours, since not doing so meant a very painful visit from the local labor leaders who were really just agents of the KGB, thugs tasked with boosting worker morale through pain and suffering. The vast Soviet military had to have its weapons, no matter the cost. And since the Soviet economy was so pathetic, forced labor was the most cost-effective method for producing the goods. *Stalin would be proud*, Oleg thought as he turned right and walked toward the police station. He wasn't going to report a crime, rather to commit one. High treason against the Union of Soviet Socialist Republics. A crime punishable by death by firing squad.

Oleg turned left just before the police station and walked to the back of the building, turned right into the parking lot where the official vehicles were kept, and stopped at the corner to make sure there were no onlookers. Satisfied he was alone and unobserved, he opened a small grate in the wall, hidden by the gutter downspout, and extracted a metal box. Flipping it open, he pulled out a thick roll of American dollars, closed the box tightly, and replaced it behind the grate, which he made sure was shut tightly.

Back on the street, he finally headed for his small apartment on the outskirts of the city. The streets were far more deserted as he neared his building, only a handful of passers-by, all of them huddling into themselves against the cold. As he rounded the final turn, he ran head-on into another pedestrian coming the other way.

"Oh, I'm terribly sorry, sir," he told the gentleman apologetically as he helped the face-down man to his feet.

"It's no problem," the man said, grabbing Oleg's hand. "In fact, I'm not the one with the problem now."

"What?" Oleg blinked, confused.

The man turned toward him. It was the restaurant owner. His left hand gripped Oleg's right arm tightly and his right hand contained a switch blade, which he snapped open. In one swift move, the man pulled Oleg toward him and ran the blade up under his ribs and into his lungs.

"That's for stealing secrets for the Americans," he whispered to the shocked Oleg.

Unable to gather air, Oleg wheezed for a moment before the man stabbed him again, this time between two other ribs and right into his heart.

"And that one is the General Secretary's little going-away present," he said as he dropped Oleg's lifeless body to the cold, slushy sidewalk.

He took Oleg's wallet and the roll of American money before leaving the body on the sidewalk to be covered by the overnight snow. And with that he hurried home. The police would take care of the body in the morning and chalk it up to a robbery gone bad. Wallet missing, body dumped, no murder weapon. And most likely no eyewitnesses. The only official record of this being a murder would appear in the annals of the KGB, buried deeply among the many accomplishments of restaurant owner and senior agent Vladimir Dostivich.

The STU-1 secure phone on Simon's desk sprang to life. The voice on the other end was not what he expected. "We have a problem," the man, one of Simon's most trusted agents, said. "When we arrived at HOPPER's apartment, he wasn't there. He's nowhere to be found. His apartment door was still locked and looked undisturbed. Has he reported to you?"

"No," answered Simon. "He's under strict orders not to unless there's a real emergency. Could he just be running behind? That happens sometimes."

"We'll stay on station for a few more minutes," the agent replied, "but we can't risk staying here too long or we'll raise suspicion. Plus, if he's been flipped..." He didn't need to finish the sentence. Walter Simon knew exactly what would happen. They had built in safety measures to isolate the US from any official involvement in the operation, but too many spies had been caught over the years for Simon to think for a moment that they were air tight.

"Give it a few minutes and get back to me. If you have to, abandon ship. We have ways to contact him for new arrangements if necessary." He hung up and sat back in his chair, the tea now getting cold on his oak desk. What the hell is HOPPER doing? Why would he be late tonight, of all nights?

Ten minutes later the phone rang again. "Sir, we have a serious problem. HOPPER is dead."

"Dead?" Simon asked. "Where?"

"A block from his apartment. Stabbed twice in the abdomen. Bled out something fierce. What do you want to do with him?"

Simon thought for a moment. The CIA hated leaving agents behind, even dead ones, but sometimes sacrifices were necessary to preserve plausible deniability. Tensions were high between Moscow and Washington, and Simon and all CIA offices were under strict instructions to keep a lid on all operations no matter what. He had to think fast.

"Leave him for now and make sure you cover your tracks. Nobody is to know you were there. The police will take him to the morgue and we can handle it from there. Get away from the scene."

The agents did as they were told, the police arrived a short time later after an anonymous caller tipped them off to the location of a dead body, and Walter Simon put into gear the means necessary to erase all records of HOPPER's involvement.

Vladimir Dostivich and his team of KGB agents had no trouble getting past the night security at the munitions factory. Cutting through the chain link fence and killing the lone security guard was easy. Dostivich never failed to see the irony of how easy it was for his own detail to get past almost any Soviet security system. He knew the men in charge were too cocky when it came to their confidence in cheap metal fences and poorly-trained men, bought off by the promise of a warm apartment and a steady supply of vodka. Everything was built to minimum specs. Which made his job easier. Within minutes, he and his team of three men had planted explosives and done enough sabotage damage to the machinery and the structure of the massive building that nobody would survive the blast that would greet them in the morning. But before they left, there was one final card to play.

The men reassembled at the back loading dock, where they had parked a cargo van. From out of the factory, the four men carried two long wood crates, placed them into the back of the van, and covered them with blankets. They drove into the cold Russian night, the load in back destined for a warmer, sunnier climate.

38

Present Day

Metallurgy had come back with the results Allison Crenshaw needed. The report on her screen gave her a clear understanding of how old the fragments from the bomb were, and that told her where it was made. According to the analysis, the bomb fragments came from a manufacturing facility in Leninsk-Kuznetsky, Russia, a town in western Siberia. That was all it said. No details of what the town made, what sort of bomb it was, or anything else that would be helpful. Then again, she reasoned, she wasn't the field agent who was going to track down the maker. She was just the backroom analyst. Field ops were for somebody else. Not her forte. She was perfectly content to be locked up in the lab, helping the guys in the field from afar.

Director Longfellow had given her explicit instructions to call as soon as she had the report in hand. He'd even given her his direct cell number. She punched the number. He answered on the first ring.

"Director Longfellow, I have your results," she started, a little intimidated to be speaking directly to the director of the FBI.

"Yes, Agent Crenshaw, what did you find?" His response was professional yet polite.

"Sir, it appears the bomb that went off in North Carolina was indeed Russian, or more accurately, Soviet manufactured around 1985 or 1986 in a town called – I hope I pronounce this right – Leninsk-Kuznetsky." She got it close enough that Longfellow understood. "It's in western Siberia."

"You're sure about this?" he asked. He had to be certain.

"Yes, sir. The metallurgy report came back conclusive."

"Alright, good work. Can you forward the report to my PDA?"

"Yes, sir. Right away. Look for it in the next few minutes."

"Thank you, Agent Crenshaw." And he hung up.

Allison slid the cell back into her lab coat and typed the instructions into the computer.

Longfellow had already left the White House after his briefing to the Joint Chiefs so he had to call the President to give him the news. President Thornhill hung up the cell and gripped it tightly as he digested what the FBI director had just told him. A Russian bomb dropped on American soil was supposed to be a relic of the Cold War. The US had won that war without either side dropping any bombs, and yet now there were charred fragments of a freshly exploded one sitting in the FBI lab.

Whenever Thornhill thought of the old Soviet empire, he remembered his days as a Marine captain in Iraq, fighting against a military with outdated Soviet equipment and soldiers taught to fight by the elite Russian Spetnez special forces soldiers and other Eastern Bloc troops. As the radar operator of a Hawk missile battery during Operation Desert Storm in 1991, Thornhill had seen the first wave of American fighters leaving Saudi Arabian airbases on their way to downtown Baghdad. He had prayed they would return safely. As it turned out, the anti-aircraft artillery and surface-to-air missiles guarding the heart of the city were obsolete and manned by inexperienced soldiers who had never encountered a force like the American Air Force. The AA fire was so erratic that if a plane were to get hit it would be simply luck of the draw. As it turned out, wave after wave of F-117's, F-18's, and F-15's had flown unmolested target practice, with only one Eagle being shot down, the only aircraft lost the first night. The US and its allies would go on to decimate the entire Iraqi military, both in the air and on the ground, in an unprecedented show of force.

In Thornhill's mind, Operation Desert Storm had been the final nail in the coffin of an already dying Soviet Union. The Berlin Wall had fallen and the Soviet economy, suffering for decades, was on the brink of collapse. When the Soviet leadership saw how poorly their equipment and the Iraqi troops they had trained had performed against an infinitely more technologically sophisticated American military, they knew the end was in sight. No longer a true global military threat, the Soviets had nothing left to stand on. The country collapsed. The Union of Soviet Socialist Republics was no longer.

But he also believed the threat was far from over. Not only was the military, though weakened, very much still in place, but in all the turmoil of the breakup much of the security surrounding the arms and weapons stores had been sacrificed. Questions immediately arose about who exactly was in charge of the military and who was keeping track of all the weapons, both nuclear and conventional. Inventories were raided and stockpiles were looted in a mass grab for power and protection. Most of the weapons were small arms that could either be used for personal protection or sold on the black market for top dollar. And because they were stolen, it was all pure profit. While the AK-47's and other small arms were a concern to everyone, the bigger worry had been the nuclear and larger conventional weapons. Both the Russians and the Americans feared they might turn up in the wrong hands.

The Russian military was more or less a fraction of the old Soviet military machine, using old equipment since Russia was too cash-strapped to manufacture many new weapons. Their tanks were obsolete, the newest one – the T-80 – over twenty years old, and even the once-feared Soviet navy was but a skeleton of its old capabilities under the Russian flag. Several subs had been lost at sea and the ones that remained were long overdue for upgrades they weren't going to get, their sonars lacking the technical sophistication of their American counterparts, and many of their torpedoes were no longer functional, victims of years in the confines of a sub in ocean conditions.

Thornhill turned his chair back around toward the desk and opened the top right drawer, extracting a small black spiral-bound phone book, which he opened to the first page. On it were listed the direct lines to all the world leaders the President spoke with on a regular basis. The book, if it fell into the wrong hands, might be used to start World War III. But in the hands of the President of the United States, it was meant to stop it. Which was exactly what Thornhill aimed to do.

He turned to the first page and dialed Vladimir Dostivich, President of Russia.

"Mr. President," Dostivich said into the cell phone, feigning cheeriness, as he set his tea down on the expansive mahogany desk. "How are things in the United States today?" He knew it was usually bad when Thornhill called him, especially at this number. Very few people even knew Dostivich carried a cell phone, especially foreign leaders, and almost nobody had the number. The last thing the Russian president wanted was for international leaders to have instant access to him. But since the days of the Cold War, the United States had always had a means to get in touch with the leader of the Soviet Union via the hotline from the White House to the Kremlin, in case of a nuclear launch issue. That tradition continued with the fall of the Iron Curtain. Some things never changed. Only the technology had been updated. Kind of like the way things were in Dostivich's home country. Nuclear war was still a very real possibility despite numerous treaties between the two countries and the new openness that followed the demise of the old Soviet regime. But now everyone just smiled a little more when talking about it.

What Dostivich relished the most about the new relationship Russia enjoyed with the world was its naïveté. The Soviet Union had fallen in name and in leadership, and officially in form of government. Communism was no longer a formal part of Russian rule, replaced with a loose representation of democracy, with its limited freedoms and openness. But many of the same players were still very much in place and working behind the scenes to see to it nothing really changed. Those in power wanted to stay there, knowing full well they would be helpless if they ever lost their seats at the table. They would be relegated to the working class, the lower class, and become victims of their own communist rule that favored only the elite. That wasn't going to happen so long as they had their way, which they were all committed to ensuring.

"Vladimir, it seems we have a little diplomatic issue that we need to discuss – what I hope will simply be a misunderstanding that can be clarified," Thornhill answered.

"Mr. President, I will be happy to help any way I can," Dostivich replied. "What seems to be the problem?"

"I'm sure you've been following the news of the recent attacks on my country and our ongoing investigation of who is behind them."

"Of course."

"Well, our FBI has determined that the bomb used in the North Carolina nuclear power plant explosion was of Soviet origin." He let the words hang in the air for a moment to gauge the Russian president's reaction. "You wouldn't happen to know anything about that, would you?"

Dostivich knew Thornhill was a straight shooter and could be a blunt diplomat. He also knew the American president didn't ask any questions to which he didn't already have the answers. But Dostivich also knew there was a difference between diplomacy and accuracy, a fine line he was about to cross.

"Mr. President," Dostivich began, "as you know, security issues have been a tough challenge for us for many years now. Our weapons have mysteriously found their way all over the world through the black market. We have tried to control as much as possible, but it has been a daunting task, to say the least."

"I completely understand, Vladimir," the President replied, "which is why I came directly to you first, to see if you may have once again been the victim of a clever and dastardly thief." Thornhill could mentally see the Russian president squirming in his leather chair. He knew enough to not totally trust Dostivich or his cronies. Publicly, he and Dostivich were best buds, always glad-handing for the cameras and sitting down cordially for diplomatic talks. But Thornhill didn't trust a word Dostivich ever spoke out of either side of his mouth. Let the State Department carry on their delusions that the old regime was long gone in present-day Russia; Thornhill wasn't fooled. He'd spent too long fighting communist ideology to not recognize the subtle signs. Even within the United States Congress there were both tenured and new Senators and Representatives who had socialist and communist leanings, and Thornhill was prepared to fight them tooth and nail. He wasn't about to play politics as usual, especially when that was what had gotten the country into the economic mess he had spent his entire first term trying somewhat in vain to clean up.

Dostivich had been prepared for this conversation for a long time. It was all part of what he had anticipated when he had agreed to the plan. He knew the American president would come calling as soon as the attacks were traced back to Soviet equipment, asking for details like this.

"Mr. President," Vladimir finally said, "let me assure you that we will do everything in our power to find out how this happened. You have the full cooperation of the Russian government. Please forward me any information your FBI thinks would be helpful and we'll add it to our investigation."

"Thank you for your cooperation," Thornhill said to the posturing Russian president. "I will have Director Longfellow send you all the working files and get in touch with your lead investigator."

Dostivich hung up from his conversation with Thornhill, tucked his cell back into his jacket pocket, and picked up the desk phone.

Retired Major General Mikhail Yenchenko, former Soviet tank commander, set his fishing pole in the mounting bracket, checking to see that it would not get yanked out if a fish suddenly bit, and answered the satellite phone resting in the worn wooden tackle box beside him.

"General, I need your help on something," Dostivich told the man on the other end of the secure line.

"Yes, Vladimir?" was all he said in response. Decades of dealing with Soviet leadership and all the ramifications of a misstep had taught him to wait for all the information before committing to anything.

"Thornhill has figured out the bomb that hit North Carolina was one of ours. It's time for your damage control efforts to kick in."

"What do you need me to do?" the general asked. He was not about to take any action without direct orders from Dostivich.

"I need you to see to it all traces of the Skat records are erased and replaced with the documents that show it was stolen. None of this can get back to us. None of it. Do whatever you need to do to make sure we point the finger away from us."

39

"We have word on the bomb in North Carolina," Martin said, pointing to his laptop screen.

"Whatcha got?" McAllister replied.

"A contact at FBI sent me a copy of the official report." Martin told him about the chemical makeup and the metallurgy analysis and the approximate location and date the bomb was made. "Looks like the Russians had something to do with it."

"Not so fast, Sherlock," McAllister cautioned. "Maybe, maybe not. A lot's changed in that area since the fall of the Soviet Union. It might be stolen property."

"Then how did they drop a bomb undetected and fly away? What sort of 'stolen property'" – he made the quotes in the air – "are we talking about here?"

"Two things. The bomb part is easy. Old Soviet weapons are all over the world now, thanks to the black market and other avenues. The flying part, however, not so much. Do me a favor and Google Russian stealth bombers. Rumor has it a while back they were nearing completion of an unmanned stealth drone capable of carrying a payload of weapons. Bombs and missiles and such. Don't know if they ever finished it."

"You're serious? Like an F-117 that doesn't need a pilot?"

"More like an X-47. We've had unmanned stealth drones for years, so about time the Russians got one, too. Probably our design, since they steal all their technology from us."

"So you're saying the Russians have the ability to drop bombs on the US and just fly away, like we did in Iraq?" he asked as he tapped keys.

"And in Afghanistan. And, yes, they probably do. But that doesn't mean that's what happened. The Russians have been playing fast and loose with their weapon stockpile ever since the fall of the Soviet Union. This might not be their idea."

"Okay, here's what I found. It's called a Skat." Martin explained what he was reading to McAllister. When he was done, McAllister decided a change of tactic was in order. He called the President.

"Yes, sir, that's exactly what I'm asking for," McAllister said over the phone. "I'm sure the CIA or the military has satellite data from the area the night of the attack. If the Russians have a stealth aircraft, no matter who's flying it, radar won't do any good. But I doubt it can go invisible. They're not that good. I have a contact within CIA and several in the Air Force, but I thought it might be faster if you turned some screws."

"I agree," the President said. "I'll call General Hanesworth and see what he can dig up."

McAllister hesitated before asking, "Can we trust him, sir?"

President Thornhill, acutely aware of why McAllister was asking, replied, "Completely. He's the one who knows about you. Your secret's safe with him."

Then-Senator James Thornhill, retired Marine and former investment banker, had been elected President of the United States as a response to the previous administration's lackadaisical attitude toward terrorism that had brought the country to the brink of another attack. To say they were soft on terror was a vast understatement. The previous administration had sat down with some of the top terror leaders, including the heads of state from many of the countries that directly sponsored terror networks, and tried to negotiate America's way to safety. What the previous President didn't understand was that sitting down for tea and crumpets was exactly what the terrorists wanted, so they could continue to train and equip their suicide bombers and other "tacticals" without interference, including in secret camps on US soil, while the American government was distracted "negotiating" nothing, because the terrorists weren't going to give in to *anything*. They took great pride in having brought the spineless American government effectively down to its knees.

President Thornhill wasn't about to continue the same tactic. He understood all too well who these terrorists were and was not going to allow another attack on US soil.

But less than six months into his term, it had happened. Multiple hits, all unanswered. And in the midst of it all, his own private team, designed to strike at the heart of terror organizations secretly and stealthily, had been taken out one by one, until only their leader remained.

Thornhill made the call to General Hanesworth, who went to work immediately on his request.

40

They ordered room service, careful to make sure the delivery man from downstairs wasn't going to kill them, and ate lunch in the confines of the room, waiting for the results from Hanesworth. Finally McAllister's phone buzzed. He put it on speakerphone and set it on the table for everyone to hear.

"Yes, Mr. President?"

"I have General Hanesworth on the other line with us here. He's calling from a secure Pentagon line. We think he's found what you were looking for. I'll let him explain. General?"

"Thank you, Mr. President," the general started. "What I have is overflight images from the night of the attack. We had a bird over the area for other reasons that night, and it happened to pick up a strange aircraft in the area of the explosion right after it happened. Flight path tracking shows it returning at a fairly high rate of speed to a small abandoned airport in southern Virginia. Seems to indicate a jet of some sort, judging from the shape and speed. I can send you the images, but it looks to us like a Russian Skat."

McAllister looked up at Martin, who was smiling. "Yes, General, please forward those to my phone. Where is the aircraft now?"

"We don't know, but I suggested to the President that we send a tac team to the airport to see if they can find it. I doubt it's still there since they probably moved it to avoid leaving a trail, but it's worth a shot."

"I agree," McAllister said. "Sir?"

Thornhill answered, "Already ordered. At the very least we can establish a link and see if they left any evidence behind by mistake. But from what we've seen so far, they don't make mistakes."

"Mr. President," McAllister said carefully, "with all due respect, everyone makes mistakes. They will mess up somewhere. It's just a matter of being ready to act when they do."

"Agreed," said the President. "I've also instructed Director Longfellow to forward the detailed summary of the metallurgy report to you, just in case you might have some insight."

McAllister checked the display. There was an envelope indicating a message. "Looks like something already popped onto my screen. I'll check out what you sent and get back to you, sir." They all hung up, and McAllister retrieved the message.

Accompanying the detailed chemical analysis of the metal and paint was a report from the CIA open source database linking the bomb to a manufacturing facility in Leninsk-Kuznetsky, Russia, a former "closed town," the report said, where the vast Soviet military machine operated largely out of sight. Along with select nuclear facilities, the existence of many conventional arms manufacturing factories was also kept a closely guarded secret. During the Cold War, the CIA had kept vast files on Soviet weapons inventory, which required a great deal of human intelligence on the ground. Some speculated the files were even better than those the bureaucratically-driven Soviets kept themselves. The hardest part had been getting spies into the manufacturing facilities to keep tabs on production. Putting Americans in place would have nearly impossible due to language and culture obstacles, so most of the intelligence was gathered by Soviet workers inside the facilities who chose to work for the Americans at great peril to themselves but great wealth once their jobs were done.

Included in the report was a PDF of a newspaper clipping from the London bureau of the Associated Press dated January 16, 1985, and headlined "Report: Soviet munitions explosion kills hundreds." The article not only reported on the explosion in Leninsk-Kuznetsky but also chronicled a series of mishaps, including one aboard the Soviet nuclear-powered submarine *Lenin* and a meltdown that had occurred in 1972 aboard another Soviet sub that was parked just off the coast of the United States at the time of the accident.

The third file was another CIA report, this one noting a discrepancy in the inventory of the Leninsk-Kuznetsky factory following the damage assessment. All the bombs had been accounted for except two, which had mysteriously disappeared during the cleanup. The Soviets had dismissed the report, claiming the bombs must have gone off during the explosion. But the CIA's own bomb damage assessment calculated that if that had happened the explosion would have been much bigger. Clearly the Soviets were covering up their mistake.

Longfellow had added an electronic note in the margin: *Our bomb?*

"Most likely," McAllister answered out loud, to no one in particular.

"Mostly likely what?" Molly asked.

McAllister snapped back into the present. "Most likely the bomb that went off in North Carolina was stolen from the old Soviet Union. But how did it get here? Martin, what's the most common port of entry for shipments from Russia into the US?"

"That would most likely be the west coast. Los Angeles and Long Beach both take shipments from there. Why?"

"It would be nearly impossible to move a bomb into the US in an airplane, even a private one. Customs would catch it. Even shipping it via FedEx or UPS would have raised suspicions and been stopped. Plus, there were two bombs, not just one. But shipping them by boat, that's a whole 'nother matter."

"What about just flying it in on board the Skat?" Martin asked.

"That would be a logistical nightmare," McAllister answered. "The Skat is a short-range aircraft, not designed for intercontinental flight, so it would have to stop for fuel along the way since it can't be refueled in the air. That means it would have to be shipped separately, just like the bombs."

"So I should be looking for two separate shipments then?" Martin asked.

"At least two. More like three or more," McAllister assessed. "The bombs could come all together, since they are relatively small and only weigh five hundred pounds a piece. But shipping an entire plane is harder. It was likely sent over in pieces, probably wings together and fuselage separately, and then assembled once it got here. So we might be talking about multiple shipments. And they might be spread out over many weeks or months so as not to arouse suspicion."

"You're not helping me much here," countered Martin.

McAllister smiled. "Doing the best I can. Call it job security."

Martin rolled his eyes and started typing. Five minutes later he popped his head back up.

"Got something," he said. "I pulled up DHS's port incident database and found a report that back in 1988 there was a raid on a cargo ship called the *China Angel* in Long Beach Harbor. The FBI had been tipped off that the ship was hauling illegal Chinese immigrants along with weapons sent to help boost the Mexican drug trade in the southwest US. A tactical team intercepted the ship once it reached port and boarded it after a brief firefight. The smugglers were taken down but all of the tac team members were killed in the operation except one, the sniper who was covering the team from the outside. Apparently they were killed inside the hold."

"Did they find any weapons?" McAllister asked.

"No. By the time backup arrived, whatever was on board the ship was gone."

"How could they have moved it out that fast? Wasn't the backup team close by?"

"Doesn't say. The timeline's not that detailed. Whoa, whoa, whoa!" Martin exclaimed. "Check this out. Take a guess at the name of the surviving sniper."

McAllister shrugged.

"Dominic Rippon."

41

Special Agent Davis answered on the first ring. "What the hell did you do to Mr. Rippon?" he asked McAllister.

"What do you mean?" he asked.

"His entire elbow is blown out!"

"Oh, yeah, that."

Davis sighed. "Yeah, that. Look, I'm going to have to –"

"Do nothing," McAllister said, cutting him off. "Because I need you to do something else for me."

"No, no, no, no, no," Davis said, shaking his head, which McAllister couldn't see over the phone. "I'm not doing anything else for you. This can't go any farther. You nearly killed one man and badly injured another. And then you took off to who knows where."

"Wait just a minute. Did you say *nearly* killed?" McAllister asked.

"Yeah, the black man sitting in the chair with the needle in his arm is now in the hospital recovering from bruising and a severe overdose of some sort of chemical."

Stanford is alive? McAllister about jumped through the phone.

"I didn't do anything to Willard Stanford," McAllister said." For your information, Agent Davis, Willard Stanford is a friend of mine, a good friend. Dominic Rippon tortured him, not me. And that's why I had to get information out of Rippon."

"You shot him in the arm to get information? About what?"

"Listen, what you know so far is just the beginning. I need to tell you about Rippon so you can understand exactly what's happening here. Then I need you to dig up as much as you can on Dominic Rippon, especially focused on the operation in Long Beach. Get back to me on this number when you've got something."

"Wait," Davis said. "I don't know who you are or what sort of mess you've created, but this can't continue. You're in serious trouble, and it's my job to haul you in. I need you to tell me exactly what's happening here."

"Agent Davis, I would love to, but it'll have to be some other time. I'm kind of in the middle of something right now and need you to help me, not arrest me. After this is all over, I'll be happy to come to your office and tell you all about it. But for now, you're going to have to trust me."

"Trust you? You expect me to trust a guy who just shot a guy in the elbow to get him to talk?"

"Yes," McAllister said flatly.

Davis chewed his cheek on the other end of the phone. The silence on the line was palpable.

"Okay," Davis finally said, "I can tell you one thing already. He's former FBI."

Then he should have reacted better to the flash bang. Guess all those years out of practice will do that to you, thought McAllister. "Good, that should make your job easier. Get back to me on the rest."

An hour later, McAllister's phone rang. It was Davis.

"I made some phone calls, and here's what I found out. Apparently Rippon resigned from the Bureau in 1992 after an investigation into a weapons sting gone bad in San Diego. He had been working with the San Diego field office and the local ATF office to track down an arms dealer who was receiving shipments from a Mexican cartel, not at all uncommon in that area. During the investigation one of the investigating agents was found shot dead. Nobody was ever charged with the killing. Soon after, Rippon resigned, citing work-related stress as the cause. From there he went to NSA, as an analyst, working on some program that remains classified. Couldn't get anyone over there to talk to me about it."

"Okay, here's what I need you to do," McAllister said, hoping Davis wouldn't be upset over what was going to sound like an order. "Rippon works, or worked, for a man named Max Preston, who owns a technology company in Costa Mesa, California. He is the head of the group responsible for the attacks. All of them. But now he's disappeared, gone into hiding. We've tried to track his cell phone via the GPS system but apparently either he's taken the battery out or he's devised some way to block the signal. He is a techy nut, after all; he could do that. We need to find him. He's the answer to everything that has happened."

"And you're thinking Rippon might know where he is?"

"Maybe. At least he might know some possibilities. I don't care how you get it out of him, but we need to know what he knows."

"What will you be doing while I'm beating up a suspect?" Davis sneered.

"Working another angle, hoping to find the source for funding the operation. Call me if you get anything."

42

Darkness had settled over the city as McAllister watched from a block away as the Stevens' limousine pulled away from the front door of his house with the tuxedo-clad senator inside. He had checked Stevens' schedule and knew he would be away at one of the many political fundraisers held every year all over the DC area. During the afternoon, McAllister had stopped by an old contact in Annapolis whose house was a few streets over from the Naval Academy and requisitioned a few "supplies" for tonight's operation. With him in the car was a Glock .40 caliber pistol with silencer and a black nylon courier bag full of ammunition and other goodies.

He left the rental car a block from Stevens' house and walked down the alleyway, careful to avoid the streetlights, until he came up along the back of the senator's residence, which was bordered by a short picket fence. He pulled the recon photos from the courier bag and, using a red lens flashlight, compared them to what he saw in front of him. They matched. Nothing had changed. He stowed the photos and pulled out the Glock. Recon had shown the house had motion sensors on the exterior lights which stood guard on the corners between the stories. He leveled the pistol and sent two silenced bullets each into the dark floodlights. He also placed a perfect shot into the light hanging by the back door. Glass popped from the impact of the rounds, so McAllister waited for reaction from neighbors. Nothing.

He climbed the fence and quickly covered the two hundred feet across the yard and around to the left side of the house, where the alarm box hung on the brick wall. Using snips, he clipped the small padlock and opened the grey plastic box. From his bag, he pulled out the instructions he had printed from an online source and had the alarm defeated in less than a minute. He closed the box and reinserted the broken lock so it would look to a casual observer like it hadn't been touched.

Back around to the rear of the house, he landed on the concrete back porch. The lock pick set worked beautifully on the back door – he'd picked so many locks over the years that it was almost habit – and he was inside in seconds, gently closing the door behind him. He found himself in a country style kitchen, the white cabinets visible in the darkness. He checked to make sure all the blinds and curtains had been closed before turning on his blue-colored LED flashlight. The last thing he needed now was a nosy neighbor calling the police after seeing the light from his flashlight scampering around the walls.

The house was eerily dark as McAllister crept from room to room, running the light over the pictures on the walls and items on tables. Stevens was an immaculate housekeeper, or whomever he hired was. McAllister entered the foyer and chose the door on the right. *Door number one,* he thought. The large double oak doors opened into an opulent living room, complete with a baby grand piano, plush couches, a low coffee table between them, and a large, unlit wood-burning fireplace on the far wall. Over the mahogany mantel hung an oil painting of a two-story log cabin set in a clearing with woods on three sides. McAllister scanned the room for a desk, but, not finding one, he moved back into the foyer.

He quietly crossed the marble floor and tried the other set of large double doors, which he discovered opened into Stevens' study. With a large oak desk, wing chairs, and another big unlit fireplace, McAllister knew he'd hit the jackpot. Stevens' laptop computer was sitting open on the desk, the screen lit, showing a log-in screen. McAllister sat in the large leather chair and pulled out his cell.

"Are you in?" Martin asked on the other end.

"Yeah, and I found his computer. But it has a password protect to get in."

"Okay, the login is probably his last name. Type that in."

He did.

"For the password, you won't get more than three tries to get it right before it locks up. Then we'll never get in. So I need you to give me the maker and serial number of the machine so I can trace it."

McAllister told him the brand name and flipped it over and read off the serial number from the bottom of the computer. A moment later, Martin had an answer.

"Okay, I was able to trace an IP address string to that computer from earlier this evening. Based on that, I was able to deduce a logarithm from various sites he visited that give me possible passwords. Based on that, I was then able to –"

"Just give me the freakin' password!" McAllister said.

"Patience, my son, patience."

"I don't have any. I'm not a doctor."

"Very funny. The password is 'lockhard1' – pretty lame if you ask me."

"I didn't. Thanks." And he hung up.

McAllister typed in the password, and the screen changed to the desktop view. For the next few minutes, he searched file after file for any keywords that might pop up in documents or e-mail. Finally he struck gold. When he had collected all the files into a folder, he inserted a thumb drive into the USB port on the side and copied the folder over. After it was done, he dragged the folder from the desktop to the recycle bin and emptied it. He knew the computer had created a trail of his actions, but he didn't care. It was okay if Stevens discovered he'd been snooping. Who was he going to tell? And maybe it would scare him a bit.

He unplugged the thumb drive and reset the computer to the login screen, just as Stevens had left it. No need to make it too easy on him. McAllister collected his bag and headed back out the door to the foyer.

And was smacked down to the ground with a forearm right to the face, landing him on his back on the marble floor, his head thumping against the hard stone. He grunted as the handle of the Glock he had stuck in his waistband dug into his back where he landed on it. Dazed and in pain, he tried to scramble to his feet to counter the attack but his feet were ripped out from beneath him and he fell flat on his belly as he felt the bag get yanked off his shoulder. Getting up again, he wheeled around in the dark, looking for his attacker. Then he heard footsteps running through the kitchen and the back door slam shut. He drew the Glock, ran to the door, flung it open, and surveyed the back yard.

Nothing. Empty.

He wiped the blood from his mouth with his sleeve and went back to retrieve the flashlight that had scooted across the foyer floor during the struggle. Whoever had attacked him had been efficient and quick and knew what do to and where to hit him. He was a pro, whoever he was. He picked up the flashlight.

And then he laughed. All that work and his attacker had missed what he was probably after, McAllister thought, as he patted his front pants pocket and felt the shape of the thumb drive.

43

The NSA had been kind enough to provide them with a safe house, although the agency didn't know it. Martin had always kept a spare set of codes to get into the secured location if worst came to worst, which it appeared was happening. McAllister had picked them up from the hotel after his adventures at Stevens' house and had headed to the remote house deep in the Maryland countryside. The house not only offered better protection than the too-public hotel, it also afforded everyone a little more privacy and room to move. Once settled, they all gathered in the kitchen to go over the events of the night and where they were so far.

Martin plugged the thumb drive into his laptop and went to work, scouring all the files not just for words on the screen that might incriminate Stevens but also for the data bits and bytes behind the words that could lead them to others. Most of all, he needed any information that McAllister could present to the President. Finally he had it.

"Check this out," he told the gathered three. "It looks like Stevens was copied on an e-mail from Preston a few months before the second attack, the one on the mall. It looks like some sort of mission launch command, giving final go orders to the players."

"Is there more?" McAllister asked.

"Yeah, there's a whole string of e-mails around the same time frame to and from. It appears that the messages were encrypted by a program that I've never seen before. Something called *Foggy Daze*. But it wasn't very effective. I didn't have any trouble getting in."

"But you're using the latest and greatest software from the NSA."

"Touché. This is stuff nobody even knows we have."

"They will one day," McAllister countered.

"Yes, but by that point we'll have jumped ahead again," Martin insisted, attempting to bolster his pride in his own work.

"Is there any indication from the messages where Preston might be now?"

"Not so far, but I'll keep looking," Martin said.

McAllister noticed Molly had drifted into the living room during the discussion, so he left Martin and Lena in the kitchen to keep working. Molly was seated on the edge of the low couch, staring absently into her folded hands.

"Mind if I sit down?" he asked carefully.

She looked up. "No. Please do," she said, forcing a smile.

"How are you holding up through all of this?" he asked as he sat down beside her.

She exhaled and went back to staring at her hands. "I'm not sure. On the one hand, I'm very angry at what's happening and more than a little scared about what's going to happen now, especially since I'm now so caught up in the middle of it all. What my uncle did was inexcusable and at the very least he should go to jail for it." She looked up at McAllister, gauging his reaction.

"And on the other hand?" he asked.

"On the other hand, he's my uncle, my dad's older brother, the man who made me laugh and always treated me like a princess when I was growing up." She looked up to the dormant ceiling fan hanging over the middle of the room.

Gordon reached over and separated Molly's hand, cradling her right hand between his own. "Having second thoughts about what you said at breakfast?" He asked, knowing he had to be careful what he said but hoping to steel her resolve.

She turned toward him and squeezed his hand. "No. My princess days have been over for a long time. Now it's time to treat Uncle Frank like the grownup he is and hold him accountable for his actions. I'm accountable for mine; he should be accountable for his."

Senator Stevens returned around midnight from the fundraiser and stumbled half drunk into his study, switching on the banker's lamp as he sat down in the burgundy leather chair behind the desk. Through the glare of the bulb he was sure he was hallucinating, as he saw what looked like a man standing by the fireplace, leaning against the mantel. Except he was real. And he spoke.

"Have a good time tonight, Senator?" said the man. "Raise lots of money for your reelection campaign?"

Stevens recognized the voice immediately and involuntarily began to sober up, fear and unease shocking his system, desperate for an adrenaline rush to sharpen his booze-dulled mind.

"Yes, quite a bit, although the final tally won't be counted until later this week," he answered. "What do you want at this time of night?" He hoped he wasn't slurring too much.

"Then let's have a drink, Senator, to your reelection." The man walked over to the mahogany sideboard across from the fireplace, grabbed two napkins, and used tongs to put ice from a silver bucket into two cut crystal tumblers. He poured scotch over the rocks in both glasses, careful to not touch the ice bucket, tongs, or liquor bottle with his bare fingers. He cradled the glasses in the napkins and carried them to the desk, reaching across the front to set Stevens' drink on the blotter. He was sure Stevens was too sloshed to notice.

Stevens eyed him suspiciously. The man caught the gaze of the slightly sloshed senator, his shirt collar open and his tie askew, a sad embodiment of the republic.

"To your reelection," the man said as he raised his glass.

Senator Stevens reached for his glass and raised it in a feigned attempt at enthusiasm. He sighed and said, "To my reelection," and took a long sip.

The man moved quickly behind the desk, catching the senator's drink before it spilled. He didn't want to leave behind any evidence. The virtually untraceable death drug sodium morphate he had dropped into the scotch began to work almost instantly, inducing severe cardiac arrest.

"Well, Senator," the man said, a sadistic glimmer in his eye, "looks like your chronic heart problems finally caught up to you."

Senator Franklin Stevens tried to speak but all he could muster was a whimper as he gripped his chest and tried in vain to breathe. In less than a minute his heart stopped, and he collapsed back into his chair, the rich burgundy leather cradling the freshly dead body of the senior senator from North Carolina, traitor.

44

"Uh, Gordon, you might want to see this," came Martin's voice from the living room. He was standing facing the TV, remote in one hand, his morning coffee in the other, and had settled on a cable news network.

"What is it?" McAllister asked, as he emerged from the kitchen carrying a mug of his own.

On the screen, police were mingling around in the background in front of Senator Stevens' house while a beautiful blonde reporter was standing just off the front yard talking into her microphone. Martin turned up the volume.

"North Carolina senator Franklin Stevens was found dead this morning in his Georgetown home, the apparent victim of a heart attack," she started. The screen changed to footage shot earlier, while it was still dark, with police and ambulance lights flashing off the white columns in front of the house. "According to early reports, police were summoned to the senator's residence around one this morning after a panic alarm was triggered. When they arrived, they found the senator slumped in his chair in his study. Paramedics arrived within minutes and tried to revive the senator but to no avail." The report went on, but McAllister had heard all he needed.

He grabbed his cell phone from its belt holder and dialed. The President answered on the first ring.

"This your work?" Thornhill asked in an irritated voice.

"No, sir," he answered, "That's why I called you immediately after I saw the news."

"Seems a bit too much of a coincidence to me," the President countered, a hint of suspicion in his voice.

"I understand, sir, but I assure you I had nothing to do with this."

The President was quiet for a moment. McAllister continued,

"Sir, I'm sure Senator Stevens' involvement in all of this got him killed, but I don't know who killed him. I was at his house last night, but he wasn't home. He had gone to a fundraiser. I got what I needed and left. But before I left, I got attacked by someone who tried to steal what I had found."

"Did they get it?"

Yes, I'm fine. Thanks for asking.

He hesitated before answering. What if the President was involved too? Was that possible? What if everything he was saying was going to be used against him? He had the take the chance.

"No, but they probably thought they did. But they'll figure it out this morning, if they haven't already."

"So what's next in your investigation?" the President asked.

He wasn't going to answer that question. Instead he asked, "What did the team find at the airport?"

"Nothing," answered Thornhill. "As you suspected, the plane was long gone, no doubt moved to another location right after the attack."

McAllister had an idea. "Sir, can Director Longfellow track down more satellite images?"

"What exactly are you looking for?"

"The new location. If the satellite was still in the area when they moved the plane, it would show up in later photos. If it left the area, at least we'd have an idea of which direction."

"Excellent. I'll ask," the President answered. "In the meantime, what's next for you?"

There it was again. Gordon had to be careful how he answered. He needed to maintain secrecy and cover but didn't want to offend the President of the United States, his boss. "Sir, you know part of our arrangement is that I don't disclose operational details to you. I just get the job done. That's the way it's always been. It gives me freedom to do what it takes. And it gives you plausible deniability. That's the way it has to be this time, too. I'll be in touch." He thumbed the end button, not waiting for Thornhill's response.

As he tucked the cell phone away, he looked up and saw Molly standing in the doorway to the kitchen. He met her stare. Finally he asked, "Did you see it too?"

"Yes," she said, not breaking eye contact, fire blazing in her pupils.

"And?" he asked, holding her gaze.

She looked down and to her left, formulating her response. Satisfied with her answer, she looked back up at him and said with firm resolve, "One more suspect out of the way." Then she turned back toward the kitchen and said, "My eggs are getting cold."

45

Homeland Security Director Henry Williams grabbed the phone as soon as the satellite photos crossed his computer screen. He arranged a meeting in the Oval Office and grabbed the printouts on the way out the door.

"Mr. President," Williams began, taking the seat Thornhill offered. Across from him sat Longfellow and James Fleming, Director of Central Intelligence, eagerly anticipating a look-see at the pictures Williams was laying out on the low table between them. Each one showed an overhead shot of the Skat. "As you'll see from the satellite images, we can trace the Skat to an abandoned airport in North Carolina, one that has been out of use for about three years now. No planes are stored there and the runway has been inactive ever since the FBO shut down operations. However," he continued, "as you can see from this thermal image," which he laid down next, "there is clearly a plane or other activity inside this hangar, which is supposed to be empty. Judging from the color contrasts – red being hot and blue being cold – I'd say the engines haven't been shut down very long. Whoever is running this operation did a lousy job of covering up the location of the plane."

Thornhill studied the photos, taking each one and examining the details. Satisfied, he set the last one down and said to Williams, "Henry, I want that plane and whoever is flying it taken out, no matter what you have to do. But keep it quiet. Coordinate with Bill to get a tac team down there. No need to alarm the neighbors. I don't want an F-15 screaming in there at mach one and dropping a five hundred pounder down the air shaft. Take them out surgically, nice and quiet. And I want the plane intact. Then quarantine it until the Air Force can get a look before the Russians insist on getting it back. They know it's here but I'll stall as long as I can before telling them we have it."

Preston was now worried. He'd just received a very disturbing phone call about the FBI lab results, pointing the fingers at the Russians. He knew they would figure it out sooner or later, most likely sooner. That part was completely expected.

As was the death Senator Stevens. His refusal to sign the impending legislation meant he had lived out his usefulness and had become a liability, a ticking time bomb. The last thing Preston needed was a blabbermouth senator who could ruin everything they'd been planning all these years. Dispatching with him had been a pre-decided alternative plan if he refused to cooperate after all the persuading. Blackmailing him would have been too obvious. Killing him was far easier and less messy. Making it look like natural causes, pure genius. Personally, Preston liked Stevens. They were both ruthless men who would stop at nothing to get what they wanted, which was what pulled them together in the first place. Their common drive had made for an excellent team during the planning phase of the operation. But that all changed when Stevens started to chicken out and waver on finishing. Stevens was standing in the way of completing the operation, and Preston wasn't going to let that happen. Easy choice: Stevens had to go.

What was not expected was Dominic's prolonged absence. He had been dispatched to take care of McAllister, the final link in the chain, which would open the patch wide for the final phase of the plan. But he had not made contact in several days, and Preston began to wonder who he was talking to and who knew what. While he had given Dominic free reign to accomplish what he needed and didn't need him to check back with him, Preston was still concerned. It wasn't like Dominic to go this long without an update, especially with his ego. He thrived on approval and would tell Preston whenever he had accomplished something significant so as to boost his importance in his own mind. Preston was sure Dominic did it to impress him, too, but he was more impressed with results. Dominic got results, and that was all that mattered. Preston wasn't in the business of handing out praise. Get the job done or you're of no use.

Preston wasn't worried about Dominic's state of health, only the status of the secrets inside his head. He didn't care if he was dead or alive, just so long as he hadn't run his mouth.

But he had to put that aside for now. There was much more to accomplish before the next phase of the plan could play out. He turned his attention back to the problem at hand: loading a nuclear missile into the Skat. The dark flying wing had been flown out of the small airport in Virginia and put inside a hangar at another abandoned airport not far from there.

The decline in the economy had resulted in less money being spent on recreational general aviation, which impacted the viability of many of smaller airports. Many of them had been so drastically hit that they had simply closed up shop. Cash-strapped counties and cities could no longer afford to maintain them when their use declined. So finding another suitable runway and storage had been fairly easy. Preston would have preferred to fly the Skat through a more circuitous route instead of straight here, but he knew the longer the plane stayed in the air the better chance satellites had of tracking it. So he had no choice but to bring it straight here.

He walked out into the cramped hangar, where the plane sat dormant, waiting for the new crew to get to work. Both the new crew and the old one, now rotting underneath the rock and dust of the Nevada desert, had been hired separately and without any knowledge of the other. This crew had no idea they were slated for the same fate as the others.

A large stainless steel crate on wheels had been rolled onto the floor near the leading edge of the left wing, the lid now open and hanging along the side of the crate. Two men, one on each end, reached into the crate and tugged on its contents. It was heavier than they anticipated. They repositioned and finally got underneath and gave it another heave. One man had the nose and the other had the stabilizing fins of the ordnance. Two other men joined them to share the weight as they lifted the projectile slowly over the edge of the crate and set it gently onto the cradle of a waiting ordnance cart. They then wheeled the cart under the Skat, ducking under the wing so they wouldn't bang their heads or scratch the delicate and valuable stealth paint. The slightest imperfection in the coating of the aircraft could give it an unacceptable radar signature, resulting in it being found and shot down before it reached its objective. Preston had made that very clear to the crew.

But it wasn't Preston's threat that scared them. It was what they were doing that frightened them the most. As they secured the weapon into the bay and attached the hooks and wiring harnesses that would give the missile its arming and release signals, they were reminded of the destructive power of the Russian Kh-31 air-to-surface missile, also knows as the AS-17 Krypton to NATO forces.

Developed during the Cold War, the Kh-31 was created as an anti-radar missile designed to hunt down enemy radar, lock onto the tracking signal, and ride it all the way down to the radar station, destroying it on impact, ironically using it against itself. The warfare version of unintended suicide. In its original design, the missile had a sixty mile range and remote arming capability, which allowed the operator to fire the missile in the general direction of the radar but out of its range. The missile would then lock onto the radar source once inside its scanning range and home in on the target. This capability allowed the aircraft that launched the missile to get away undetected while still destroying the target.

That was its original intent – which had nothing to do with why Preston was loading this one onboard the Skat. He had chosen it because it was one of only a handful of missiles that would fit inside the bay of the small aircraft. This particular missile was a far cry from the one that had left the Soviet Union in July of 1988, bound for Long Beach Harbor and points beyond. The outer skin and control system were original, but the guts of the missile, including its powerful explosive charge had been removed, replaced with a far more lethal payload: a nuclear warhead.

The modifications had required a great deal of expertise, including substantial engineering know-how from a former Soviet weapons researcher who had defected in the mid-1980's. Dr. Vladimir Mikhail Kuchon had come to the United States on a scientific exchange program that was supposed to last a month. Two weeks into his stay, Kuchon and the CIA carried out a plan they had been cooking up for months, involving a sudden disappearance, stays in a series of safe houses, and eventually a full defection to the United States. After the government learned all they could from Kuchon, he was given a new identity and a new life, but that didn't stop very powerful people from finding him and recruiting him to do their dirty work. He was blackmailed and threatened, much the way he would have been treated if he had just stayed in the Soviet Union, and made to divulge nuclear and weapons guidance secrets to men who should never have learned them. Once he had spilled enough of his knowledge, he was murdered, a case that mysteriously went unsolved since his body was never found and there was no other material evidence. Officially his murder was pure speculation. Unofficially he was dead.

Preston watched as the crew finished the loading procedure and carefully closed the bomb bay doors, completing the smooth-skinned underbelly that would keep the UAV away from prying radar. The last phase was finally underway.

46

The FBI tactical team spread out into their rehearsed positions around the perimeter of the small airfield, just outside the fence, taking cover among overgrown bushes and tall grass, long since neglected after the last private planes left. The team had left their vehicles out of sight a half mile away and hiked the distance to the abandoned airstrip. Still air surrounded the team, their breath fogged by the chill. The airport was dark, except for two lights hanging high atop telephone poles in the empty and cracked parking lot. The plan was to avoid that area and keep to the shadows.

Once the proper hangar had been identified, the team's first element, made up of three black-clad agents, made its way to the corrugated metal building and set up right by the small exterior exit door along the side perpendicular to the large aircraft door. One member flipped on his night vision goggles and peeked inside the dark hangar. And saw nothing. The entire hangar looked empty from his vantage point. He signaled to the two other agents what he saw and then motioned for them to move forward toward the aircraft entrance. Creeping around the front of the hangar, they again peered inside using night vision and got the same result: the hangar was completely empty. It was time to break radio silence.

"Cobra One, this is Cobra Three," he said into the thin, clear microphone hanging just off the edge of his mouth. "Target building is empty. No sign of anyone."

Before Cobra One could respond, a sudden jet blast almost knocked the remaining members stationed just outside the perimeter fence near the far end of the runway off their feet, as close as they were to the tail of the plane. With almost instantaneous motion, the Skat, which had been sitting quietly, invisible in the darkness, roared to life and began its rev up to full throttle, ready to take to the air. The high pitched whine of the powerful single engine spun up and the black airplane began to roll, slowly at first, until it suddenly sprang to life and hurtled down the concrete strip, the engine plume no longer visible as it lifted off into the dark night sky.

47

The melodious ringing of the phone on the Resolute Desk brought Thornhill back to the present. He had been thinking about the events of the evening and his mind had wandered. He stabbed the speaker phone button.

"Mr. President," came the call from DHS Director Williams, "we have a problem."

The President had been sitting behind his desk in the Oval Office waiting to get an update on the operation. He could tell this was not going to be good. "What is it, Henry?" he asked, not sure he wanted to know the answer.

"Sir, the Skat and the crew got away."

The President leaned forward on his elbows. "What do you mean it got away?" he asked incredulously. "They were faster than you?"

"No, sir. They were gone when we got there," Williams answered.

"Where is the plane now?"

"In the air."

"What?" the President exclaimed. "You mean to tell me it's airborne?"

"Yes, sir," Williams answered tentatively, "but we are able to track it. Which is why I'm calling you."

The President didn't like the tone of where this was going. "Explain."

"Sir, if our data is correct, the plane is headed right toward Washington, DC."

Thornhill had to answer calmly. After all, he was President of the United States; he had to be in control, at least on the outside. "Henry, do you have a probable target?" he asked, already guessing the answer.

"No, sir, but I would not be surprised if it's the Capitol or the White House. I've already alerted the Air Force and they are coordinating with us to get data uplinked to the birds patrolling the no-fly zone around DC."

Suddenly a pair of Secret Service agents burst into the Oval Office and sprinted toward the President. They were there to take him to a secure location, either the bunker deep below the White House or to another prearranged facility, depending on how much time they had.

"Henry," he said into the phone, as he stood and raised his hand to acknowledge the first agent, "call me back on my cell." And he hung up.

48

The bird began its pre-loaded flight by heading almost directly east, followed by a jog to the north, its onboard brain constantly relaying data from the GPS into the flight control computer, which made ever so subtle adjustments to the wings to stabilize the aircraft and guide it to target.

Preston had taken on all the responsibilities himself, once he had disposed of the support team. As before in the desert, he had gathered everyone in the office after the bomb had been loaded and the aircraft preparation finished. But this time he'd simply poisoned the celebratory champagne instead of gunning them all down. Without Dominic to help him, it would have been harder to dispose of the bodies, so they would probably die where they fell and stay there. And since he wanted to leave behind as little evidence as possible, that meant he was better off with poison than with bullets, which could be easily traced back to his gun. After the meeting concluded and everyone else was dead, all that was left to do was upload the flight plan into the flight computer and set the time to execute. Then he opened the hangar door, started the clock on the

Skat, and drove his black SUV out of the gate and into the night before the FBI team that he knew was surely on its way would be arriving.

And now his programming was proving fruitful as the Skat made a sweeping left turn and climbed to 20,000 feet, its passive targeting system scanning the ground nearly four miles below. So far no radars had tried to light it up, which was not surprising since the plotted route was designed to take the stealth aircraft beyond the range of most ground-based radars until it got closer to the DC airspace. Once inside, it would make quick evasive maneuvers if it was lit up. Otherwise, it would continue on its original flight path all the way up until missile launch.

McAllister watched the FBI team from his perch in a big oak tree a hundred yards from the fence. Darkness had hidden him in the leaf-bare tree, plus nobody ever thinks to look up. He could have been wearing a neon sign, and the agent who walked right below him wouldn't have noticed. Gordon had moved into position right before the team arrived and seen the Skat sitting on the runway through his night vision goggles. He felt bad for the team members who had been caught off guard when the engine fired. They had not flipped down their goggles before the noise caught them off guard, practically knocking them over.

The team was pulling heavy black body bags from the hangar's office and loading them into the back of a big Suburban. In total, three bodies had been removed before McAllister slid silently to the ground and scurried off into the darkness.

Four F-16s lifted off from Langley Air Force Base en route to join four other Falcons already in the air on station inside the Flight Restriction Zone. Within minutes the fighters were all inside the FRZ and patrolling their respective sections, with orders to be looking for the Skat. Pre-flight briefings had been put together hastily but because of time they had been relayed to the pilots over the radio as they were flying toward the patrol area. With the Skat already in the air, they didn't have time to sit around and discuss the mission over coffee.

The Falcons were staggered at different altitudes, each covering two thousand feet, actively scanning their respective areas with full power on their radars. They didn't care if the Skat spotted them; it didn't have defensive weapons so it couldn't shoot back. All that mattered was that they could find the Skat. And shoot it down. Maybe. The orders had been to locate the bird and relay its location to the ground station and wait for orders. The well-trained pilots all thought the process would take too long. Once the missile was airborne on its way to the target, it would be too late. They had argued for different rules of engagement, but the commanding general had been clear: the orders he had received from above were to spot it and report it. Nothing more. The rest would be decided over his head.

Preston turned onto the two lane state highway and headed south through the woods toward the North Carolina border. He was fairly confident the authorities didn't know where he was because the SUV he was driving was registered in a phony name, so even if they knew the plate the cops would have no reason to pull him over. He settled into the leather seat and flipped on the satellite radio to a classical station. Soon he would tune to the news to get the latest from his operation. But for now he was content enjoying not only the music but also the irony that the same basic technology that allowed him to partake of Beethoven's Ninth Symphony also afforded him the luxury of sending a nuclear missile streaking toward Washington, DC without endangering himself.

49

"Eyes on target!" came the call from the pilot of the lead Falcon. Having exhausted his search inside the FRZ, he received permission to move farther south in hopes he could intercept the Skat before it entered the restricted airspace – and close enough to attack its target.

Radar searching having proven fruitless against a stealth plane, he had descended below 15,000 feet so he could look up toward the gray clouds covering the night sky, hoping the contrast would reveal the form of the black flying wing. Finally he caught a glimpse of motion off his right side, contrasted exactly as he had anticipated. Now flying alongside the aircraft, he couldn't believe he was this close to a plane whose goal was a target somewhere in the nation's capitol.

"Viper One, stand by," came the voice from the control tower. He was sure the controller had to check with whoever was in charge before he could authorize any action.

The Skat almost looked like a monster, its black wings stretched out and the hunched back with a mouth in front and a stubby tail concealing the engine exhaust. It reminded the Falcon pilot of a miniature B-2.

Thornhill punched the button on his cell phone. "General, what do you have to report?"

"Mr. President, we have the target aircraft in sight. What are your orders, sir?"

"How close is it to DC?"

"Just outside the fifteen mile mark, sir."

"Do we know what's on board yet?"

"No, sir, we're still working on the possibilities. We have to assume it's nuclear until we learn otherwise."

"I thought you said this bird can't carry nuclear weapons?" the President said.

"That's correct, sir, assuming it hasn't been modified – either the plane or the weapon. In theory, it could be carrying a conventional bomb or missile that has been modified to carry a nuclear warhead. It's not unheard of. And it's very possible."

The President was well aware of the dangers nuclear weapons posed. But he was also aware of the safeties built into the nuclear weapons to avoid an accidental discharge with devastating effects.

"Just so we're clear, General," the President said, "if we don't shoot it down it could wreak incredible destruction on the entire DC area. But if we shoot it down, the weapon could still go off. Correct?"

"That's correct, Mr. President."

He didn't have a choice. The "safest" alternative was to blow it out of the sky and risk the nuclear device detonating in spite of their best efforts. But letting that plan fly all the way to DC and then wipe out millions of people was unacceptable.

"General," Thornhill said, "Shoot it down."

The F-16 pilot received the order and pulled back into position behind the Skat, close enough to keep the plane in range but far enough to be clear of any debris that could fly up his air intake when the plane exploded. He knew a radar guided AMRAAM would be useless against the stealth bird because it wouldn't be able to lock its radar seeker onto target. So he had to get right behind the plane and hope the heat-seeking AIM-7 Sidewinders could lock onto the small heat signature coming directly off the engine exhaust nozzles.

The seeker head in the Sidewinder on the under-wing launch rail found its target and sent a warbling sound into the pilot's helmet, letting him know to fire. He thumbed the release button on top of the control stick and had to close his eyes momentarily as the air-to-air missile lit its rocket motor and zipped out from beneath his left wing, on its way down range toward the Skat.

"Come on, baby, hit your mark," the pilot willed the missile.

It worked. The black airplane, almost invisible against the night, burst into a fireball and lit up the sky in a cloud of smoke and flame, the wings tumbling violently from either side, streaming lines of burning jet fuel in all directions.

50

Preston looked at his watch and tuned to an all news station, hoping to hear good news. Instead it was on a commercial for some sort of debt refinance company touting how you could get out of debt in under ten years with a home equity loan. He missed his Beethoven. After three more commercials, the headlines reader's voice announced, "We have breaking news out of Washington this hour as the Air Force has apparently shot down a plane that had wandered into the no-fly zone that surrounds the city."

Preston's eyes went wide. *Shot down?! What? How?*

The announcer continued. "Air Force spokesman Major General Jeffrey Langston told reporters that the small private plane had wandered into the airspace inside the Flight Restriction Zone that surrounds the Capitol and White House without authorization and refused to comply with directives to turn around. According to Langston, when the pilot refused to comply, the Air Force was left with no choice but to order it shot down. The plane was only a few miles from the White House and Capitol Building."

Preston was livid. How in the *hell* had that happened? He pulled the SUV to the side of the road and skidded to a halt on the gravel shoulder. He had to think. What was next? His entire life's goal had just evaporated thanks to some jet jockey who probably thought he was pretty hot stuff now after saving the nation's capitol from sure destruction. Well, Max Preston wasn't done yet, no sir.

He gunned the motor and pulled back onto the road, kicking gravel up behind him.

McAllister's cell rang as he was headed back to the hotel. It was Martin.

"Go."

"I just found our connection." Martin almost sounded enthusiastic. McAllister was stunned.

"And?" he pressed.

"Okay, guess who was Senator Stevens' biggest single contributor last election?"

"Are you going to make me work for this or just give me what I need?"

"Patience, grasshopper," Martin countered.

McAllister did not have the patience for this right now, but he had to play Martin's game long enough to get what he needed.

Martin continued, "Through two front companies, the good senator's reelection campaign received nearly ten million dollars from one – drum roll, please – Max Preston, terrorist extraordinaire."

"Okay, that explains their connection, but how does that explain the terror acts?"

"Once again, I'm getting to that."

McAllister could almost see the smirk on Martin's face over the phone. He hated when he got like this. The only upside was the egomaniac was usually right.

Martin continued, "Apparently the Senate was supposed to be voting on some environmental legislation that had already been passed by the House but was almost sure to be vetoed by the President. He didn't like some of the provisions in the bill and wasn't going to let them slide through. Stevens' vote would have created the two thirds majority they needed to override the veto."

"What did Preston have to gain by it?" McAllister asked as he drove.

"Looks like he was up for a huge contract on the west coast to create more windmill farms."

"But he runs a computer company. How does that tie together?"

"I cross referenced his name in the California state records and found he has applied for a business license for a new eco company specializing in wind turbines and solar panel production. Looks like he's diversifying a bit."

"So let's think this one through," McAllister said. "Preston is a business man, a very wealthy one. He's already made millions from the computer industry and will likely continue to. But now he wants to get into something that doesn't make any money. The wind turbine industry is losing money hand over fist with no end in sight. Why would he want to invest in a losing battle?"

"Maybe he likes the challenge," Martin hypothesized.

"Unlikely," McAllister answered. "Unless…"

"Unless, what?"

"Unless he intends to corner the market."

"What do you mean? There are lots of turbine companies."

"Not the turbine market," McAllister said. "The energy market. Remember, he tried to take out a nuclear facility."

"Okay, but what about the attack on the mall?"

McAllister thought for a moment. Why the mall? What did Preston hope to accomplish by attacking civilians in a shopping center?

"Control."

"What?" Martin asked.

"Control."

"Control of what?"

"Everything. Control of everything."

"What are you talking about?" Martin wondered if McAllister had lost his mind.

"Where's the Vice President right now?"

"Where are you going with this, Gordon?"

"Just answer my question. Where is the Vice President?"

Martin tapped a few keys on the computer and pulled up the White House travel itinerary. "On personal time, no further details provided. But he did take a small Secret Service protection with him."

"He had to, but I bet he didn't like them tagging along. I think I might know where he is. Can you get a hold of the crime scene photos from Stevens' house?"

"Already downloaded them. What do you need?"

"Do any of them show the painting over the fireplace?"

"Let me check." Martin pulled up the file and scrolled through the photos. "Yeah, here's one. It's a cabin in the woods."

"Ask Molly if she knows where that cabin is in real life. She's probably been there."

"It's in western North Carolina," she said. McAllister hadn't realized he was on speaker phone. "It's a hunting lodge. We used to go there for the weekend a couple times each summer. It wasn't all that long ago, so I can probably get you there."

"Good. I'll be by to pick you up in less than an hour. Martin, hop on the satellite and see if you can find it. That's where Preston's headed. And so am I."

McAllister clicked off the phone and dialed the President's cell out in the car.

"Mr. President, are you out of earshot?"

"Yes, why?" Thornhill asked, not sure he wanted to know the answer given the events of the past hour.

"I know who's behind all this and why, but you're not going to believe me."

"Why shouldn't I believe you?" Thornhill asked. "This whole thing's be a cluster since the beginning. It can't get any worse."

"Yes, it can," McAllister countered. "Sir, what I'm going to tell you might put you in more danger."

"Then why are you talking to me?"

"Because you need to know and I need your authorization and promise about something." He explained his plan and where he was going to Thornhill.

When McAllister was finished, the President said, "What help can I give you?"

"None," McAllister said. "This is personal now."

"Wait a minute," Thornhill said. "You can't make this personal. You've worked all these years for this office because you don't take things personally. It's a job for you. But now you want to make it personal?"

"Sir, Max Preston took out most of my team members and has tried to kill me. I didn't make this personal – he did. So now I'm going to personally take care of it."

James Thornhill, President of the United States, was silent for a moment as he ran everything through one more time in his head.

"Take him out," he finally said. "But leave Lancaster for me."

51

Vice President Thomas Lancaster nursed his second scotch on the rocks, the ice having barely begun to melt from the first one, as he stared out from the wood rocker into the woods behind the log cabin. A lone bulb hanging just outside the back door illuminated the plank floored porch. A crisp wind blew through the trees and across the clearing, but he barely noticed, bundled as he was against the night inside a long black overcoat covering his suit. Marine Two had barely taken off from depositing him at the cabin before he was out on the porch with his first drink. The Secret Service had been given very strict instructions to leave him alone on the porch. They were welcome to protect from a safe distance, even scour the woods for what the VP regarded as "squirrel hunts" – as if an irate rodent, or whatever they were, would suddenly rise up and start catapulting acorns or some such nonsense. But no one was to come close to him unless something dangerous occurred.

His cell chirped. He extracted it from inside his suit jacket pocket and answered but said nothing, only listened. Then he hung up. He had all the information he needed.

Preston wound his way from the state highway to the local roads and finally to the gravel drive that cut a path through the tall trees to the cabin. He was greeted about halfway down the almost one mile gravel road by a pair of Secret Service agents decked out in jeans, boots, and winter coats, with gloveless hands poised to instantly reach for hidden weapons. Preston slowed the vehicle and rolled down the driver side window, careful to keep his hands where the agents could see them.

"Max Preston to see the Vice President," he told the approaching agent.

"Sir, please open the back of the vehicle," the agent instructed him.

Preston frowned before reaching down to hit the hatch release button.

The other agent walked around the back of the SUV and parted the tailgate into window and door, scanned the inside, lifted the carpet and spare tire cover, put it all back together, and closed it up. He then opened the back passenger side door and searched the back seat. Finding nothing, he nodded to the first agent, who waved Preston on.

"Mr. Vice President," said the agent assigned to Lancaster, "Mr. Preston has arrived."

"Thank you, Mark," Lancaster said as he rose from the chair and headed back inside.

A few minutes later, Preston, having been thoroughly searched for weapons by the agent standing on the front porch, walked in the front door. Lancaster did not shake his hand, but instead greeted him with a scowl as he motioned for Mark to leave them alone. Lancaster waited for the agent to close the door behind him before speaking.

"You fucked up, Max."

Preston started to protest but Lancaster put up his hand and stopped him.

"Don't even start with me, Max. You promised me this plan would work. Years – *decades* – of preparation and hard work boiled down to three attacks, one of which worked, another missed, and the third was a colossal failure. This is unacceptable. And now we have a leak. This whole thing is blowing up in our faces."

"Tom," Preston started.

"Don't 'Tom' me!" Lancaster shouted as he got right up in Preston's face. "It's Mr. Vice President to you, you idiot! How dare you call me by my first name after what happened tonight! "

Preston wanted desperately to take a step back, give himself some breathing room, distance himself. But he dared not now. Instead, he steeled himself and met Lancaster's glare with steady eye contact.

"How was I supposed to know they would find the second airport so fast?" Preston countered. "I built in enough time that they shouldn't have been there that soon."

Lancaster considered the man standing before him for a moment, looking him up and down. He turned and walked toward the fireplace, the logs inside beginning to die, and extracted the poker from the rack on the stone hearth. He pulled back the screen and prodded at the logs for a moment, sending sparks up the flue, until the top log rolled slightly and caught. Finally he spoke.

"That's not like you, Max. You don't normally make excuses. Normally you own up to your failures. Why now?"

Preston swallowed before answering. "I don't normally *fail*, that's why. Screwing up is fairly new to me."

"Yes, it is," Lancaster said. "Which is why I think there's more to it. We've known each other for how long now?"

"Over twenty years."

"Yes, twenty-two to be exact. And in all that time you've rarely fucked up anything. Your company is going strong. You're making a killing in the market. You've done everything right. But now this...." He let his voice trail off to see if Preston had a response.

Preston only stood there and blinked. He was clearly terrified of the man before him holding not only a poker but Preston's very life in his right hand. This kind of fear was foreign to a man who had always been in total control of everything. The grip he held so tightly to his life was slipping away right in front of him, and it was like watching a train wreck – except he wasn't a witness. He was the sole passenger in the very front car, about to collide with a high speed freight coming head-on the other way. His whole adult life had been leading up to this point, an event that was supposed to define him from this point forward. But it was all slipping away, draining the life out of his dream.

"You do realize," Lancaster continued, "that you're finished, done, end of story, right? This is it for you. Once they figure you were mixed up in all of this they'll take away everything and throw you in jail for the rest of your life."

"What about you?" Preston asked. "You don't think they'll take you down, too?"

"Oh, they'll try. Of course they will. But I've built up enough layers of insulation that they'll have a hard time pinning anything on me. I'm so far removed from the process they'll never have any idea."

"Not if I tell them," Preston threatened.

Lancaster turned back from the fire and looked directly at Preston, his own fire burning in his eyes. "You do and you're life will be such hell that death won't come soon enough."

Preston was running out of options and he knew it. Lancaster had him by the nuts and was ready to squeeze as hard as he could at the least provocation. He and Lancaster had created the perfect plan! A stealth aircraft to deliver a nuclear missile to take out the entire government – the President, Congress, the Supreme Court, all three branches – with one fell swoop, leaving the Vice President to take over an unstable country, impose Marshal Law, and usher in his radical sweeping changes, all designed for total control. Even the original Constitution would evaporate in the explosion, instantly bringing into question any legal claims anyone had on the presidency other than the Vice President, the logical successor. Nobody would stand in his way!

But it had failed. Miserably. What the hell was he supposed to do now? Plans had been made and agreements had been reached about what the country would look like after the nuclear fallout had settled. People had been promised important positions.

And now it had come down to this. Man versus man. Political ideologies had been rudely tossed out the window, replaced with pure survival. Tiger instinct. Darwin was right.

"Max, I don't want you to feel too bad," Lancaster finally said. "So I'm going to give you one last chance to redeem yourself."

Preston was immediately suspicious but silently hopeful. "What do I have to do?" he asked warily.

"It's simple, really. I'm guessing McAllister has figured out where you are. He's a smart guy and generally puts two and two together pretty quickly. Which means he's probably on his way out here as we speak."

"To kill us?"

"No," Lancaster said smugly, "to kill you. He's smart enough to know that killing the Vice President of the United States would be suicide, especially since he has no official ties to the government, which means the Secret Service won't even let him through the front door. But he wants you dead, I'm sure. You killed his team. And you tried to kill him."

"So what do you want me to do about it?"

"Come on, Max. You're a bright boy," Lancaster said.

Preston hated when Lancaster talked down to him that way, especially after all had done to help get him on the ticket in the first place, not to mention all the time and money he had invested to get him elected.

"Yes, I am, Mr. Vice President," Preston hissed. "But why don't you spell it out for me anyway, just to make sure I get my orders straight and don't screw up again."

"Alright, it's simple," Lancaster stated. "When McAllister arrives, you take him out once and for all. End this thing right here."

"And where are you going to be?"

"Safely back in Washington, DC, where nobody will suspect a thing," Lancaster said as he opened the door to let his Secret Service protection detail back in before Preston got any ideas about killing him right there on the spot. He would rather let McAllister unwittingly do his dirty work. "Mark, I need to be on the road in five."

"Yes, sir," the agent said and gave the instructions over the microphone inside his sleeve.

52

Gordon picked up Molly, and they headed toward the cabin. In the trunk was some equipment he had grabbed before they left the safe house, including weapons and night vision goggles. This was going to be a nighttime assault, even though it was technically morning since it was past midnight. Along the way, he briefed Molly on his plan. She was to guide him to the cabin and then stay in the car, cell phone turned on, and wait for him to return. He was going to take out Preston and then they would head back to the safe house. In, out, done.

Martin had uploaded the latest satellite images to McAllister's phone. They were a couple years old but still accurate. McAllister knew Preston would be watching the front door and the driveway so he'd have to find a back way in. Between the satellite pictures and a local map he'd picked up at a gas station along the way, he figured out a way in that might work. It would require a bit of a hike but was worth it if it meant accomplishing the mission, a mantra that had kept him alive all these years in far more dangerous settings.

McAllister pulled the car off the road and in among some trees and killed the engine. Molly made sure her cell phone was on and getting decent reception before McAllister got out and grabbed his gear. Dressed in a dark jacket, black hoody not only for concealment but also to fend off the cold wind, blue jeans, and black combat boots, he slung the backpack over his shoulder and headed off into the woods. He had installed fresh batteries in the night vision goggles so he wasn't worried about their running out of juice. He flipped them on and was able to better navigate between the trees and see what was under foot. The overcast sky worked against him for this part of the hike, concealing the moonlight, but would work to his advantage if he had to cross the clearing. The barren trees allowed what little light there was to filter through and assist the light sensors in the night vision goggles to guide him, yet anyone without artificial assistance wouldn't be able to spot him approaching.

Using the satellite images on his phone, he navigated through the forest, carefully on the lookout for booby traps and trip wires. He highly doubted Stevens or Lancaster had rigged the woods, but he wasn't willing to take a chance, slack off, and get killed for inattentiveness. He knew all too well from experience that missing details can cost an operation and a life. Sweating the small stuff was often the difference between life and death.

Within minutes he neared the edge of the woods and could make out the edge of the clearing up ahead and the two-story cabin beyond, with lights turned on both upstairs and down. He stopped and hunkered down fifty feet back from the tree line and scanned visually for movement, then slowed his breathing so he could hear clearly any sounds that might indicate the presence of guards or dogs. There was no hurry to get to the cabin, so he waited until he was fully convinced it was safe before moving forward into the meadow. A small creek bed ran parallel with the edge of the trees about twenty feet inside the meadow. McAllister edged slowly toward it, and seeing it was dry, lowered himself into the creek bed and settled to resurvey the area for threats. Once again satisfied he was alone, he pulled the Glock from its concealed holster, checked that a round was chambered, and took a deep breath. Moving across the meadow was going to leave him completely exposed, with no chance for cover until he reached the cabin: hostile territory. So he had to be prepared for a firefight the moment he moved from the creek bed. And that meant running as fast as he could, gun at the ready.

He focused his attention on the cabin windows, checking for movement and shadows that might give away the locations of anyone inside. The curtains were all drawn, so he could not get a complete view. But it also meant that anyone inside most likely couldn't see him either. Not spotting anything useful, he next located the door. Molly had given him a verbal description of the cabin and drawn out a rough sketch of the floor plan on a sheet of printer paper, which he pulled out of his back pocket and unfolded. Now that he was within sight of the structure, he could compare the drawing and the cabin and decide whether his initial plan of attack was still the best. It was. He folded the diagram back up and put it back in his pocket. One final check and...

Crap! In a sudden bolt of thought, McAllister realized why the cabin looked so familiar to him now but hadn't when he saw the picture hanging over the fireplace. The view in the picture was of the *front* of the cabin. But McAllister was looking at the *back* – the same view as he had envisioned in his dream, the horrible recurring nightmare in which he tried to storm the mysterious cabin in the woods, only to have every one of his shots either go wide or bounce harmlessly off his target. That was this cabin! But in the dream there were guards all along the balcony that wrapped around the second floor. Tonight there were none. Was that a good sign or a bad one? Maybe since the dream took place during the daytime, it had served as a warning that he should attack at night. After a shiver, McAllister shook the thoughts from his head. Whatever the omen, good or bad, he was here now and had a job to do.

He steeled himself against the negative thoughts, hoisted himself out of the creek bed, and set out at a dead sprint across the meadow, headed for the cabin's back door. Running as silently as possible while at full speed, his lungs burning against the cold night air, he was on high alert for threats in front of him as he got closer to the door. Nearing the cabin, he leapt up onto the wood plank porch and landed as quietly as possible, careful not to disturb the boards or run into the pair of rocking chairs and table set out next to the door. With a quick scan left and right, he was sure nobody had seen him make his run. He crouched low and took a quick peek into the bottom corner of the window beside the door where there was a small gap in the curtain. Inside the room, there was a lamp turned on sitting on an end table by a long tartan plaid couch. Two other lamps lit the room from opposite corners, giving the interior a warm glow. On the far side of the room was a fireplace with a small fire burning on the grate.

And standing by the wet bar on the left side of the room was one Max Preston, pouring himself what looked like scotch on the rocks. McAllister couldn't get a good look at the entire room, but Preston seemed to be alone. He slid away from the window and over to the door. It was a single wooden door, no storm door, so he knew he could open it with one motion. There was no deadbolt, so he'd only have to worry about the one layer of lock, which he could easily kick in. He had originally toyed with the idea of coming in through an upstairs window, since coming in the back door might be too expected, but he quickly discarded the idea when Molly told him the upstairs floors sometimes squeaked, which would give him away before he could get into position, nullifying the advantage of surprise. Instead he chose the simple route: the door.

With a step back and a swift and forceful kick, McAllister smashed the door from its frame, sending it swinging violently on its hinges as it opened wide. Before it could snap back, McAllister leaped into the room and leveled his gun at Preston, who turned and dropped his drink, the glass shattering on the hardwood floor, spilling liquor at his feet.

"Max Preston?" McAllister asked, already knowing the answer.

Preston composed himself, smiled, and answered, "Mr. McAllister, I presume. Code name ZEBRA. I've been expecting you. Please, have a seat," he said as he gestured toward the couch.

McAllister looked down the gun sites and said, "No, thanks. This isn't a social visit."

"I see," said Preston, feigning disappointment. "Perhaps I can offer you a drink then?"

"Thanks, but alcohol affects my ability to shoot straight, a skill I'll probably need tonight," McAllister said.

"So that's why you're here?" Preston asked mockingly. "To kill me?"

"That is kinda what I do," McAllister answered.

"But not without cause, I would imagine. You see, Gordon – do you mind if I call you Gordon?" Preston asked, turning to get a replacement glass. McAllister didn't respond. "Anyway, I know enough about you to know you don't kill indiscriminately. Each one of your *hits* has been for reason. Just cause, you might call it. Justified in your mind. You're a patriot, Gordon, just like me."

"Just like you?" McAllister said, keeping the gun trained on Preston as he inched across the room toward him, slowly closing the distance to increase his accuracy. "How do you figure?"

"We both want what's best for this country. We just have a different idea of what that is," Preston explained.

"Yeah, we definitely disagree on that," McAllister said. "I don't believe killing innocent people and nuking Washington D. C. is very patriotic. I'd call that terrorism or murder."

"So if you kill me right here, right now would that be patriotic?" Preston asked.

"No," came a new voice from across the room, "that would be stupid."

McAllister turned to train his gun on the new threat: the supposedly dead Peter Jacobs standing just inside the back door, with a pistol pointed at Molly's head.

53

Vice President Lancaster's plane touched down at Andrews Air Force Base and was greeted by the limo and small motorcade that would take him to his residence on the grounds of the United States Naval Observatory. However, partway there the motorcade took an unexpected turn.

"What's going on?" demanded Lancaster to the Secret Service agent in the back of the car with him.

"Sir, we've been told to take you to the White House."

"Under whose orders?"

"The President's, sir."

Lancaster knew he couldn't defy the order, much as he wanted to. Any wrong move now would make him look guilty and blow any chance he had of covering up the whole incident and his connection to it all. He dialed Preston's cell. It rang several times and went to voicemail, which meant McAllister had already gotten to him. He hung up and didn't leave a message.

McAllister had to think fast, decide quickly what to do. Peter showing up was not part of the plan. Molly had watched him die. Or so she claimed. Had she been part of the plot all along, used to lure McAllister into the killing zone so Peter could take him out once and for all? Or had she been duped, too, Peter's death staged to fool her into believing he'd been killed so he could disappear and orchestrate everything from behind the scenes? Either way, Peter was now on the wrong side and apparently had been for quite some time.

"Surprised?" Peter said with a smirk.

"A bit," McAllister answered, not losing focus on the gun sites trained on Peter, but watching Preston to his left in his peripheral vision. "Especially since the NYPD ruled your death as a homicide. Guess they missed that one."

"Guess so," Peter replied.

"So what do we do from here?" McAllister asked down the barrel of the Glock.

"It's simple," the newly alive Peter said. "You drop your gun, and we talk about what to do next."

McAllister laughed. "Drop my gun? Why? So you can kill me with only one shot instead of risking a miss and getting shot yourself? I trained you on that tactic myself. Why would you think I'd fall for it? Not gonna happen. But it was a worthwhile suggestion, if you think I've gone senile."

"How about this, then?" Peter countered. "I kill you with one shot and then kill Molly. She can't do anything, since she's unarmed. Two shots, one for each of you. Neat and tidy."

"You wouldn't get it off in time. Your gun's aimed the wrong direction. Besides, then what do you do with Preston?" McAllister asked. "I'm sure he might have a few things to say to the FBI, Secret Service, and DHS once this whole thing is over."

"Oh, yes, Preston," Peter said, annoyed. "He could prove to be a problem, especially if he spills his guts like Dominic did. Guess I'll have to dispatch with him, too. Might make staging a bit tricky, but it can be done. I can make it look like self defense if I work at it."

Preston blinked and looked helplessly at McAllister then back to Peter.

"So you've been the ring leader all along?" McAllister asked Peter.

He laughed. "No way. I'm not that smart. This goes much higher than me." Peter thought for a second. "Normally, I'd keep that a secret. But since that secret is going to die with you, I can tell you."

"Wait, let me guess," McAllister said. "Vice President Lancaster."

"Impressive. You've been doing your homework," Peter answered. Molly started to squirm a bit, and Peter tightened his grip on her, making sure she completely shielded him except for his face.

"Didn't have to look far. You know the types of resources I have at my disposal."

"You mean Martin?" Peter sighed. "He's been a royal pain in the ass ever since you contacted him. Every time I turned around he was digging up something else. Where did you hide him, anyway? I haven't been able to track him down lately."

McAllister was surprised at Peter's arrogance. Didn't he know McAllister could take him out right where he stood before he could get a shot off? McAllister had trained him, for Christ's sake.

"I got the whole puzzle pieced together," McAllister said, "as far as who was involved. My main question is why."

"Why what," Peter asked.

"Why do it?" McAllister answered. "What do you get out of destroying Washington, DC?"

"It's not what I get out of it, you fool. It's what the country gets out of it. Sure I stand to make a fortune and be set for life. But more importantly, the country will be a better place."

"How so?" he asked.

"You don't get it, do you?"

"Apparently not," McAllister said impatiently. He wanted to get the explanation before he pulled the trigger. "Enlighten me."

"You see, that's just it. Enlightenment," Peter said. "This whole thing is about waking up the world to the real threat."

"Which is?"

"Democracy."

"I don't follow," McAllister said.

"Of course you don't. You're too damn patriotic."

McAllister was thinking this conversation was starting to sound all too familiar.

Peter continued. "Democracy has too many loopholes, too many opportunities for the wrong outcome. Putting decisions in the hands of the people means risking bad decisions, mistakes. Civilization can't last that way. At least not good civilization. Put the decision-making process into the hands of the smartest people in society and it can thrive."

"Are you talking about a dictatorship?" McAllister asked.

"We prefer the term benevolent dictatorship," Peter said.

"In the United States."

"Of course. It's the only way the country will last. It's the only way we'll save our environment and heal the world."

McAllister's brain shifted into overdrive. "Are you talking about environmentalism?"

"Ding, ding, ding!" Peter said mockingly. "Now you're getting it."

"But can't you just save the planet without destroying the country and the freedoms we all enjoy?"

"You're so naïve, Gordon. It's those *freedoms* that have put us in the position we're in now. Unbridled capitalism has allowed companies to rape the world with no recourse for the people who get hurt. The rain forest problem, the hole in the ozone layer, global warming, all problems caused by man-made pollution."

"And you don't think we have the resources now to fix them?" McAllister said.

Peter laughed. "No! That's the problem! To fix the problem you have to get rid of the cause. The cause is capitalism!"

McAllister tightened his grip on the Glock. The room was getting warmer, causing his palm to sweat. "So this is really all about control and getting *rid* of freedom then."

Peter nodded. "It always has been. Environmentalism is just the effect. The cause is our system of government. Get rid of it and replace it with something more effective."

"Communism," McAllister said.

"Exactly. But socialism has to come first," Peter said. "The American people won't stand for a direct switch to communism. It's too harsh, too radical for step one. They have to be led along by the hand slowly through socialism first so they won't see communism coming."

"Which is why the left in this country has been slowly dripping socialist policies into the system for decades, right?" McAllister said.

"Yes, ever since Woodrow Wilson. But the process has been taking too long. We're decades behind where we want to be. We're done wasting time. It needs to happen now before the country realizes what happened. Once they catch wind, we'll never win. The slow drip no longer works."

"How does blowing up Washington help you?"

"Simple," Peter said, again adjusting behind Molly. "Take out the entire government and what happens? Think about it?"

McAllister pondered the question for a moment. "The Vice President takes over and in effect becomes the government."

"Exactly," Peter said.

"But what do you and Preston get out of it?"

"Protection and wealth. Communism is never about the working class. They get screwed every time. It's about the elite, the powerful, the decision makers. Hobnob with the powerful and you're in, a life of luxury at the expense of the schmucks who let you get away with it."

The room was suddenly still and quiet, except for the popping of the burning logs in the fireplace. McAllister shifted his glance back and forth between Preston and Peter, holding Molly tight as a shield, the barrel of his gun against her right temple.

"So what's it going to be, Gordon?" Peter finally asked, bringing everyone back into the room. "You want part of the action?"

McAllister once again tightened his grip on the pistol. "Peter, do you know what the penalty is for treason against the United States?"

"Yes, death," Peter answered. "But it hasn't been carried out since the Rosenburgs were gassed for selling secrets to the Soviets. Every other traitor has been put in prison."

"Until now," McAllister said. And squeezed the trigger, instantly launching a 9mm hollow-point round spinning across the room. Peter's head exploded out the back as the bullet blew out his skull, splattering brain and blood on the wall behind him. His body involuntarily released its grip on Molly as he fell down and backwards, the gun dropping from his hand, clattering harmlessly to the floor.

McAllister lowered the gun and looked at the terrified Molly still standing frozen where Peter had held her captive. "I'm pretty sure he's dead this time," he said.

54

President Thornhill tucked his cell phone back inside his grey suit jacket as Lancaster was ushered into the Oval Office. The Secret Service agents started to leave, but Thornhill stopped them and instructed them to stay. Seated on the couches that surrounded both sides of the low coffee table were the attorney general and the directors of FBI, CIA, and Homeland Security.

"Tom," the President said, "I'd offer you a seat, but they seem to all be taken. Besides, you probably don't feel much like sitting down at this point."

"Why is that, Mr. President?" asked the Vice President of the United States, trying to look stoic.

"I just got off the phone with a reliable source who confirmed that your associate, Peter Jacobs, was killed in a hunting accident in the woods of North Carolina. That's unfortunate. You must be heartbroken at the news of such a tragedy."

"Peter who?" Lancaster asked.

Thornhill smiled wryly. "Peter who. That's very nice, Tom. Maybe you should try Hollywood next, since your political career is over."

"Excuse me?" he asked, trying to mask his anger.

Thornhill approached the slightly shorter Lancaster and stood toe to toe with him, their noses almost touching.

He said slowly, "Tom, I have waited for this day for a very long time. You have been a pain in my ass ever since the party forced me to select you as my VP candidate. You weren't even on my list, but the party heads insisted on it. Let him run with you, they said. It'll get the moderate votes, they said. I didn't believe them then and I still don't. I didn't need the moderate votes, and you nearly cost me the election.

"But we're not talking about an election here now, are we?" he continued. "Nope, we're talking about getting rid of a pox, a roach, a varmint, one who has impeded the American people's agenda far too long. Now I get to get rid of you once and for all. I know all about your connections to the terror attack at the malls in St. Louis and across the country and the bomb at the nuclear plant in North Carolina. And I know all about the plot to kill me and nuke Washington, DC. And so do the four other men who are sitting here right now," he said, pointing behind him toward the couches. "Tom, you're done," the President said, spittle forming at the corners of his mouth. "If you think you can take out this government that easily and take over and have it all for yourself, you don't know much about the history of this country. And you *damn* sure don't know anything about me. This will not go away quietly, Tom. I have instructed the attorney general to bring you up on charges of treason. And I will personally testify at your trial. You can count on that."

Thornhill held the penetrating stare for a moment before turning back toward his desk. Lancaster started to speak. The President wheeled back around, the fire furiously burning in his eyes as he put his hand up. "Shut up, Tom! Save it for your trial."

He waved the Secret Service agents over, and they escorted the Vice President unceremoniously from the Oval Office.

Epilogue

Six Months Later

Gordon McAllister sat alone on his screened-in back porch, cold beer in hand, watching the deer frolic in the wooded yard below and enjoying the warm summer evening as he contemplated what had happened. His window, carpet, and garage door had been repaired, and the house – and his life – was back to normal.

Max Preston had been sentenced to life in prison for treason after a speedy trial. McAllister figured Preston wouldn't last very long in prison, even if the government tried their best to protect him. Someone would get to him and permanently shut him up before he spilled what McAllister was sure would be the rest of the details. Most likely about a dozen senators would want him shut up, and fast.

Former Vice President Lancaster's trial did indeed feature testimony by President Thornhill. Attempts by Democrat operatives and the media to bring up dirt in Thornhill's past to impeach his testimony failed miserably, and Lancaster was sentenced to life without parole for his involvement in an attempt to murder thousands of innocent American citizens and government officials, including the attempted assassination of the President of the United States. Gordon was sure both cases, especially Lancaster's, would go all the way to the Supreme Court. It was the first time a sitting Vice President had been accused of crimes against his country. Gordon didn't like the sentence, but he figure recommending the death penalty would have been a political nightmare, not just to Thornhill but to any future administrations.

Willard Stanford had recovered fully from the grueling torture inflicted at the hands of Dominic Rippon. The drugs had not been potent enough to cause any permanent damage, so he was back on his feet and diving into international affairs in short order.

Meanwhile, Dominic, sensing his own demise, turned into a gold mine of evidence, testifying for the prosecution at both trials in exchange for full immunity from everything. He and the FBI worked out a mutually beneficial informant arrangement that allowed him to stay out of prison but kept a tight leash on his activities. The NSA also got to tap into his knowledge, once again enlisting his services on an as-needed basis, with certain security measures put in place to keep him out of things where his nose didn't belong.

The body of Peter Jacobs was returned to his family for burial, accompanied by an official looking police report stating he had accidentally shot himself while on a hunting trip in the woods of North Carolina. The ballistics information included in the report pointed the finger at a Remington 30.06 hunting rifle. His family would never know the difference.

The Russians, continuing to deny any involvement in the attack, did indeed want what was left of the destroyed Skat back but decided to send only a small contingency to examine the pieces the CIA had carefully recovered from the crash debris field, which was spread across several miles. The FAA and NTSB had been called to the crash site immediately to form a tight perimeter around and divert prying cameras from the real crash. They had put on a good show and convinced the media of the original story.

Covering up McAllister's involvement in the whole mess proved to be a bit trickier than normal, given the Vice President's knowledge of the covert operation. But Thornhill had called in more than a few favors to make sure both Lancaster and Preston understood the seriousness of what might "accidentally" happen to them if word leaked out about how things had really played out. So far they were cooperating.

Congress launched its own internal investigation into the connections between the government and environmental extremist groups, looking for any and all campaign contributions to senators and representatives who had voted for legislation. The American people in poll after poll thought the investigation was laughable at best, like criminals trying to prosecute themselves, but the farce that was the legislative branch trudged on anyway. Behind the scenes, however, the FBI was taking all the evidence Congress dug up and adding it to their own to compile a complete list, which would be passed along to federal prosecutors. Several lobbyists and heads of environmental groups had quickly and quietly resigned under pressure of being hauled up before the Senate to testify. Instead they pled the fifth and trundled off into hiding. Gordon was sure they would reappear in another form on down the road.

Martin went back to work in his cube at the NSA with a promotion and a new assistant, Lena. Rumor had it they had bought a house and were talking marriage.

McAllister Management, Inc. had picked up several new clients and business was good, despite the down economy. Failing companies were dumping ineffective upper management left and right, paving the way for Gordon to step in with timely replacements. And he was glad to be back in the saddle. After all, he really preferred recruiting executives over killing people.

The cell phone on the glass top table next him vibrated. He picked it up and looked at the caller ID. And smiled.

"Hello?" he said wryly.

"Hey, what does it take for a girl to get a ride home from the airport?" asked Molly.

"I'll be right there."

Acknowledgements

Authors don't work alone. While only one name appears on the cover, many people contributed to the success of this endeavor. Without them, Gordon McAllister would still be stuck in my head, confined to an endless misery of never getting to shoot anyone. And he would never have met Molly. What a sad existence that would have been!

First, for her technical assistance, thanks to former FBI Special Agent Nicole Duckworth. Her details of the Bureau's crime lab and forensics operations helped me get inside Allison Crenshaw's head and gain some semblance of credibility in an area almost completely foreign to me.

To *New York Times* best-selling thriller author John Lutz, for his priceless advice and willingness to take valuable time out of his own very busy writing schedule to review the manuscript of an untested author. His insight and encouragement gave me the boost I needed to convince myself I could actually write this darn thing.

To Holly Broyles and Beth-Renee Pawley, who read early manuscripts and pointed out everything that was wrong with them.

That's why it's called a draft, so that all the big mistakes can go floating out the window. Many of their suggestions for improvement found their way into the finished product. Beth-Renee's nursing savvy and craftiness led to the tragic demise of Senator Stevens. If the details of how it happened are wrong, it's my fault.

To Michelle Argyle, author of the new thriller *Monarch*, who read the whole manuscript in great detail, offering valuable advice along the way, including a suggestion to chop about 20,000 words. I fought her on it, but she was right. Consider yourself lucky you didn't have to read that part after all.

To the staff at Facebook, for keeping me connected with friends who followed this project from start to finish, affording me hourly input during the writing process and allowing the creative juices to flow unsquelched. Social media does wonders for the creative process.

To Melissa Williams, cover artist extraordinaire, thanks for taking my lame first attempt at a cover and turning it into a wickedly cool work of art.

Copious thanks to Jeff Stewart and all the volunteers at non-profit coffee shop Java Journey in Hickory, North Carolina, for letting me make permanent impressions in the cushion of the leather chair in the corner as I pounded my keyboard day after day, downing delicious mochas and cappuccinos along the way. Yes, this is a caffeine-fueled book, which might explain the rapid pace at the end.

To the many people I have met over the years who served in our armed forces. Not only do I appreciate your service to our country to allow us the freedom they earned for us, but on a more selfish note I have learned a whole lot about military protocol and operations and how these men and women work tirelessly day in and day out to keep us safe. Freedom is the most expensive thing in the world.

To the authors of many valuable articles and studies that show just how far left we have come as a country, especially in regards to the environment. Socialism is pounding on the door, soon to be followed by communism if we aren't careful, and our government is shamelessly shoving it open. We must stay vigilant if we are to preserve the American way of life.

My most endearing appreciation goes to my wonderful wife, Stephanie, who read and re-read the entire manuscript over and over, wrote big red notes (most of which were absolutely dead on) in the margin, and encouraged me to plow through, especially in down times, when I wanted to tear the whole thing up and forget it. She kept my finger off the delete key. She is a storyline genius and offered several suggestions that found their way into the plot.

And, of course, I can't forget you, the reader. Without you, there would be no point in writing the book in the first place. Why write something no one is going to read? Special thanks go to you for taking a chance on a first-time novelist. I hope it was worth the price of admission.

Finally, a closing thought to all my dear friends who begged and pleaded to be written in as characters and killed off: here, drink this.

Made in the USA
San Bernardino, CA
22 April 2014